Percy
and Two Other Fools

Other books by Michael J. Merry

The Golden Altar (2002)
El Altar de Oro (2008) (Spanish)
The Reluctant Colonel (2010)
The Education of Santiago O'Grady (2014)
'Guten Tag, Mr. Churchill' (2016)
Galleón and Seven Other Tales (2017)
The Tomb Robber (2018)

Percy
and Two Other Fools

Michael J. Merry

ISBN: 978-0-359-21164-7

PublishNation LLC
www.publishnation.net

This story is dedicated to my wife and family:

Mariela Esther Merry

Michael J. P. Merry

James B. V. Merry

Jennifer Merry

'Cuidate de los que saben escribir, pues tienen el poder de enamorate siquiera tocarte'
(Old Spanish saying)

With thanks to:

James Michael Merry – Photography
Martin Bonacia – Cover conception
Georgina Hunter Gordon – Editorial assistance
Jason Merry – For being Jason

Contents

Observation

When I set out to write this book, I had no idea of the suffering and pain that many of the quarter million indigenous peoples of Brazil have put up with. Tribes are described as indigenous when they maintain traditions of a previous culture associated with a given region. Research has opened my eyes, and I have found that unfortunately, mistreatment continues to this day.

However, the exploitation of these jungle dwellers is slowly being eliminated thanks to the United Nations Working Group on Indigenous Populations, the Brazilian Government's Bureau of Indian Affairs and several private organizations such as Survival International.

We may only hope that eventually, modern mankind will stop trying to convert everyone on earth to their own image and allow these tribes to live as they wish on lands where they and their ancestors were born.

Michael J. Merry, October 2018

CHAPTER I

The mysterious disappearance
of Percy Fawcett*

In 1925, twenty-seven years ago to the day, Percy Harrison Fawcett DSO, vanished while exploring the forests of the Mato Grosso in north-eastern Brazil. A fellow officer upon learning of his disappearance a few years later, wrote a mock epitaph:

Percy Fawcett, he has gone
To explore the Amazon.
With a dog, a horse, and two old mules,
Percy, and two other fools,
Crossed the ocean, climbed a hill,
In the untamed jungles of Brazil.
No one saw where Percy went,
Bones were found, all broke and bent
Wild natives said that they were beaten,
Put in a pot and all were eaten.
There in Brazil, the very middle,
The Mato Grosso hides its riddle.

No trace has ever been found of Fawcett or his accomplices.

* From 'The Westminster Gazette', April 25th, 1952

This extract from the Gazette article contains the only epitaph ever written for Fawcett, a Lieutenant Colonel in the Royal Artillery. He had served in Ceylon and retired in 1910 to concentrate on his surveying adventures. Returning to the army in 1914, he commanded an artillery brigade in Flanders. In 1925 he obtained financing from a group of London bankers, known only as 'The Glove', for an expedition to the Mato Grosso in Brazil.

1

Fawcett was looking to solve the mystery of a mythical place he called, 'Z'. João da Silva Guimarães, wrote in 1753 that he had discovered the ruins of a City and described it in detail without providing a specific location. This, thought Fawcett, might be his 'Z'. Perhaps it contained riches? They would see.

Many famous explorers wanted to go with him, including T. E. Lawrence (Lawrence of Arabia) but he took his son and a friend, Raleigh Rimmell, instead.

On 20 April 1925 his final journey started from Cuiaba. An experienced traveler, Fawcett had items such as canned foods, powdered milk, guns, flares, as well as a chronometer and sextant. Along with his son and Rimmell, he took two horses, a pair of dogs, and eight mules. Assuming the mules could carry 200lbs. each and that two would be unloaded at all times, Fawcett's group carried 1,200lbs. plus another 400lbs. on the horses. A great deal of equipment, at the start at least. They carried their own backpacks and had two local porters with them. What happened then? Nobody knows for sure. Bones and a compass were found. The bones were submitted to a detailed forensic examination and determined they were not those of Fawcett or any of his party. The compass, it turned out, was left at Fawcett's base camp and not taken with him into the Mato Grosso.

Several stories have surfaced, bought back by searchers over the years. An American explorer by the name of George Miller Dyott claimed in 1927 that he had found evidence of Fawcett being murdered by Aloique Indians, but his story was unconvincing.

Back in 1931, Aloha Wanderwell took her seaplane to the Matto Grosso seeking Fawcett. She had to make an emergency landing and was obliged to live with the Bororo tribe for 6 weeks before abandoning her attempt.

Fawcett wrote a last letter to his wife from Dead Horse Camp before he headed into the jungle. In it he said the hardships were great, his coordinates were not always accurate and that he was worried about Rimmell, Jack's friend, who was accompanying them. Indeed, the camp, named for a spot where his horse had died on an expedition in 1920, was listed in one report as being 11.43S 54.35W. In another, sent to the North American Newspaper Alliance, he gave the coordinates as 13.43S and 54.35W. Perhaps this was a deliberate attempt to prevent his notes being used to find where he was exploring.

Still, many theorize that local Indians murdered them. There were several tribes nearby at the time: the Kayapo, the last tribe to have seen them, and the Arumás and Suyás. The Kayapo elders had a story passed down that said three explorers traveled east, and after four days they noticed no more smoke from their camp fires. It's said a very violent tribe, the Piripkura, known as 'the Butterfly people', were the most likely killers. Still, it's plausible that they died of natural causes in the Brazilian jungle.

Fawcett's fate may never be known for sure but modern investigative methods have shown his theory of a mysterious City is not a total fantasy. Archeologists now say the Amazon and Mato Grosso were home too many bustling settlements hundreds of years before the arrival of European explorers.*

What is not general knowledge is that Raleigh Rimmell wrote a note to his father which was sent along with the one Fawcett penned to his wife, from Dead Horse Camp. The contents of that letter lead to the modern expedition undertaken in 2018 which is described in this book.

CHAPTER II

Anatomy of a gunshot

- The odds are you won't pay any attention to the distant sound of a gunshot.
- Few people ever hear a bullet whizzing past them.
- A miniscule percentage of the population are struck by projectiles.

Take a moment from what you are doing, put your hands together, and pray you are never included in the last statistic!

The majority of gunshot wounds in the world can be attributed to the AK47, the Kalashnikov Model 1947, Soviet assault rifle, the most widely used shoulder weapon in existence. Mikhail Kalashnikov, who designed the accepted version in 1947 made it simple to operate, rugged, reliable under trying conditions. It fires a 7.62-mm round and its cyclic rate of fire is 600 rounds a minute. The AK47 and its successors are the weapon of choice for 90% of guerrilla and nationalist movements worldwide. Its nick-name speaks for itself. They call it "The Evil Rifle".

These guns and the bullets they fire are not the deadly accurate weapons seen in popular films where one shot drops the victim and a small hole, with a circle of blood appears on the shirt. They're untidy and do a lot of damage that cannot immediately be seen. A bullet can punch its way into the human body quite effectively. There's a reason the basic use for guns has remained the same for centuries: They work. When a bullet hits you, the momentum transfers to your flesh. The bullet usually tumbles and creates cavities, causing a serious wound.

Of course! You can use body armor. Kevlar for instance. But behind the Kevlar is your flesh, blood, and bones. The armor will not 'stop' a small caliber round, although it may prevent penetration. A bullet's momentum continues however, and this itself can cause serious injuries. The Kevlar Kick, it's called. Without body armor the round pushes through your body at 900 MPH. So fast it forces tissue in front of it as it penetrates. If it doesn't hit anything except flesh, it may go right through the body.

Then all that has to be done is stop the bleeding and get to a medical facility quickly. You're lucky! Few casualties receive nice, clean wounds. You'll probably suffer shock, but the facility can control that. Pain is something else.

After the first impact people react differently.

Some say they noticed nothing. Others experienced a burning sensation. Many tell of the force of the round and described it as "being hit by a sledgehammer wielded by Superman on steroids". So, a 'clean wound', all the way through, perhaps to a leg or arm, while not at all pleasant, promises a good chance of recovery after a few weeks in a hospital. Providing, of course no complications arise.

Complications? Indeed! Perhaps an infection? It takes time to get casualties to where they can be treated in sanitary conditions. Meanwhile, jungle dirt, brick dust, and other contaminants can get into a wound and create havoc.

If a bone is broken the chances of infection rise considerably.

Fever perhaps? Difficult to control unless in a hospital and very dangerous for the patient. There's a secondary consideration as well. A wounded person requires human and mechanical resources for transportation. Then medical staff for immediate and then ongoing care. All in all, getting shot creates problems not only for the victim but for many others performing ancillary tasks who become involved in the overall predicament.

It's not a good idea to get shot for all the above reasons. However, if you are unlucky enough to suffer such a wound, be ready for the consequences!

CHAPTER III

'Consequences of an ambush'

The British Army Jungle Warfare (JWS) School is in Seria, Brunei. Here the men attending are put through the Operational Tracking Instructors Course. They have an exchange arrangement with other friendly nations. In Hawaii the US Army School for instance, and with Brazil. This is an extremely important one. There, the Jungle Warfare Training Center–Centro de Instrução de Guerra na Selva (CIGS), also known as the Colonel Jorge Teixeira Center, is based in Manaus. Most of its support members are local men, mainly privates, corporals, and sergeants. They are adapted to the conditions of life inside the forest and can perform many activities. Foreign attendees at the School describe their impressive skills in jungle survival.

Earlier in his seven-year career, Staff Sergeant John Pullen had attended Hawaii, and two years previously he had spent six months as an instructor at CIGS. He had enjoyed that assignment. Manaus is a lively City, and he was befriended by Thiago Perez who, like himself, had been assigned to the school. He was a five- stripe First Sergeant from, Dantos a tiny village on the headwaters of the Xingu river near Porto de Mos, a long way south-west of Manaus. The high point of Pullen's time at CIGS had been during a week's leave when he visited Dantos with Perez.

He had had had trained anti-poaching units in Kenya and worked with US Special Forces pirate hunting in the Gulf of Aden and Guardafui Channel. In Nigeria he fought Boko Haram and in Tunisia the Daesh. Now, as perhaps the most highly trained jungle warfare soldier in the British forces, he was attached to the Army Training Support Unit Belize (BATSUB), in Belize. Pullen spoke a little Portuguese and Spanish plus a smattering of Somali.

There, the Army quietly maintained a highly trained force of men available for immediate dispatch to anywhere in the area to support friendly forces asking for assistance and cooperation. Lately however, along with the Belize Defense Forces, a special group patrolled the border with Mexico to eradicate the growing drug smuggling operations. Shipments from Colombia come in small boats, landing on the isolated beaches of Corozal Bay and cross west towards the Rio Hondo, bordering the State of Quintana Roo. From there they go north to the Mexico/USA border. The Colombian cartels prefer this route rather than chancing the more eastern route between Cuba and Haiti where the chance of interdiction grows as the low-profile vessels (LPV's) push north. These craft, designed to ride low in the water, are specifically designed for smuggling illicit cargo such as drugs, weapons and cash. They float just above the surface to reduce their radar signature and have multiple outboard motors which allow them to travel at high speeds. The vessels have camouflage paint jobs that blend with the water color. These days they seem to be favored over the previously used submersibles and semi-submersibles which were not always mechanically reliable. These new craft also have specially elongated bows, allowing them to carry over three tons of drugs. This delivery method was projected to displace the Bahamas string of islands as the preferred way to get illegal cargo into the United States. That was until the BATSUB Special Group became involved. Then things changed.

The Belize Defense Forces realized it was impossible to patrol the entire Corozal Bay coastline to combat this new threat. They also knew drugs would have to be taken cross country in northern Belize to arrive close to the highways in Mexico which would allow swift transportation north. So, it was decided to concentrate efforts along the northern Hondo. They formed the Special Group, and it moved from Price Barracks at Ladyville to a small base camp near Douglas on the river. The unit, consisting of thirty men, would live there for three months at a time. They would send out their four, five-man patrols every week to camp close to the waterway and attempt to intercept drug shipments using satellite intelligence reports. These patrols included a BATSUB jungle warfare expert and four local soldiers. From the start they were very successful. In the first two months of operations they were responsible for capturing two tons of cocaine, arresting more than forty smugglers, and killing a further twelve who fought instead of surrendering.

The Colombia cartels became angry and sent more men to increase security for shipments. Their partners in Mexico augmented protection on their side of the river and provided heavy firepower should any drug crossing be challenged. The Mexican army got into the act and increased their presence in the area and many short and sharp battles were fought between the cooperating forces against the smugglers.

On the night of Thursday January 18th, 2018 Staff Sergeant John Pullen was leading a five-man patrol which had set an ambush on the banks of the Rio Hondo, ten miles west of Orange Walk. The crossing spot would give any smugglers a straight shot at the town of Nicolas Bravo on Mexico's Highway 186, and on north westward to Mexico City, and beyond to the U.S. border.

They had been camped out for two days. The thick bush along the river gave them ample cover from the trail running down to its banks from a road to the east. The previous night they had scrutinized three rafts, towed by a wave-runner, make a practice run from the Mexico shore to a bare patch of earth on the Belize side on the waterway where the track ended. They were sure as they gazed out over the water that a shipment would arrive the next evening.

Pullen and his group were familiar with the procedure. A pickup loaded with packaged drugs would come down the trail from the eastern road preceded by a motorcyclist who would dismount at the landing space and signal the opposite bank with a flashlight. Rafts would cross the seventy-yard wide river, and three men would unload the truck while a six-man security details would offer cover for the operation.

Pullen's patrol realized these days, with the increased manpower the smugglers employed, there could be a fire-fight and casualties. They were well paid to deliver their cargo's and would fight to earn the bonus a successful delivery would bring.

Tonight, the men would set a 'near side' ambush. When the trucks stopped, and all their personnel were on the ground, a Spanish speaking patrol member would call upon the smugglers to surrender. Should they do so, they would be disarmed, and the patrol would call in reinforcements to secure them and remove the cargo. If they decided to fight it out, then all five patrol members would launch incendiary grenades which would ignite the drugs. If there were any survivors, the L85A2's were ready. Once the area was secure, a radio message with coordinates would be sent to BATSUB operations headquarters to be passed on to the Mexican army who hopefully, might capture the rafts and the receiving crews.

It seemed like a fool-proof method, and indeed it had been up to that night. But as Robert Luis Stevenson once said *'Sooner or later, everyone sits down to a banquet of consequences'.*

John Pullen knew most of what could be taught regarding survival and fighting in the jungle. Fifty years beforehand, the battle for Plaman Mapu, Borneo had been fought. That fight convinced the British army that a specialized group of soldiers trained in jungle warfare should be raised. Based on this decision, Pullen, along with an elite group, had been trained and then seen combat in Nigeria, fighting Boko Haram and in Tunisia against Daesh. Before BATSUB he had been in Somalia after pirates. Pullen and four others, dressed in their MTP combat uniforms, crouched by the side of the narrow trail leading to the Hondo. This was the fifth operation he had headed, and he felt confident of its success. He and his small group had the knowledge to pull off the ambush and they would do so quickly, efficiently and safely. Once it was over, his three months were finished, and they would be trucked back to Ladyville to find out what awaited him next.

There was the sound of a muffled exhaust and a Suzuki RMX450 off-road bike came into view. Its rider must have known the terrain because it showed no lights and headed unerringly to the landing area by the river and stopped. He removed his helmet and looked carefully around but didn't notice the prepared ambush. He took two items from a pocket, one a small walkie-talkie, and spoke into it. Then he dismounted and walked to the river edge and scanned the water. The other turned out to be a flashlight, and he keyed it in the direction of the other bank. A long and a short flash were seen, and a marine motor started. The wave-runner was being readied. Headlights could now be seen coming down the path and a heavily loaded pickup came into view. It halted a few yards from the river and a group of armed men fanned out and took up positions around the vehicle. Three others climbed on to the cargo bed and threw off a covering tarp.

Pullen tapped the shoulder of the man next to him and signaled with his fingers that there were ten smugglers in all. He nodded and passed on the message, readying his incendiary grenade, and sure the others would be doing the same. Then he tapped his companion's shoulder.

The soldier shouted out loudly in Spanish *"Alto! No te muevas. Baja las armas y pon tus manos en el aire o disparemos.*"*

Right away one of the security group leveled an AK47 at the sound of the voice and opened fire, other smugglers did the same. The rounds were high, the attacked men not knowing the exact position of the patrol. Five thermite grenades came flying from the forest, landing in and around the truck and exploding with bright flashes. Whatever happened, the cargo would be destroyed. The patrol returned fire from their well-prepared positions and immediately half a dozen smugglers were hit. Four threw their arms into the air, two of them not quick enough to avoid the final fusillade from the L85A2's the patrol members carried. It was now light as the drug cargo burned and as he stood up, Pullen noted the wave-runner cut loose the two rafts and gun its engine, turning for the opposite shore. He raised his rifle and picked out the passenger on the runner. As he fired, the man opened up with a wild burst of rifle fire and rounds whizzed past his ear. Then a locomotive crashed into him, knocking him to the ground. As he struggled to rise, he noticed a burning sensation in his left arm and he dropped his weapon and stepped backwards. Everything spun around, and he fell down, dazed and confused. He didn't realize it at the time, but he had become a statistic in the three categories covering gunshot wounds.

a) *The odds are you won't pay any attention to the distant sound of a gunshot.*
b) *Few people ever hear the sound of a bullet whizzing past them.*
c) *A miniscule percentage of the population are struck by projectiles.*

He had noticed shots, heard a bullet pass close and then been struck. However, he was still alive. Twenty minutes later a very sore, and soon to be unconscious, Staff Sergeant Pullen received a pain shot, was placed on a stretcher, and trucked back to Price Barracks.

* 'Stop. Don't move. Throw down your arms, put your hands in the air or we'll shoot.'

CHAPTER IV

'A nice clean wound'

There was a light touch on his forehead.

"The doctor is here Staff Pullen."

Pullen opened his eyes for the first time in twelve hours and peered upwards into the dark face of a Medical Orderly.

"He's conscious Sir."

Turning his head slightly hurt like hell but he observed one of the Medical Center doctors come into view and blinked in acknowledge.

"Awake at last eh Staff? I'm Major Teith. Doc to you. Well, you had a good rest that's for sure! I'll tell you what happened because you were out when you arrived here last night. The medics gave you a shot when they arrived at the ambush site. You were apparently in a lot of pain and suffering from a bullet wound in your left arm and blunt trauma of the left chest where an AK round struck your Osprey vest. I'll show you that later. Anyway, the Osprey prevented it from penetrating. You have bruising on your upper left torso and a nice clean penetration wound about four inches above your left elbow. The round passed through and hit a few blood vessels but nothing else. It's just below the skin surface and should clear up in a few weeks. We need to check you out now to view how things are progressing. You had surgery for the wound last night and we did x-rays on the blunt trauma, but they show no broken bones. You have an IV in your right arm, we've been pumping anti-biotics through that as well as glucose. Shock has vanished, so we have to feed you in a few minutes. You will be hurting for a few days that's a given. Those Osprey's stop a bullet from going through, but the trauma is problematic. However, better than a sharp stick in the eye as they say. Now, I'll be on my rounds. I'll be back about fourteen hundred hours. There are two of your boys waiting to see you. Eat first. The orderlies can clean you up and you may talk with them for five minutes. Then sleep until I get back, and we'll see what has to be done. You were lucky Staff. The band you intercepted were all killed. By the way, the Mexicans picked up a man on the west bank of the Hondo when we told them what happened. He had a 5.56 wound. Probably lose his leg. Those HandK's pack a hell of a punch! Just relax Staff. I'll be back."

He saw crowns on the doctor's shoulders. A Major indeed! Very VIP.

"Ok Staff. Let's get started."

Pullen glanced up and noticed the orderly who had woken him up, standing by the bed.

"I'm Corporal Desmond. 'Des' for short. I'll be taking care of you. The Combat Medical Technician who came in with you said he put on a pressure bandage and gave you a half a cup of salt and soda solution when you complained of being thirsty. You've been here since about nine last night, it's eight in the morning here now. I'm sure you want something to drink so I've got tea here. Drink that and we'll get you clean. In ten minutes, when you're ready, your mates can come in for a bit. Then it's breakfast and rest, rest, and more rest. You've got a clean wound. No problems as long as we keep an eye on it. The bruising is severe. I'll get a mirror and you can see it when we wash you. Don't worry about it too much, it's ugly and hurts but it will clear up in a week or so. Better than a penetration wound let me tell you! Here's the tea."

He helped Pullen sit up and drink. His mouth was very dry, and he had a headache, but he was alive. That was the important thing. They cleaned him up and put on pajamas. Then they let in two of the patrol members who had been with him. Together, they re-hashed the action and he was told that they recovered ten bodies. The Mexican's had captured the man on the jet-ski that he had shot. A good night's work, except for his wounding. When they were shooed out five minutes later, he was exhausted. He managed to eat some toast and scrambled eggs and they showed him the bruises. Then he fell asleep. Major Teith came back at 215pm. Captain Donavon, the Special Group commander, arrived with him. Donavon extended a hand and Pullen shook it.

"Well done Staff Pullen, another shipment destroyed! Sorry about the wounds. Preliminary reports clear you and the patrol from any wrongdoing regarding the deaths of the smugglers. They were warned, and they decided to fight it out. Poor decision! Your injuries sustained in the conflict were thankfully, not life threatening. Nasty but recoverable. We received a note from the Mexicans thanking us for our assistance. They said the rafts were of an advanced design and not immediately replaceable."

"You, Staff are getting a Mention in Dispatches for what you did. The Belize Prime Minister is also sending a personal letter of thanks. Those rafts were very valuable! Finally, you are getting leave. You've been here for eight months under constant pressure, you need a rest from that and time to recover from your wounds. So, it's thirty days at home for you. Major Teith will tell you when you go, and I'll be in frequently to check on how things are progressing." He turned to Teith. "He's all yours Major."

"Staff. We have to monitor everything, but I would guess two weeks will get you out of here, proving we have no complications. I do not expect any. You, for your part must stay quiet for a few days until we are sure the bullet wound is on its way to healing. After that is sorted out, the rehabilitation people take over and you'll be pushed and pulled every day to loosen up those bruised muscles and make sure the arm is completely functional. Like Major Donovan, I'll be around all the time. Any questions?"

"No Sir." He said, saluting.

"Good." Turning, the two Majors both returned the salute and walked out.

"Congratulations on the MID Staff! When you're ready, I'll make sure we've got the insignia for your uniform. Speaking of which, you definitely need new MTP's. Yours were covered in blood and we destroyed them. Plenty of time. Now get some sleep!"

Pullen knew he was hurting and did what Des had said. He slept. Then he woke, and he slept again on and off for four days. After that he began to recover, and the medical reports confirmed that things were going well. The wound had scabbed over, and the lurid bruises were slowly losing some of their brightness. Everything still hurt, but he was sure he was getting better. He was eating well and after a week, actually craved for a Belikin Lighthouse lager, something Desmond smuggled in for him the next day.

CHAPTER V

'Home, for a while'

Two weeks later, February 4th, Pullen boarded an army 'Atlas' transport aircraft returning from a re-supply mission, to the garrison at Mildenhall in Suffolk. Convenient for Pullen who lived in Southwold. He arrived at nine on Monday morning February 5th and after buying a cheap cellular telephone at the base store and activating it, he checked in with the Royal Anglian Regiment. They were based in Bury St. Edmonds, close to the airfield. He had his large bag taken there for storage. Once he learned of the army's plans for him, he could have it sent to where he needed it. He took his smaller duffle and walked outside to wait at the bus stop. It didn't take long. A BMW pulled up and the passenger window was lowered. He could see the driver looking across at him. Young, pretty, and like many before her, seemingly fascinated by the tall, tanned, blue eyed, Staff Sergeant wearing a cold weather parka with the hood down on his shoulders.

"I'm going to Lowestoft. Can I give you a lift?"

"Thank you, Madam. I'm for Southwold so anywhere close would be appreciated."

"Put your bag in the back and climb aboard."

He did as he was told, hiding a smile. The car felt warm, and he could sense the expensive perfume. He waited for her to open the conversation.

"What a great suntan you have!"

"Well, you know the army. They send you to the all the best resorts!"

"I bet you weren't at any resort! You're too thin! All they do is feed you at those places. I know, I took a cruise out of Miami last year and gained five pounds! No. You were somewhere hot, and it wasn't a luxury hotel. Am I right?"

"Yes Ma'am, correct."

"So, where were you?"

He realized where the conversation was going, and having played the game many times before, he knew all the responses. He faced her.

"Ma'am. You are aware this is Mildenhall, and it's a military base. Therefore, you must realize that all personnel are warned about foreign spies and how they entice innocent young servicemen to give up secrets. I have to inform you, I won't spill the beans without a struggle!"

She laughed and offered her hand to him.

"I'm Audrey. I just dropped off my husband, Captain Steven Williamson. He's on his way to Germany for a month. Accountant he is. Checks all the pennies and makes sure no one is paying too much for toilet paper. Glamorous job that! I bet you have a more interesting duty?"

"I'm John. Now I'm convinced you are an enemy agent! OK I give in! I'm on leave from Belize. Hence the suntan."

"I guessed it would be something like that!" She sighed.

"You look the part. My bloke joined the Defense Technical Undergraduate Scheme and became an officer who checks receipts. Just my luck. Anyway, I'll go through Thetford and Halesworth, drop you and turn north to Lowestoft. Do you have a place to stay?"

"Yes Ma'am. I do."

"Because I've got an apartment on Water Lane near the college. It will be lonely for a few weeks if you get what I mean."

Pullen understood exactly what she had in mind.

"Ma'am. I'm staying at The Swan Hotel. My brother and his family are meeting me there. We haven't seen each other for a year so I'll be busy. Thanks for the offer. I only wish circumstances were different!" He meant that when he said it, but he knew he was in no condition for a couple of weeks of strenuous exercise!

"Oh well. Never mind. I thought it might be too good to be true."

"The lift is appreciated, anyway."

"I'll drop you in Halesworth. By the station. You can get a cab to Southwold."

The next hour passed by with few words exchanged between them. Pulled again thanked her as he alighted in Halesworth and looked about for a taxi. The driver he found was happy to pick up a ten-mile fare.

As they left the town, Pullen shook his head and thought how easy it could have been. However, he had to get back to normal, and needed rest. He hoped the mention of the Swan Hotel would put Audrey off the scent if she tried to find him. The Swan was a good mile from where he was going.

From the taxi he called his mother. She was very pleased to hear he would soon be home. In Southwold it was cold as he had himself dropped off near the pier. He wanted to look at the sea. Walking quickly, he arrived at the house shortly before twelve. His elderly mother, who lived alone in a cottage in Trinity Close, was there to greet him.

"John! It's been two years! How are you?"

She ushered him in and had him leave his bag in the small hallway. "Come into the kitchen, I've had the kettle on for half an hour waiting."

They sat at the wooden table and Pullen explained that he had been Somalia and then Central America on training missions. No combat he assured her. He had however, been involved in a traffic accident and had slightly hurt his arm, nothing else. The last thing he wanted was for his mother to worry. He spun a few tales of spiders and snakes in the bush but carefully refrained from mentioning any of the fierce engagements which he had been part of. She relaxed and laughed as they sipped their tea.

"I see you have two medals John."

"Yes mum. That's the Order of Belize and that silver oak leaf on it is a 'Mention in Dispatches'. They give these to foreigners who served there, nothing else." He purposely bent the truth to keep her from fretting about him. It had been awarded for the accumulative actions during his service there. It was the second highest medal for non-Belizeans.

John Pullen had left home to join the army at seventeen and a half and had been back only twice in the past six years. His father, a Fire Brigade Assistant Divisional Officer, had died at a factory blaze twenty years previously. He didn't remember much about him, but he had left the cottage paid for and his mother collected a good pension from the Government for his service. Pullen allotted her two hundred pounds a month, money she said was not needed and had been deposited in an account to be given to him when she eventually passed.

She had her gardening and the Woman's Institute which kept her busy. She was friendly with the neighbors, all elderly and gossiped with them a few hours a week. It was a quiet life, but she was content, looking forward to Pullen's monthly letter he always sent.

It was warm and cozy in the house and after eating a crab sandwich for lunch, he walked to the small, second bedroom and after unpacking, slept until almost six o'clock. His mother was watching TV when he glanced into the living room. She muted the remote and asked what he wanted to do. He said he would grab something to eat and would sleep some more. She served him baked chicken and vegetables and sat with him, drinking tea, while he ate.

"John. You seem tired. Finish up here and get some rest. Tomorrow you can decide what you want to do." That's what he appreciated about his mum, she didn't bother him with demands or questions. He was happy at home in an environment like that. He wandered off to bed and slept the clock round until nine the next morning.

"Can I get you some breakfast" asked his mother when he finally got out of bed.

"Thanks mum, eggs and bacon, please."

"There's today's newspaper on the table there. Have a read while I get things cooking here. Will you be here for lunch? I have to go to the shops later."

"I thought I might go by St. Edmonds and afterwards drop in for a pint at the Lord Nelson and get something at the bar there. Back about one thirty, and I'll need a nap. What about dinner tonight?"

His mother looked pleased. "How about liver and onions John? You always liked that as a boy! Say about six?"

"Fine mum. Haven't had that for years. Something to enjoy for a change!"

He read the Southwold Gazette while waiting for his food and smiled as he examined the benign articles. Dawdling over his meal, he pulled up his sleeve and looked at the bullet wound. The angry inflammation had vanished and there was just a reddish dent in the skin where the round had gone in and a bigger indentation where it had exited. He washed up his crockery, despite the protests of his mother who said she would take care of things. He got up dried everything and let her put it away.

After a shower and a careful examination of his bruises which seemed to be improving, he dressed and walked to the cemetery at St. Edmund's and spent five minutes there. It was a short walk to the Lord Nelson. The time was eleven thirty. A cold but bright day and quiet as one might expect in an English seaside town in early February. As he turned the corner from Trinity to East Street, an ancient, but shiny, black Rolls Royce passed him and parked outside the Lord Nelson. A driver, wearing a cap sat in the front seat. In front of the pub a man in a tweed jacket alighted and went through the door.

Pullen arrived and saw the pub was almost empty. He ambled through to the snug bar at the rear and entered. The only person there was the stranger he had seen coming in with the tweed coat. He sat at the bar speaking on his cellphone. A bartender appeared, and Pullen ordered an Adnams Broadside. It was a little cold in the bar, but he noticed an electric heater in one corner doing its best to change things so early in the day. He was wearing an old army olive green commando jersey over a heavy T shirt and green light-weight army trousers. It happened to be the only jersey he owned. Jungle warfare postings were all warm weather.

His beer arrived, and he sipped it, relishing the almost forgotten taste of a locally brewed ale. When he raised his head, the stranger nodded at him.

"A little chilly don't you think? Sun's out so perhaps it'll get warmer."

"Yes Sir. I'm not used to this climate myself. I prefer it a lot hotter."

"Well Southwold is blessed by good weather starting around April. Will you be here then?

"'Fraid not. I've only two weeks before I return."

He smiled at the man, wondering who he was. Somehow, he seemed familiar. He appeared to be in his late forties, showed no gray in his hair and was slimly built. Then as he turned to speak he could see clearly his tie. It was silk, and the red castles showed clearly against the blue background. Royal Anglian Regiment, Pullen's outfit.

The man spoke again. "Would you by any chance be in the armed forces young man?"

Pullen grinned. "Yes sir. John Pullen, Staff Sergeant. On detached service from 1st Battalion Royal Anglian."

The man stood and held out his hand. "Pleased to meet you Staff Pullen. I'm The Viscount Lynn. Sid to you."

Then Pullen realized that Lynn was one of the largest Suffolk landowners and said to be a very rich man. He had been Major General, The Viscount Lynn, Commanding Officer of the Regiment, seven years before when he had first volunteered.

"Thank you, Sir. You were in command when I joined up in two thousand eleven. I did my basic and was fortunate to be picked for jungle warfare. I've been all over the place in warm climates, but this is only the third time I've been home in those seven years. It's strange."

"John. I'm going to call you John because the last thing we need is military protocol interrupting a quiet pint! So, it's Sid and John OK?"

"Yes sir, I mean yes Sid." Lynn smiled.

"I'm an amateur detective John. You're not just visiting here. This isn't somewhere most people would pick in February. You sat down gingerly when you came in, I noticed that. The left arm, you favor it slightly, not letting it take any weight. My guess is that you were sent on leave to recover from an accident of some sort or another? Somewhere warm from your color. You're jungle warfare, detached duty. How am I doing?" He gazed directly into Pullen's suntanned face and nodded.

Pullen had to laugh. "Well Sid, you hit the nail on the head. A clean AK47 round through my left arm and bruising from a Kevlar kick left chest. It's all clearing up nicely and I'll be back on full duty in two weeks."

"I know the drill. Call Regiment and see what's happening. They'll ask Special Forces for a status report and if they need a JW expert anywhere. Of course, they always want them! There's so few of you. Then off you go and the cycle will start again. Was this the first wound?"

"Yes, and hopefully the last!"

The Viscount raised his hand, and the bartender pulled two pints.

Lynn looked at Pullen. "John. I have security clearances so please don't worry about speaking with me. So you'll be comfortable, I'll give you a direct number to the Regiment's present Commander. His name is Major General Sir William Fredericks. If you wish you can mention my name and ask him if you may speak freely with me."

"I'm sure who you are Sir. I don't need to call."

"Thank you, John. Your confidence is appreciated."

He examined Pullen carefully, seemingly trying to make up his mind about something. Then he nodded and commenced speaking.

"In a few minutes my associate, Sir Paul Soames should arrive. Paul is with the Diplomatic Corps. Permanent Under Secretary. He lives close to my place at Reydon. Believe it or not, there's no pub there! That's why we meet here at the Lord Nelson! Anyway, for the past year we've been planning an expedition to the Mato Grosso in Brazil. I would think you attended CIGS and that you know the country. We are well advanced in our work and the departure date has been set for the 1st. It's been decided our party should consist of nine persons, no more. Paul and I, two guides, three very experienced canoe-men doubling as porters. That leaves two places to fill. We have excellent relations with the Government of Brazil and all the necessary permissions to explore in the area are in place. The Brazilians insist we take security in the form of jungle experts. Have you ever heard of a soldier by the name of Thiago Perez? He's an instructor at CIGS and our Brazilian contact says he is the best. They are arranging to get him assigned to us on detached service."

"I know Thiago well. I traveled home with him to Dantos near the Xingu River when we were at the school. A good soldier!"

"It's a small world John! Now, I haven't told you what we will be doing. It's all to do with a fellow called Lt. Colonel Percy Harrison Fawcett. He disappeared in the Mato Grosso in 1925 and despite quite a few expeditions to search for him. Nothing has been found." He paused.

"On 20 April 1925 his expedition departed from Cuiabá. It was Fawcett and his son Jack and a friend of Jack's, Raleigh Rimmell, neither had any jungle experience and were criticized in some English newspapers as 'fools and glory seekers'. In addition, there were two Brazilian laborers', two horses, eight mules, and a pair of dogs. A last letter was dated 29 May 1925 saying he was ready to go into unexplored territory with only Jack and Rimmell. They would cross the Upper Xingu, a southeastern tributary of the Amazon, and head east, never to be seen again. Many people assume local Indians killed them. One tribe has a story the three traveled to the east, and after four days they noticed no more smoke from camp fires." He signaled to the bartender.

"There are a lot of stories from the region about the tribes. Some are said to be very unfriendly, and another takes care of a giant pink Dolphin in a river. These are all tales and there's nothing firm." The drinks arrived.

"I became interested in the story as a young boy at Wellington and a fellow pupil Paul Soames, took up the challenge and is now an expert on Brazil and the Fawcett matter. He's studied archeology and Pre-Colombian history. I myself got into Sandhurst and joined the army, Paul was accepted at Cambridge and after, chose the Diplomatic Corps. He married the daughter of the Brazilian Ambassador. They are divorced now but still on excellent terms. She lives in Sao Paulo. One of their sons David, is an up-and-coming light in the Brazilian Ministry of the Interior, the other Victor, is a Major in some secret military organization. Most fortunate for us!"

Lynn sat back and sipped his beer, looking quietly across at his companion. "Where are you staying John?"

"Around the corner. My mother has a house there. I don't see her very often."

"That's the soldiers life John. That's the way it is."

"Yes. You're right. I must say though I'm happy with my lot. The service had been fair with me."

They heard a door open and a moment later when Pullen turned around he observed a very fit looking man coming into the bar.

"Hello Sid! I see you and your friend have full glasses! Let Harry get me one and you can do introductions." He waved at the bartender and turned back to them. He extended a hand to Pullen.

"I'm Paul Soames. God morning."

"This is Staff Sergeant John Pullen, Paul. We've been talking."

"Pleased to meet you sir." Said Pullen, taking the outstretched hand.

"Paul to you John. Now, tell me, what have you two been plotting?"

"John's from my Regiment. He's a specialist in jungle warfare. He met Thiago Perez and has been to the Xingu! How about that?"

"Ahhh! The plot thickens!"

"Yes, indeed it does Paul. Now we should, I believe, get to know John better. Then let's have lunch. Depending upon our talk perhaps we can move forward a little more with our project. I've given John the background so let's ask him a few questions that we don't have answers for yet.

They sat at the bar and sipped their beer for the next hour, quizzing Pullen about his jungle experience, and especially about Brazil. Soames then talked about the mission.

He told Pullen they were in the provisioning process and he was not surprised to find that they had been purchasing the best of equipment and supplies. The area they wished to explore happened to be in the northeast part of Mato Grosso state. Numerous waterways meet there to form the Xingu river. Surrounding the river are 2.64 million hectares of land that form the Xingu National Park and Indigenous Peoples Preserve. This was where Percy Fawcett was lost and where they would look for him.

Gear would go to Manaus and then by boat down the Amazon for about 800 miles. Then down the Xingu river through the Xingu National Park. The boat would anchor there and act as a base camp while the expedition took canoes along a tributary of the Xingu, the Olgo.

Harry, the barman, bought out menus.

Lynn recommended the Halibut, and they ordered still sitting at the bar. As they ate, Lynn told Pullen of the dangers involved. He said there had been quite a few expeditions looking for Fawcett. Legends say as many as a hundred men had died in the jungle, and a quite a few had vanished without a trace. These were stories with no verification whatsoever. In 1996, a team of Fawcett-hunters led by a wealthy businessman named James Lynch was captured by an unfriendly tribe and held for ransom. They only escaped with their lives after giving up $30,000 worth of equipment.

"Now you see why we need security." He eyed Soames who nodded.

"John. For the past twelve months Paul and myself have been on a regime of exercise to get fit. After all, we are both in our early '50s so we needed to make sure we are strong enough to face the Matto Grosso. We both run about four miles every day and spend another hour lifting weights and doing other cardio workouts. The last time we visited a doctor he was amazed at our stress tests. We passed with flying colors. So, we believe we have the strength and resistance to hold up on this trip. Twice a week we go canoeing on the Blythe. We paddle about ten miles and then back again. We're ready!" He looked at Pullen.

"One last thing. We have formed a corporation which is used for all business associated with the expedition. It's called FADE for Fawcett Discovery Expedition. Purchases of equipment, other expenses, in fact everything goes through the corporation. Would you consider joining us John? I can arrange things with the Regiment if you are willing?"

Pullen held out a hand and Lynn and Soames, took it. "Good, now let's get down to business! We have all the permits and the boat, porters and guides, will be ready for us on arrival at Manaus. All the equipment and supplies are at my place, Reydon Hall. You John must see those. I'm thinking it might be a good idea if you move in with us. Paul can do the same starting tonight. In that way we are all close together and can solve and problems that come up while we pack and check everything. When we get to Manaus we will run through the equipment with the men. Once on the river-boat it will take about five days to travel down to the Xingu. On the way we open the containers for a last check, and to have everything ready. The guides and porters were recruited by Thiago from his hometown of Dantos." He took a notebook from his jacket pocket and consulted it. "Let me have your number John. I'll call before I send the car to your place later. One last thing, I'll be taking lots of photographs and video starting tomorrow. We will need a good record of the expedition. Don't get worried when I whip out my little digital Fujifilm X100F. It will give us everything we need. I'm taking a Sony Coolpix as well, as backup. They can be downloaded to our laptops whenever we have time. Now, you must say your goodbye's. I'll drop Paul off and send my driver for you, say five o'clock. You can rest and pack your stuff. We'll meet for dinner at seven at Reydon Hall. Completely casual so don't bring anything formal."

They finished their beers and Pullen walked back to Trinity Close. His mother was watching the television but turned it off as he came through the door.

"Hello John. How's the Lord Nelson?"

"Good mum. I met Viscount Lynn there. He was the Commanding Officer when I joined the Regiment."

"I didn't realize you were friends with him John. You never mentioned it?"

"No mum. I'm not a mate of his. He was the General! Anyway, He's asked me to join him on a trip to Brazil. Detached duty. They want me to move over to Reydon Hall this afternoon that's where all the planning is being done and it's a lot of work. Moving out at five today. I'll only be five miles away, so we'll keep in touch."

"Well. If you say so John. You must promise to call me though!"

"I will mum, don't worry!"

It was almost two o'clock, and he felt tired. He retired to his bedroom and dropped off until about four thirty. His cell-phone range at ten to five. It was Lynn saying the car would arrive in fifteen minutes. He said goodbye to his mother and walked to the end of Trinity Close carrying his bags. As he turned the corner the Rolls stopped, and the driver helped him put his luggage in the trunk.

"I'm Douglas Sir. It's a short ride to the Hall. Station Road then up to Wangford. You know the way having lived here."

After a ten-minute ride they entered a large driveway off the Wangford Road, passing under a latticed arch of wrought iron in the form of a line of deer jumping. It was a good two hundred yards to the Hall, a classical Georgian residence. Pullen counted twenty windows across the second-floor level.

Sid Lynn stood in the magnificent doorway waiting. "Hello John. Welcome to Reydon Hall."

"What a beautiful house! Georgian style isn't it?"

"Right. Built by James Gibbs in 1750. You would recognize his name if I mentioned he designed Burlington House on Piccadilly. Wonderful old place the Hall! Now come in, Douglas will take the bags, and I'll show you everything."

They entered into a large reception area furnished with comfortable armchairs and couches. There was a smaller partitioned space off to the right which Lynn said was the library. Dark leather volumes lined the walls and there was a long table in the center topped with an antique world globe. A wide staircase lead to the second story. Off to the left was a formal dining room and through a passage to the rear, several closed doors lined the route. They came out of the shaded passageway and onto a beautiful indoor terrace with a huge fireplace and French doors overlooking the striking hedged gardens.

"Not much in the way of flowers right now John, but in spring and summer there's a fine view here. Back there about half a mile are the farm buildings, stables and cottages that house many of our laborers. Back in 2013 my father died, and I inherited. It's a big job the estate. Father knew a little, but we had a professional Manager. I then retired after serving nearly 30 years to oversee things. I'm still learning. Our son Albert, finished his agricultural degree at Reading University over a year back and is now working on a farm in Queensland to get experience. When he returns, he'll assist Herbert Smith, the present Manager. At least one person in the family will understand what he's doing in the future."

He took Pullen to one side and through a hallway. There he paused. There was a digital lock on the door. Lynn used the number pad to enter a code, and they walked through into a huge space that contained all kinds of equipment laid out in rows.

"Here we are then. It's all ready to pack but I want you to examine every item first and let me know what you think. It should take a couple of days. I've spoken to General Fredericks at Regiment. He has no problems seconding you to us for up to four months. He'll take care of the Ministry of Defense side and you'll have orders delivered here tomorrow. Very efficient is Fred! Paul should arrive in a few minutes. Douglas can take you up to your room now. Please treat the house as your own! As well as Douglas, who takes care of all my personal needs, we have Cook. That's with a capital letter 'C'! A housekeeper, and Maria who is my wife's helper. You'll meet Anastasia at dinner tonight. Cook will barbeque steaks and Paul will complain when he is told he can't help!" He laughed.

"We'll eat outside, it's a bit chilly but I have commercial patio heaters that adapt halogen fire tubes as heating elements, and they can produce up to 1500 watts. It'll probably be warm enough but make sure you put a sweater on and remember, it's informal. Come down about seven and we'll have a drink on the inside terrace and eat afterwards."

Pullen followed Douglas up the stairs. He noticed a stairlift installed to one side. His room was at the back of the house and had been obviously aired out. There was fresh bed linen and an electric blanket on the bed. Bottled water stood on the night table and the room had its own bathroom and shower. Douglas took off his sweater, rested on the pillow and looked at his watch. It was five thirty. He set the alarm for half-past six, leaned back, and slept.

He was awake before his alarm sounded. It felt cold. A thermostat on the wall showed the temperature was 9 Celsius, about 48 Fahrenheit. He turned it up to 25, close to what he was used to at 77. The room soon got warmer. Taking his toiletry bag, he cleaned his teeth and tidied up in the bathroom. The large window looked out over the rear of the property and the gardens. They gave way to a wood and beyond he saw buildings, and cottages in the distance. Visibility was lessening now that the sun had dropped below the horizon and he stood watching as it became dark and stars appeared in the sky. He checked his watch and noticed it was five minutes before seven. Time to go downstairs. Lights were on and he walked slowly back through the passage he had been through earlier and on onto the terrace. There were overhead spotlights illuminating the paintings on the walls. His gaze was drawn to the fireplace where a wood fire burned. It was a noisy blaze, and he walked across to where it spluttered. Sap dripped from the wood and spat as the flames consumed the logs. A piece of a green branch cracked as the heat reached it and sparks flew up the chimney. He was enjoying the spectacle when a voice called to him.

"I love a fire at this time of day don't you Staff Sergeant Pullen?"

He turned and for the first time saw someone sitting in the shadows. He couldn't see clearly in the gloom, but he realized it had to be Lynn's wife.

"Lady Anastasia. My apologies, I didn't see anyone when I came into the room." He lowered his head in a slight bow.

"Beautifully done sir! You chose exactly the right words! I always sit over here when we have a fire. From the shade you get quite a different perspective than if you are close. Besides, I'm scared that one of those cinders will come leaping out and set me ablaze! I bet I was doing what you were, enjoying the fireworks!"

"Yes, you're correct."

She rolled towards him in the electric wheelchair where she was sitting. Holding out her hand looked up at him.

"I'm Anastasia, Sid's wife. You are John Pullen." He took the hand.

"Sorry about this." She indicated her extended right leg. "Been riding all my life and never had an accident, then three weeks back I had a small fall and was told to use this contraption for a month. After that I can be up and about again. The doctor's say nothing's broken but there's ligament bruising."

"My sympathies. What a great house you have. This is the room that's captured my heart though. The fire is magnificent.!"

"Douglas does it. He's good at most things but fires bring out his special skills. Let me get you a drink."

She spun the chair around towards a low bar. "What's it to be John?"

"A beer please."

She reached forward and opened a small refrigerator. Taking out a bottle of Corona beer she held it out to him. "I bet you don't want a glass?"

"Correct. This is fine thanks."

"So. You are to join Sid and Paul on their journey. I've been helping with ordering items and correspondence, there's so much to do! My husband says you're a jungle expert, so I have one request to make." Moving forward she took his hand.

"Please take care of him!" Pullen could hear the anxiety in her voice.

"Anastasia. Your husband was a soldier. I'll be there but I assure you he won't need to be babied. His kind never does. Take my word for it!"

"Thank you. I'll not mention that again."

"What won't you mention my dear?" Said Lynn, walking into the terrace.

"About being careful Sid. That's all. Now, your usual?"

"Yes please. John, I see you've met Anastasia. Amongst her many talents is the ability to make a wonderful Martini!"

They watched as she did just that. Preparing the drink on the bar and finally shaking the silver container and pouring it into a glass. Lynn took it and sat down next to Pullen.

"Can I get one as well Annie?" said Soames, who walked in carrying a manila envelope.

"Of course, my dear. Here we go." She repeated her manipulations and handed him his drink.

27

"Thank you. Here comes Cook with the makings." He indicated an aproned man pushing a rolling cart loaded with dishes, making his way across the room. "Hold on Cook, I'll open up for you."

He opened the glass doors, and the cart was pushed through to the terrace. Pullen noticed the heaters outside, glowing and throwing off warmth.

"Thank you, Sir Paul. Now I'll take care of things and you may return to your Martini."

Soames came back in grumbling. "Bloody Cook. Won't let me help with the barbeque!"

Anastasia spoke. "That's because you burned the chicken that time! How are you to be trusted after that?"

They all smiled.

Soames sipped his Martini and addressed Pullen.

"Now it's time to tell John a little more about the Fawcett story. I gave you a brief outline of what is known. Fawcett wrote a last letter that was dated 29 May 1925, to his wife from what he called 'Dead Horse Camp'. He said he was ready to go into unexplored territory with only Jack and Raleigh. A runner delivered that message but what is not generally knowledge is that along with that correspondence, Raleigh Rimmell also sent a letter. We didn't know for sure, but we surmised that Fawcett may well have asked him if he wanted to send a note home along with his own. As it turned out, he did."

Pullen looked up, surprised. "Rimmell?"

"Yes, he had been sick. a foot infection. He wrote to his father and sent the letter with the same messenger. The contents were not made known to Fawcett. I have a copy of that letter right here." He held up the brown manila envelope.

"The father kept it and it was passed on with other family documents when he died in 1937. It passed to Raleigh's brother's son who thought nothing of it and left it inside an old chest in the attic of his house in Halesworth, which you know is ten miles west of here. I traveled there about two years back on a hunch and made enquiries. As Sid has told you, Fawcett has been an interest of both of us since boyhood. Anyway, Drake Rimmell, a retired local surveyor, was only too happy to help. He said he had a letter from Raleigh in his possession. He's close to ninety years old but still very sharp. Although I confirmed it was Fawcett I was interested in, he extracted a promise from me. I agreed that anything we found of Raleigh's, would be returned to him and failing us encountering any hard relics, I would provide him with the full story. He in return wouldn't mention the letter to anyone."

He glanced at his audience.

"The letter convinced us to move forward and mount this expedition. Take a look."

He handed it to Pullen who opened it and read the single sheet.

'Dear Father

We are on the north Xingu. Fawcett says this is 'Dead Horse Camp'. A terrible name in my opinion. But I am accustomed to his idiosyncrasies. We are camped at the mouth of a small river with four tiny islands in the rocky estuary, we leave with the mules tomorrow to follow the river and I only wish we had access to canoe's. My sign is R >. My feet are a little better but still painful. I hope I can keep up on the journey. This must be a short note as the messenger leaves momentarily. I'll say goodbye now and trust I can write upon our triumphant return from discovering 'Z'.

Your Loving son, Raleigh.'

Pullen looked up from the page with an inquisitive glance at Soames and Lynn. It was the Viscount, after a brief glance at Soames, who spoke.

"Yes. I can guess what you are thinking. First, Raleigh Rimmell was not happy with Fawcett's leadership. You know what that means John as a military man. If men have no confidence in their leader things go wrong. Two criticisms are leveled in the letter. The name of the camp and the fact that they were using foot power and mules, instead of canoe's. Rimmell has given us a clue as to where they were headed. Remember 'R arrow'? Seems like Raleigh intended to leave marks along the route. We will have to wait. All the headings Fawcett wrote in his last letter have turned out to be erroneous or outright false. Four islands at the mouth of a small river? We have access to satellite mapping of the whole region. There are dozens of rivers in approximately the area Fawcett said he was. None open at their mouth to four small islands."

He sat back and indicated Soames to continue. Sir Paul spoke.

"The fact that we are unable to find our four tiny islands is not a disaster. Over the past 90 years the river has changed as do all waterways in this area. Everything depends on the rainfall and we believe that at some time, a particularly heavy fall of water could, could have washed a small island away. We located two sites where there's three atolls'. Only one river mouth seems to be 'rocky' so that's the target. The river is called the Olgo. Now, the reference to 'Z'. Based on Fawcett's research he formulated an idea that there existed a 'lost City' he named 'Z' in in the Mato Grosso region of Brazil. He thought a civilization once existed there and that there may be ruins surviving. Fawcett also found a document known as Manuscript 512, written after explorations made in Bahia state, and housed at the National Library of Rio de Janeiro. It is believed to be compiled by Portuguese bandits headed by João da Silva Guimarães. In 1753, he wrote that he had discovered the ruins of a City containing arches, a statue, and a temple with hieroglyphics; the City is described in detail without providing a specific location. This could be similar to 'Z'. I believe that if 'Z' exists, it must be near water. That's a prerequisite for any population.

Soames walked to the bar and poured what remained of the Martini mix into his glass.

"So, there we have it. I must say we have not shared all this information with the Brazilian Ministry of the Interior. We made our original requests based on an expedition to find Fawcett's remains, nothing more. However, anything else we encounter would of course be a bonus."

He drained his glass as Cook opened the terrace and walked over to the group.

"M'Lord, m'Lady, gentlemen. The meal is ready to serve." They followed him onto the outdoor terrace. It was warm with the two large heaters blazing and four floodlights in the corners shone brightly upwards, bouncing off the trees to provide light over the whole area. A rustic wooden table was laid with bone white dinner plates flanked by forks and large, sharp-looking, steak knives. There was a colorful salad in a wooden bowl and toasted bread on a flat tray. Red and white bottles of wine stood at the tables end along with glasses. The odor of the charcoal roasted meat was delicious.

Cook carried the platter of steaks and charred vegetables to the table and placed it in the middle. He addressed Lynn. "With your permission my Lord. All steaks are broiled medium. If anyone wants theirs cooked more, please let me know now and It will merely take two minutes."

No one did, and they sat down together to enjoy the meal. Lynn spoke.

"The meat is from our farm. This batch we set to age after Christmas. We have a fridge dedicated for that. You don't want any other foods close; the meat can pick up their flavors. We installed a small electric fan inside to circulate the air. Then meat goes on a wire rack elevated over a drip tray. Close up the 'fridge and leave it. Wait six weeks, open up, and there you are! They should now have that 'dry-aged' flavor.

They did! Pullen couldn't remember eating such beef since living in Brazil and feasting on steaks cooked over a wood fire at Thiago's village. They were very, very good. The mixed salad and toasted bread brushed with cheese completed the feast. The red wine was a Medoc and the white, Californian.

They left business alone meanwhile and Lynn spoke of the farm and how it was run. He said they had a very experienced Manager who ran the actual operations and that he was kept busy with the many tasks he had to perform. The Manager was charged with the financial operation of the farm, the personnel, many of whom had worked for the Viscount's family for generations. There was a need to study the regulations from the Government and the EU. Health and safety were another of his responsibilities and he had to arrange marketing of the farm produce with buyers. The present Manager, Herbert Smith, the son of workers on the estate, received his Farm Business Management from the Royal Agricultural College at Cirencester. His education was financed by the estate. He had been in his job for thirty years and Lynn said they were very satisfied with his work. For a moment, conversation lagged and then Anastasia, ever the astute hostess, turned to her husband.

"Sid, tell Paul and John about the Gurkha, the one that you knew from Nepal." She looked pleadingly at him and he smiled at the memory.

"Ah yes! That's an example of selflessness if ever there was one! Well, back in the late-eighties I had just been promoted to Major and I was sent to in Nepal to work for three months with the Gurkha's at Kaphara Camp. It's the main recruitment center and the place where the annual selection course takes place. Now that's a story on its own! Anyway, one day, after the final day of try-outs, I attended a dinner at which Agansing Rai was given the honorary rank of Captain. Rai had been a 24-year-old corporal in the fifth Royal Gurkha Rifles during the campaign against the Japanese in Burma in June 1944. During the fighting around Imphal, he and his men, who had already taken heavy casualties, were ordered to capture an area covered by the fire of two machine-gun posts. The first post could only be approached by attacking up a hill in view of the enemy. Rai stormed it single-handed, killing three of the four crew. He then took on the second, killing the defenders. For this he was awarded the Victoria Cross. It's an enormous honor to meet a recipient of our highest award for valor, so few are awarded and so few recipients are left alive. Anyway, as an honored guest I was fortunate enough to sit beside him during dinner, and to enjoy his company afterwards. I suppose you might say we became friends, a new Major, and the VC recipient. He told me he had been to London several times, the first in 1946 to march in the Victory Parade. He went back again, four times, to attend VC reunions. He explained how he had met the Queen during her visit to Nepal in 1986. Here he pulled me close and whispered 'Sahib, it was a great honor to meet Her Majesty. Do you know? She is the same height as myself!' I managed to keep a straight face as he shook his head in wonder. 'I believed she was a giant Sahib, to rule all those lands and their people. But she was as I am. What a strange world!' Well, I kept in touch with Agansing, and when he came again for a VC reunion, his final one in 1993, I invited him to dine with the Regiment. Had him driven up from London and we enjoyed a pleasant evening. He was a prince amongst men! You John, know how rare it is to meet such a person?"

"Yes I do. You are fortunate."

"Well, he died in 2000 and in 2004 his family contacted the auction house, Spink to sell his medal. He had told his family that they should do this and use the money to help educate Gurkha children. I contacted Lord Ashcroft who collect's VC's and told him about it. He paid about a hundred and fifteen thousand pounds for the award! Which goes to show the value of the medal in a monetary sense.

There was little to say, and the group remained silent for a few minutes before Anastasia, ever the perfect host, asked Paul Soames about his life as a diplomat.

He sat back in his chair holding his Medoc. "I spent much of my career in London at the Foreign Office. My job was to meet with foreign representatives and leaders, listen to their requests and report on them to my superiors. Some were very astute and obviously had their citizens necessities in mind. Other were dangerous lunatics who should have been in a mental institution instead of running a country." His audience waited in anticipation.

"I spoke once to a diplomat who served in Uganda. He told me that before taking up his post in the mid-seventies, he met with the ex-commanding officer of the King's African Rifles. He heard the man knew Idi Amin and that he had been a sergeant-major. This, according to the CO, was considered great progress in a regiment where intelligence was not necessarily looked upon as a virtue. He was popular with the English officers, who appreciated his skill on the rugby field, unquestioning obedience and touching devotion to all things British. Also, the fact that he was very naive amused them. He said the CO suggested Amin open a bank account. He did so and deposited £10. In a few hours he wrote nearly £2,000 worth of checks. A preview of his talent with figures." He paused for effect.

"President Amin, as you know, was deposed in '79. He lived until 2003 in exile in Saudi Arabia. A strange man by all accounts. He drained his glass. "Well, we must be awake early, breakfast at 8, to start going over our equipment so I must ask to be excused and get off to bed."

Lynn moved to Pullen's side. "John, I've asked Douglas to put a couple of items in your room. You appear to be traveling light and these will help. Just wear the track suits for daily use, as I said, we are very informal here."

Pullen thanked him and they all made their way upstairs, Anastasia seated on the stair lift and being teased by Lynn. Pullen felt very tired and slept until his alarm sounded at 630am.

CHAPTER VI

Taking inventory

Pullen climbed out of bed and collected his running shoes and one of the dark blue tracksuits Lynn had left for him. He walked downstairs and found Douglas in the reception area.

"Going out Sir? I'll get the door. If you take the drive almost to the gates, you'll notice a trail to the right. Follow that along the wall all the way. The wall will give way where the Hall grounds end, to fencing. Turn right again and keep going. There may be a few puddles around but it's a good track. There'll be cattle on your right. Go past them to a few sheds. The track runs behind. Just keep straight, and after about two miles you'll find the stables and see the house. Come around the back through the wood and the garden and I'll make sure the terrace door is open. It's five miles overall. His Lordship and Sir Paul do that run every day."

"Thanks. I'll try not to get lost. He returned in just under an hour after running through the breaking dawn, his breath making huge clouds in the cold air. He made his way up to his room for a shower and came down again shortly before eight.

There was a buffet breakfast laid. Soames was already eating.

"Morning John. Grab a bite and then get going. Sid took toast and coffee up to Anastasia. He'll be down in a minute."

Pullen helped himself to eggs and bacon and sat opposite Soames.

"Today we must examine everything. Take it one item at a time and if you notice something that needs to be changed, just let us know. You're the professional and we'll listen to anything you suggest. Ah! Here's Sid now. Ready to start?"

They finished their breakfast and Lynn lead them to the equipment room. He unlocked the door, and they walked in to the large space. The first item had to be the canoe's. There were three.

"Nice eh?" Said Lynn. "Esquif Cargo Models, seventeen feet long and three feet eight wide. They can carry 1,000 pounds. Construction is of T-Formex. Better than Royalex we were told. Its biggest use is for canoes. Lighter than aluminum, quieter and more slippery over rocks. They weigh about 95 lbs. unloaded. We'll take repair kits with epoxy resin, in case of problems. These boats were made in Canada originally, but we had them modified for our needs here.

"They carry three people. Note the molded seats. They support the back, a big plus when paddling. Between the crew, on the deck, are box rails. Special containers slot right into these for loading and unloading. They don't move around, and the containers are light-weight and waterproof. Glance over to your right." He indicated to a stacked pile of a dozen, differently shaped, transparent cannisters marked with letters and numbers. "Each one is different, so they fit in their respective canoes in their assigned place. You drop in the cannister, slide it into place and the lid can be removed. You load it and, lock the lid back in position. They will take liquids or solid items. Very adaptable and the best on the market. These canoes cost about four thousand pounds each. Note the tubing around the bottom of those two? It's flexible and is held in place by catches. It holds gas needed for the generator. As with most of our equipment, Paul made financial arrangements with the manufacturer's in exchange for them associating their items with the expedition." Pullen was impressed.

"Each canoe has six paddles. Three for redundancy. They store in those clips there." He indicated the inside the hull. "Just below the top ridge of the shell, three catches. These hold a fifteen-foot fiberglass pole, one each side. They slot in and you flip the catch up which keeps them firmly in place. We may need them to fend ourselves off rocks or narrow banks. The boats have a light-weight anchors and a hundred feet of line. The design is suited for use on fast-flowing rivers. So that's the canoes. Any comments?"

"They are just what's needed. Congratulations!"

"Thank you. Now the tents. We expect to camp on the river banks each evening. Unfortunately, the satellite pictures do not provide us with an unobstructed view of the Olgo river. It's possible to guess where it goes but the tree cover is too thick to check under the overhang. We will find our own camp-sites." They moved over to three packs next to the canoes.

"These are Marmot Limelite's. Sleep three person and they weigh only 7lbs. Waterproof and insect proof. All clips and fastenings are color-coded for easy erection. Doors at front and rear. Sleeping bags and air-mattresses separate." They sauntered forward towards a box closed with a combination padlock.

"Let me open this and you can look." He pushed three keys in turn and unlocked the box. Inside resting on a sheet of foam were two shotguns and two pistols. Pullen recognized them immediately.

"I know those! Combat shotgun's. Benelli M4 with an Eotech 552 sight. 3-position extendable buttstock. Rounds go into a feed tube and not a magazine. Very good if you use the 9mm fill for the shells. The pistols are Glock 17's. They hold 17 rounds. New military issue those and surely the best available."

"Glad you approve John. You and Thiago carry the shotguns on this trip, just in case." He closed the padlock, randomly moving the keys, and they moved forward.

"Over here is the generator. One canoe has a special rack for it. It's an Earthquake IG800, weighing 21 pounds. It can charge our two laptops and the satellite phone. We must have it for communications. It can give fourteen hours of use for each gallon of gas. Fuel will be stored inside the two canoes with tubes. They hold five gallons. It's a 30-pound extra weight in each, but we need it. It offers us 140 hours of power. Plenty for what we need."

Pullen realized how important communications were and felt sure the excess was necessary.

"These are Condor Bolo machete's." Lynn touched a large basket of the implements. By the side stood a smaller container. "Ka-Bar Becker personal knives."

They came to the end of the first row. "Here we have clothing. Thiago provided measurements for the people in Brazil. There's two of everything for everyone. Shirts and undershirts, pants and socks. There will be rain but it's no use lugging rainwear. Just use large plastic garbage bags when necessary. All clothing is made of special breathable materials, no water retaining cotton. Use your own boots. People are funny about foot-wear, so we left it up to them. Here we have fishing line, hooks and lures. Plenty of fish in the rivers. They say the red piranhas are good to eat! These here are first aid packs. Specially made up for us by the Royal Army Medical Corps. No x-ray machine in them! They have drugs, needles thread, lots of pills and indigestion tablets, diarrhea and constipation capsules. Eye drops, band-aids and bandages, splints and snake bite kits. In that last box over there's a selection from the Poundland Store! A bunch of cheap merchandise. Machetes, knives, combs, mirrors, line and hooks, hammers, nails, tobacco, packs of cigarettes, ear rings, broaches and all kinds of other junk."

Pullen thought of the hazards they would meet and wondered if the trinkets would help. He shuddered. Lynn continued and pointed out row upon row of small packages and cartons. "Food!"

They strode across to the largest area laid out.

"The military has asked us to field test several items for them, and in return we pay nothing for our supplies. What we are looking at is very new. See these soups. They have the liquid in the container. Pull this tab and shake, then heat. A lot of energy bars. Breakfast, lunch, and dinner. Canned meat in light-weight containers. Chicken, and beef. Six dozen each. A special mac and cheese pack that completely integrates. There's six dozen of those. Dehydrated fruit in airtight plastic bags. Flour to make pancakes and dried eggs. Cooking oil. Stabilized mayonnaise, ketchup and mustard. Salt and pepper and hot sauce. Thiago said his people loved that! Dried milk in packets. Mix with water. Same for tea and coffee. There are plenty of purification tablets and we will take fresh stuff along with us. We also have gas lighters and back-up matches." Everything was in cartons.

Finally, they came to a stack of towels. To one side were pots, pans and hygiene products and a carton labeled 'Platypus light-weight water containers' He realized these would be filled at their destination. A gravity filter stood on top of the carton.

That was all the displayed goods. Remaining were the half a dozen Unit Load Devices (ULD's) that would hold everything and go directly onto the aircraft. Four were of a standard size, but two were obviously for the canoe's and much longer and narrower.

"Well, John, what do you think?"

"It appears fine. I would like to spend the rest of the day here and go over everything. Perhaps I can find an item we could have overlooked. You never know. I am a fresh set of eyes and might notice something. In any case, you two have done a tremendous job."

"Thanks John. I have to give credit to Anastasia for her help with the logistics. I should tell you than when we complete our mission we need to get equipment back here. We have had requests from several museums to purchase items. The canoes especially will command a big price if we succeed. Anything that goes with us, in fact, has a value as an exhibit and should be of great importance to any establishment. A draw for visitors. Most of the other things will be made available to smaller institutions for a price. Believe me there's quite a waiting list! Now, Paul and I must get to our exercise on the river. We'll meet here at one o'clock and keep talking."

Soames held up his hand. "One thing John. Please check the first aid boxes. Neither Sid or I have much experience with those. You might find we missed something."

They said their goodbyes and Pullen settled down to do a thorough examination. He returned to the boats. The Esquif's were beautifully made and very sturdy. He noted the canoes were numbered 1 through 3. Crossing to the transparent cannisters, he searched for a matching number painted on the side. He saw one reading. 'Boat #1. stern'. So, this seemed to be a container for the #1 canoe and would fit in the rear. He examined the others and saw 'Boat number' and the words, stern, midships or bow.

He took the Boat #1 stern cannister, finding it fitted into the stern of the #1 canoe and slid into place on the rails. Clever method of storage and easy to tell what went where. The paddles and spares clipped inside the hull.

The tents were equipped with color-coded poles and stakes, each one coinciding with a similarly colored area of the tent, a clever and speedy way to put up the structure. When he examined the insect nets, each had a small repair kit to fix any tears.

There were two satellite telephones in cases. Iridium models working off the low altitude LEO satellites. These were necessary for both navigation and communications. He checked the pile of miscellaneous equipment and then the first aid boxes, a large one and a smaller one. He opened the first kit. Inside were a multitude of anti-bacterial and pressure bandages, burn spray, splints, eye spray, and various aspirin-like tablets. Rubber gloves, and a suture kit. Space blankets and disinfectants. Only missing oxygen, he thought!

He wanted to examine the food items, but he had no hurry to do that.

They had, in Pullen's estimation, missed two things. A good pair of binoculars was one. The second was a method whereby everything could be fitted into the ULD's and loaded on the aircraft in a way similar to that of the canoe cannisters. He sat on the floor to think about a solution to the ULD's. It came to him immediately. Use the same method as the color-coded cannisters. Easy enough, only need to order the tabs.

He would wait for the others in the Library. He walked over, and a thought came to him. Pulling out an encyclopedia from the many books, he turned to "F" and found Fawcett. He read for two hours, using the references to find other interesting volumes with information that Lynn had accumulated. Finally, he realized he felt hungry.

Pullen exited the room and made his way to the terrace. Douglas was laying out a tureen of soup. There were sandwiches and fruit as well as a tin tub of cold beer on the table.

"His Lordship and Sir Paul are back from exercise Sir. They will be down momentarily. May I open you a beer?"

"Thank you, a lager please."

He sat down with a frosty glass in his hand and waited for the others to arrive. He didn't wait long.

Sid and Paul came onto the terrace wearing the same track suits as Pullen.

"Hello John," said Lynn. "Seems like you finished. Here's the combination to the storage room door and the arms chest. We always keep them locked." He handed over a card with numbers on it which Pullen put into his pocket.

"Thanks. I covered everything. I've a couple of ideas."

"Good, let's get a beer and talk before we eat." Douglas bought them cans of lager.

"First. Binoculars are needed, 10x40's should do it."

"Right, we missed that!" Said Paul. "I'll ask Anastasia to find up a supplier this afternoon and get an overnight deliver. What else John?"

"Getting the right items into the correct ULD. We need to tag each item, probably with a stick-on, color-coded tab that matched the ULD's into which it would be loaded. Easy enough, just have to purchase the tabs. They make special heavy duty one's I'm sure. That way everything can be tagged before we pack things. Let's be sure it all fits where it should. I'll keep a list of what is where, and we will know how to unload in an orderly manner."

"Great idea. Get moving as soon as we get the tabs. Now later today I must go with Sid to Norwich to talk about the army sponsorship details."

They strolled to the table and helped themselves to pea soup and a sandwich.

"I want to go over the food this afternoon while you are out. We should do a content check to ensure we get the calories needed."

"John, I would appreciate you entertaining Anastasia this evening." Lynn looked at Douglas. "Please tell Cook only two for dinner. Seven for drinks and half-past the hour to eat. We will be down in fifteen minutes so have the car ready please."

"Yes, My Lord" Douglas left, presumably to give the kitchen instructions and ready the car.

"OK John, we must dress and be on our way. Rest and then do whatever is needed. You've got the storage room lock combo, so we'll leave you to it. Won't see you until the morning for breakfast, those army people will want to be wined and dined tonight!" The two departed and Pullen retired to his room. The run had tired him, but he realized he had to be fit again before they left. He slept for two hours and then put on his running clothes and completed another circuit of the estate. When he got back, he showered and dressed and walked downstairs to check to inventory again.

He was interested in the food and the calories they would require. His years of experience told him that each member of the team would need 1800/2400 calories daily. They could expect to paddle a lot so probably something over 2000 would be best. A can of Spam was about 200, but a similar sized can of corned beef was almost 500. He checked the abbreviated label on the army cans. Beef came in at 400 and chicken 200. Not a lot of variety but lots of nourishment. The packs of peanuts and raisins were listed at 200 calories. Dried soup had 130 and the crackers about 80. The mac and cheese had a heavy 400 per pack. From what he could see they had sufficient food. He thought the only problem might be liquid intake. His training told him they would have to be hydrated. The Platypus bottles were light and refillable with treated water. They wouldn't be a problem.

His watch registered six forty-five. He closed up and walked to the terrace. The usual fire blazed, and he took a lager from the small fridge and sat down to watch it crackle.

The wood today was not as green and burned more quietly. But occasionally, when flames found a pocket of resin, there was a tremendous crack. After one such explosion he heard a squeak as Anastasia arrived in her wheelchair.

"Ah! That's was a good one!" She said as she rolled the chair close to where he sat.

"Make me a Martini, John please. Douglas is dealing with an emergency right now. The small lightbulb in the pantry burned out, and he drove to Southwold to find a replacement. I told him to use a bigger one, but he's very frugal and insisted on at 25 watt and not a 40 watt."

Pullen handed her the Martini. "Thank you, John. I'm sorry but no male company today."

"Please! Being in the army means that there's few ladies to be seen. Sure, you read in the papers about women being accepted into combat units. However, we haven't had any assigned to jungle warfare yet. I suppose we will sooner or later as things change. For now, all evening's in the jungle are confined to sitting with Staff Sergeants eating canned food and drinking river water. Besides, there be more of the same in a week when we get on our way."

"Well then I'll do my best to amuse you. I have been told, in the strictest confidence mind you, we will be having Beef Wellington! Cook is magnificent! I'm sure there'll be grilled Brussels sprouts and creamy mashed potatoes with it. I picked out a Chateauneuf du Pape, Sid has a few bottles of the 2009. It's the best. A special treat for us. Something to anticipate!"

"Well, I'm afraid my skills with wine are not very developed so I'll take your word for it. As for the Wellington, the closest to that dish I ever had at home was my mother's meat pie!"

Anastasia laughed and swallowed her Martini.

"One more please John. You have a great touch with the vermouth. Just the merest hint as it should be. Open a beer, you must be thirsty after your run."

Pullen opened a lager and sipped it.

"How did you know I ran again this afternoon?"

"My office is at the front of the building and I saw you start out shortly before four o'clock. Do you run twice every day?"

"I will be doing so now. We are short of time and I was laid up for a few weeks. I need to be in shape again quickly. Running and then going out with your husband and Paul to paddle, starting tomorrow, should do it."

"Sid said you were wounded?"

"Yes. Careless really. I stood up to take a shot at a passenger on a wave runner getting away from our ambush. Hit him, but he had already pulled the trigger of his AK. Probably had no idea where the rounds would go, but he got lucky. I was struck in the upper chest, but the Kevlar body armor stopped it. As I fell, another round hit my arm above the left elbow. Hardly noticed it! The one the vest blocked hurt more. Thought I had been in a car accident. I'm OK now but I'll be more careful in future."

"Show me the arm John. I've never seen a bullet wound."

"Not much to see. It didn't bump into anything important, just made a hole."

He rolled up the sleeve of his sweater and showed her the slight dent where the round had entered.

"Well, it's clearing up nicely. Does it hurt?"

"No. The doctor said the redness would clear up in a month. Already been three weeks so not long to go now. Like I said, the other thing hurt a lot more."

"Well, I won't ask to see that!" She laughed. "Why did you join up at such a young age John? Sid said you volunteered before eighteen?"

"It's a long story. Not very interesting. I was hurt for a couple of years but like everything else, I managed to keep going."

"What happened?"

"I got a scholarship to Norwich school. It's in the Cathedral grounds there. I took the bus from here every day from when I turned eleven until I reached seventeen. Of course, there was a girl. We met when we were five at Southwold primary and became good friends. There never was any romance, but Daisy was special. She developed a rare form of motor neuron sickness, they call it Lou Gehrig disease, at eight. After that came the wheelchair. Daisy, that was her name. Fitted exactly. Like a little piece of sunshine, and I pushed her everywhere. I never thought of Daisy having an impediment. She was kind and so easy to be with. She helped me with my school work and came to the rugby games. I'd pick her up, and we'd go on the bus

Saturday mornings in the winter into Norwich. She lived a few doors away from me and comforted me when my dad got killed when I was six. Every day she would come to the house when we finished school. Did our homework and then off for a walk down to the pier or along the front. There was always something to do. In the last term at school she got a cold, the cold became pneumonia, and she died. I didn't have any idea what to do. They had a funeral, and that was that. Twelve years and it finished in two weeks."

He stopped speaking and drank from his can of lager.

"I had to get away. So, one day I took the bus into Norwich and joined the Anglican Regiment. Brilliant idea! I had no time to think. Only become a good soldier. The boys called me 'smiley'. You know how people are? I rarely smiled and never laughed, hence the moniker. Still don't, but I lost the nickname when in special training. I'm over any grief now. It took a while. On Monday I visited St. Edmunds. It was all the same at the cemetery. Didn't shed a tear, but I did say a prayer."

"Poor John! She stretched out a hand and took his. There's nothing anyone can say about losses. It's something the individual themselves must handle. Sure, it's nice to talk to someone. It helps to find a diversion. It seems the army was yours. Tell me about when you joined? I've only ever heard a Major General's side of things!"

"You're right. I was so busy I didn't dwell on anything for the first three months. Then, when it seemed things might slow down, I applied for JWS School in Seria, Brunei, the Operational Tracking Instructors Course. That was the hardest thing I have ever done. I became a lance-corporal and the youngest soldier on the course which consisted of Sergeants and 2nd Lieutenants. We ate from the land and the rivers. All kinds of rodents and fish on the good days! When we found no food, we made do with termites and ants! We did river patrols with the Gurkhas, what a hard lot they were! Twelve weeks and we didn't sleep under a roof. Had to make our own 'nests', and they needed to be waterproof. We watched out constantly for the 'enemy', whichever infantry regiment was there at the time. They would be told more or less where we were and sent out to try to capture us. By the end of the course we never got trapped or surprised. The instructors were incredibly knowledgeable and made sure we understood everything before we started the next step." He softly put her hand back on the arm of the wheelchair and drank some beer.

"I traveled to Kenya after that. To the Maasai Mara Reserve. It's about 175 miles from Nairobi City, the capital. I was attached to the Elite Anti-Poaching Unit. Our group consisted of four-man patrols assigned to specific areas of the Reserve. Because the poachers were very mobile, we often had to chase them all over the place. They are nasty people, even murdering conservationists at times. It was our job to capture them, but I must say the Kenyan canine unit 'Maseto Sampei' who worked with us didn't show much patience when they refused to provide information. The bloodhounds they patrolled with were smart animals and could follow a scent when we couldn't see a trail. Once they cornered a poacher, the 'dog boys' only asked once before dishing out punishment. I spent a year there and learned a lot." The fire spat and crackled as Pullen talked.

"After that I got assigned to the U.S. 25th Infantry Division Jungle Warfare School at Oahu, Hawaii. I learned how the Americans work in the bush. Then on to Somalia. Special Operations they called it. We were after Al-Shabab who are affiliated with Al-Qaeda and have been at war with the Somali Government since 2006. We fought them in Mogadishu and outside in the bush when they ran to hide." He shook his head, remembering the danger there.

"Then came Brazil and the CIGS at Manaus. That's where I learned more about the jungle than anywhere else. I was an instructor but honestly, many of the local men from the area were more familiar with it than myself! Then I met Thiago Perez. You've probably heard his name mentioned as he's security for our expedition. Spent a week with him near where we will be exploring." He smiled thinking about that vacation.

"Finally, I went to Belize with the Anti-Narcotics action group. 'Action' being the explanatory word. Lots of action all the time. That's where I got wounded and sent home for a bit. Now you know absolutely everything, and I've been talking far too long!"

"I'm fascinated John. All I know about is meetings and parades. Trips to London to the war office and all that. You were on the sharp end."

Cook arrived. "Dinner is served. I believe you want to handle the wine? It's in the bottle, not decanted." He bowed slightly and retired.

Pullen stood to push her over to the table, but she held up a hand.

"It's two days short of a month so I'd like to try to walk, if you'll help John?"

"Of course." He helped her stand.

"Hold on a moment before start. Have to get used to being on my feet."

She waited and then said she was ready. Leaning on him they made their way slowly outside into the warmth of the patio heaters and to her chair.

"There. How's that?"

"Fine! My first steps. Thank you for the help John." She smiled at him and he blushed.

At that moment Cook came onto the terrace holding a cell phone.

"Pardon the interruption m'Lady. His Lordship said he needed to speak to you right away."

"Thank you.

She took the telephone and Pullen settled back in his chair and watched her while she spoke.

Viscountess Anastasia Lynn was a most attractive lady. He judged to be in her early forties'. Her hair was a dark mahogany color, cut straight above the shoulders and with a fringe that hung below the middle parting. Blue eyes, high cheekbones and a medium mouth. A perfect complexion as one might expect from a woman living in the country. Tonight, she wore a white silk blouse with a mock-turtle neck under a royal blue cardigan. Black moccasins peeped from under her dark trousers.

He had just finished his scrutiny when she put the 'phone down and looked across at him.

"Sorry John. That's Sid. He forgot the name of the water container supplier. Platypus of course! The army said they had something similar if we wanted to test them. I don't think we do. Anyway, let's drink a glass of this Chateauneuf. It's a Roger Saubon 2009. We had a bottle at Christmas and it made an excellent impression. Here, let me help you." She reached across, and their hands bumped as he extended the glass, and Pullen felt it hadn't been an accident.

"I'm afraid I don't get to sit down at a table very often. I must seem very clumsy!"

"Not at all. Let's take a glance at this Wellington, shall we? Can you remove the lid and see what we are to eat?"

Pullen lifted the silver dome revealing a steaming roll of flaky pastry. He took the serving knife and expertly cut slices at an angle, not breaking the remaining crust. He served them both and then offered the grilled sprouts and the dish of creamy potatoes, lightly browned on top

"Now that's clever! I thought you said you didn't sit at tables often. I can never slice Wellington like that!"

"Funny isn't it? I've carved up so many rabbits, chickens, deer and other stuff. It's no use hacking at it. Cut carefully and serve. There are not always the comforts of home, but I've found soldiers like to carve meat and poultry and make it as tidy as possible. Brings a little civilization to sometimes unpleasant situations."

"Try it John. Cook has been masterful with this. Melts in your mouth."

It did. The filet, wrapped in mushrooms and prosciutto, and covered with the puff pastry, had been prepared by and expert. They sipped the wine and barely exchanged a word while they ate dinner.

Finally, they sat back and stared across at each other.

"That's the best meal I've had in ages! I must say thanks to Cook."

"He'll be in momentarily to offer desert. Frankly, I couldn't eat another thing. How about going inside and finishing the wine? There's a couple of glasses remaining."

At that moment Cook did as Anastasia had predicted and entered to ask about cheese or fruit which they both refused. When he had cleared the table, Pullen stood and helped her back towards the wheelchair.

"No John. Let me sit in an armchair please. It's been a few weeks and I want to be comfortable. The leg appears to be fine so hopefully it's mended and all I need is therapy."

He helped her inside and poured the remaining Chateauneuf into their glasses.

"Sid told me there's a son?"

"Yes, that's Albert. He's in Australia learning to manage an Estate for two years. He'll finish by December and then come back here to work for Herbert Smith. We must have someone in the family running things one day. Sid is a good organizer but Estate Management these days is specialized, and he knows it. Herbert has been with us for about thirty years and is getting on nowadays. So, the next Manager will be Albert."

"What keeps you busy here?"

"I do the household accounts and I'm the person at the supermarket. Before I met Sid, I worked as with UK Theatre as Assistant to the Director. I learned a lot there. We were always at receptions and dinners and Sid found me at one of these. I loved the job, but he needed me here and so I gave it up and here I am." She looked up at him.

"There are guests at least one day a week, usually two. Other landowners, military, friends from the Lords, people he represents and local politicians. Quite a selection. It keeps me on my toes. There's three horses in the stables, I ride as much as I can. In the winter the weather dictates the day and hour. The Estate is large and riding and observing what's going on sometimes helps Herbert's people. Trees down in winter, dried up ponds and things like that. There's deer in the woods and plenty of rabbits. The river gets fished only by Sid and his friends, so it's well stocked with roach, perch and trout. We go up to town once a month. Sid is a hereditary peer and sit's in the Lords. He's very businesslike about that! All in all, I manage to keep busy."

She sipped her wine and smiled at him. The fire seemed lower in the grate now and the crackling and snaps came less frequently.

"Are you happy with your life John?" Anastasia asked.

"I suppose so. It's never boring if that's what you mean."

"What about women? It would seem your environment makes relationships difficult?"

"There always have been and there always will be, women. Some are attracted to the uniform. Others to our reputation as fighters. Most are not the kind you marry, a few are married already, many of them are a lot of fun! You don't need to look very hard, they'll find you quickly enough. Doesn't matter where. In the jungle, in the city. They're there if you need them."

Anastasia laughed. "Staff Sergeant Pullen, I never expected such a frank reply! I was beginning to think you were like one of the ancient warriors with principles and customs of knighthood. Bravery, courtesy, honor and gallantry toward women. Now I see you are a modern soldier with up-to-date views. Good for you!"

She reached out and touched his hand. "Don't change John. It's nice to meet an honest man. You've no secrets, you say everything with those blue eyes!"

They heard the main door open and a minute later Sid came into the room. He kissed Anastasia on the cheek and greeted Pullen.

"Bit of luck! Didn't need stay and buy dinner, so we are back early. How about the Wellington?"

They described the meal and how good the wine turned out to be. Pullen felt tired and asked to be excused. They said goodnight and walked slowly up the stairs to his room remembering what he had said to Anastasia. *'Most are not the kind you marry, some are married already, many of them are a lot of fun! You don't need to look very hard, they'll find you quickly enough.'* Fortunate Lynn returned so early he thought to himself as he climbed into bed. So much for the strong silent type, *'You've no secrets, you say everything with those blue eyes.'* Pullen was surprised he had been caught out so easily.

Chapter VII

The hangar in Manaus

For the next two weeks they trained every day, running and then paddling on the river. Sid Lynn always seemed to have his camera in his hand to record events. They readied the supplies and packed them in color-coded canisters. These were placed into the prepared airline pods and were dispatched to Manaus. The Brazilians had earmarked a hangar to store everything until they arrived before sending it aboard the chartered river-boat.

On Thursday, March 1st, Price drove them to London from where they would fly to Miami and on to Manaus. Late afternoon they were met at Heathrow by the BAC special attention team and taken to the VIP lounge before departure. They had been upgraded to First Class on the 777 300 and slept well on the overnight trip. Then they continued down to Manaus on an American Airlines flight, the five-hour journey allowing them to view the Brazilian jungle six miles beneath them. A daunting sight!

Paul's son, Major Victor Soames waited for them with transportation and drove to the Bachelor Officers Quarters at the Logistics Support Base where they would stay before boarding the charter boat.

Victor parked while they dropped off their things and then took them to the Officers Club for lunch. When they had finished Paul stayed with his son and Lynn and Pullen returned to the BOQ to rest. Thiago would pick them up for drinks at seven and they could enjoy a reunion.

Pullen needed to sleep. After all those hours on an aircraft, it felt good to settle down in the quietness of the BOQ and take it easy. He awoke at 630pm and showered before making his way to the Quarters entrance.

Thiago stood outside, and they shook hands. He didn't seem to have changed over the past couple of years. Lynn turned up and was introduced. A taxi had been hired, and it took them along Ave. Sao

Jorge, which Pullen remembered well. They parked at the Betel Grill, a popular typical restaurant. Thiago was friendly with the owners and had called ahead. They sat down, ordered Brahma beers and five minutes later, Paul and Victor, arrived.

"My brother David is unable to come. Tied up in Sao Paulo. No worry, we are here and that's what counts!"

It turned out to be an interesting evening, firstly as Pullen and Thiago told their stories of the CIGS school and the vacation they had took to Dantos on the Xingu. The Brazilian First Sergeant explained to them the deadly Piranhas and the delicious Surubim, a zebra striped delicacy sought after by restaurants all over the country. He spoke about how river dolphins were occasionally seen, and giant otters lived along the banks. Jaguars hunted the otters and were not always victorious! River rays abounded, and care had to be taken when walking in shallow waters. Birds were plentiful. Kingfishers, and terms, herons, and doves, all fed from the river. Victor Soames listened to everything but said very little. He asked his father if they could talk after the dinner and Paul Soames agreed.

They ate and drank more beer and then returned to the BOQ in a taxi after agreeing to be ready at eight in the morning and go to the warehouse to check the equipment. Paul and Victor walked to a rest area a few minutes from the hangar. "Dad, you'll have a satellite telephone with you on this trip. It's not secure. Don't, under any circumstances, say anything confidential on a call. There are only a couple of channels for this type of communication and we don't know if they are monitored. I've prepared a list here with three innocuous phrases on it. By the side is the real meaning that I'll understand if you use those expressions. Provide me GPS coordinates but add 3 to each and every figure. I'll know what to do. Only in an extreme emergency speak in the clear. Otherwise use the list, please! If you call, I'll advise David immediately, so he'll be updated." He passed over a small card.

Soames of course agreed, and they left for their respective sleeping places.

They arrived at the Base just after eight on March 3rd. Thiago stayed at the gate to await his men. The hanger contained their gear and equipped with pens and pads they checked off each container. All appeared to be in order.

The rest of the party turned up and Thiago made introductions. There were the two guides and canoe men, Abilio, Dimas, Erico, Gencio, and Marcelo. All spoke a little English, having been employed for a few weeks most years for specialized tasks at the school. They seemed to be a happy group. All wore simple T-shirts and shorts along with flip-flops. Not one measured over five-foot-five, but all were heavily muscled. They exuded confidence and laughed and smiled as they were introduced. They had often worked with foreign invitees to CIGS and knew exactly how to behave. Pullen breathed a sigh of relief.

Lynn took charge. Having been an army officer he understood organization. He talked for ten minutes outlining what they would be doing. The next two days they would check all the equipment and then, on the third day, move everything to the chartered river-boat. They would leave Manaus on the morning of Friday, March 6th. The journey would take five days. He would address them again when they were aboard the vessel.

Then Thiago stood up and explained that the boat had ample sleeping quarters and storage space. The shallow draft vessel had a Captain, an Engineer and two crew members. They would meet tomorrow when he would bring them to the Base and show them what they were taking, and they could all get familiar with each other. Right now the equipment check was important. In a day or so, they would get an idea of where they were going and what they would do when they got there. From now on they would eat, work and sleep in the hanger. Bunk beds were provided, along with a refrigerator filled with cold snacks and drinks. The mission had to be a secret. They were to speak to nobody about it. Money would be advanced tomorrow, so they could send it to their families if they wished. They had been advised of their contracted terms before accepting the job and would receive any monies owed when they finished. Everyone had to fill out a standard Brazilian army form with their social details and next of kin, in case of accidents.

The men were pleased when they were told about the advance of cash. Only when employed at the school did they have a chance to make real money. Living at Dantos, their village, they fished, grew corn, occasionally acted as guides for fishing groups and were called in by CIGS for special assignments, but that employment came only two or three times yearly. Now they had funds for extras. Work started immediately.

They unpacked the pods and then the cannisters, one at a time so everyone could see where they were stored and what they had. The exercise had to be repeated twice more before they left on Friday. All pods would go to the boat fully loaded and once aboard, opened and made ready for their arrival at the destination on Tuesday, March 10th.

Uniforms were issued. Apart from a few minor alterations, they were fine, and everyone seemed happy. During the day, Pullen, Lynn, and Soames, took each item out and explained how it would be used. They would supervise the packing and repacking over and over during the next days to ensure they all understood their specific jobs. They all needed to be familiar with the canoes and how they would be loaded. Which pod and cannister went where and how the cannisters fit into the vessels. Color codes simplified the task. A truckload of sand came to the hanger, and the tents were pitched and taken down several times. The second day they learned to load canoes and pitch tents while blindfolded. Amazingly enough, after only two practice runs, they were able to accomplish both tasks.

On the third day, Victor Soames, and Thiago, bought in a Medic from CIGS who opened up the aid boxes and explained what they contained. When to use the drugs, and how to give injections in an emergency.

They started the generator and were shown how to refill it from the tubes built into the canoes. The satellite telephones were also tested and given approval. Soames showed them how repairs were made to the boats using the patch sets and epoxy resin. They learned how to weave netting into a damaged mosquito nets and how the air mattresses fit in into the Marmot Limelite's.

By the Thursday afternoon they were ready. Thiago arrived with a visitor, Captain Tomas, of the 'Vista' river-boat. The men asked a few questions, and all were explained satisfactorily by the sailor.

The below deck area had air conditioning. Not for the comfort of the passengers, for she rarely carried any, but to keep cargo cool. The long hold space, empty now except for the expeditions pods would hold their sleeping bags. Food consisted of simple dinners of rice and meat or chicken with pasta. Breakfast, cereal, juice, and coffee, lunch would be sandwiches. There were two bathrooms aboard, but they were told usually crew just dangled over the side of the boat. Anchoring late at night and getting underway before dawn each morning, the 800 miles to the Xingu should take about four days. They would travel 200 miles a day, fifteen hours at a speed of 13/14 knots. When they got to the river Paru, they expected to head south to the Xingu. There navigation became complicated. Their flat-bottomed boat drew only two feet of water. However, the constantly changing terrain made a joke of navigation charts. It was six hundred miles to where they were going, to the mouth of the Olgo, deep in the Mato Grosso. Keeping to mid-channel they hoped to avoid sandbanks or other hazards. The guides would help. Past Porto de Moz the river traffic decreased. The river became wider there but at Belo Monte it shrank to where a well thrown stone might reach the other bank. Then west and pass Altamira. Way down river they would start their search for the inlet they were seeking. Captain Thomas checked the cargo and examined the official documentation that gave the group permission to explore in the Mato Grosso. Satisfied he said they would be underway early in the morning, and not to worry about being sea-sick!

Victor Soames arranged for a catered dinner of Feijoada, Brazilian bean stew, a favorite for everyone, that evening. A case of ice cold beer provided refreshment. They sat around talking, and at nine, bedded down on their cots. They could expect transportation to the boat at dawn. At seven o'clock on Friday 6th the 'Vista' would push off from the Base dock and headed east along the Amazon.

Major Victor Soames at 27, was a star of the Agência Brasileira de Inteligência; (ABIN), the successor organization to the Serviço Nacional de Informações (SNI) or National Information Service. His analytical skills had enabled the Government to detain and deport eight people from two separate cells set up by ISIS in Sao Paulo and Rio de Janeiro. Before that he had gone undercover and mapped the infamous *favela* of Vila Cruzeiro, pinpointing the houses of the slum leadership. This allowed successful raids on the area and resulted in the arrest of over one hundred wanted criminals. When assigned a specific case, he could call on any military command for assistance. That help would be immediately forthcoming.

The expedition that his father lead seemed very interesting. When he first heard of it he did his research and learned everything about Percy Fawcett. Access to secret Government files provided never before seen information about the lost City of what Fawcett called 'Z'. Known to the Brazilian security forces as 'Kupic' from inscriptions found in Manuscript 512, this old document, discovered in the library archives at Rio de Janeiro in 1920, originally arrived in Rio de Janeiro in 1754 and is about a Portuguese voyage into the Amazon interior in 1743.

Soames spent two days reading every paper available, and when he finished, he sat in his office and used a sophisticated computer program to analyze the information. He added his own observations and ran it again and was surprised with the results.

These were his conclusions:

- There could be 'some kind' of metropolis within 5 miles of the Olgo river.
- The structure had been abandoned in the late 1650s after an earthquake and fire.
- Trees and brush made it almost invisible.
- Emeralds were rumored to have been found in the ruins and a silver mine might be close.
- The City's protectors were a fierce tribe, the Piripkura.

By this time the expedition had left England, and Soames had no further chance to speak to his father. He thought very carefully, but finally decided that the information he now possessed had been generated by a computer program and as such, not 'written in stone'. Perhaps he might tell his Dad all about it, but what good would that do? The expedition, so he understood, was to find out what happened to Fawcett. Perhaps it might be best if he left it at that.

However, being an imaginative and very astute man, involved in an intelligence gathering service, he realized the information about the expedition and the possibility of a lost City filled with riches, would not take long to flow along the Amazon. It would soon become general knowledge in the settlements that lined it as well as into the *favelas* of Rio and Sao Paulo. He knew who might act on the news. The *favelas* would probably have no interest, the big cities being too distant for any action from them.

No, it had to be the head of the Amazon Mafia, Benicio Renatto, who would get the intelligence, and if Soames hunch was correct, act on it. After all, he had the resources. He owned boats, men, guns, and money. On top of this he was recognized as a very clever man.

What might he do to cash in on this windfall? He didn't have all the information and therefore must get close to the expedition.

Follow it to be sure where it went?

He had to take care not to be seen. A guide who happened to be familiar with the area?

How might he keep his acquisition of such a man, secret? After a while he realized the guide must be picked up along the way so as not to reveal any details of their destination. Where could Renatto get someone like this? Why in Altamira, the most dangerous town on the Xingu!

Soames made a call to Altamira. A trusted friend from his days at AMAN, the *Academia Militar das Agulhas Negras** worked in the City and could be relied upon to keep a secret. They spoke for thirty minutes and when the conversation ended, Major Soames knew he'd done everything possible to help his father's expedition.

He hoped that would be sufficient to protect them. However, he realized the security accompanying them was top class and that both guards had attended the CIGS course in Manaus, said to be amongst the best in the world.

Black Needles Military Academy

CHAPTER VIII

'The 'Patrão*'

It was six forty-five on the morning of March 6th. Seated on a large balcony at his riverfront residence just south of Manaus, Benicio Renatto known as '*o Patrão'*, sipped his coffee as he sat listening to the man in front of him and looking out at the river.

"At six thirty today the *'Vista'* left the dock. It's headed east along the river towards Santarém, Porto de Moz and Altamira. I got a call confirming this. As you are aware, they told the Government they are seeking the whereabouts of an English explorer called Fawcett, lost since 1925. I received the final key piece of information last night from the La Fortaleza**. As you said, there's an ulterior motive."

The speaker, Gustavo Lorenzo, was the principal Lieutenant of the *Patrão,* who operated a large Amazon freight corporation and incidentally, also ran the most successful piracy operation on the river.

"Good. Very good, Gustavo. Now, what is the secret?

"The word is that a City called 'Z' exists down there somewhere *Patrão.* It's said to be near the Olgo, a small tributary of the Xingu."

"I knew it of course! There had to be a reason for all that money being spent. Tell the launch I'll meet them downriver. I need exercise. Sitting here is not good for me. Can you arrange the helicopter?"

"Yes, *Patrão.*"

"Then that's what I'll do. It will be in a few days. I'll fly to Porto de Moz Monday. You will stay and make sure all is well here. I'll take a satellite 'phone."

"We are using the 60ft launch?"

"Yes *Patrão. The Touro Bravo. Escorpião*** is Captain.*"

*Boss
**The Fortress
***Scorpion

56

They both smirked. Cezar *'o Escorpião'* Costa was one of Gustavo's first recruits to their operation. Renatto had paid a municipal judge a large sum to find him not guilty of robbery, a crime that would have meant five years in jail. *Escorpião,* a vicious, sadistic criminal happened to be an excellent boatman, exactly what was needed for their growing enterprise. He had a reputation of being completely reliable as they both knew.

The launch was a hybrid design the company used for employee outings. An ideal craft for their mission, *'Touro Bravo'* would easily hold the men required for the job. It had plenty of space for stores and was fully air-conditioned for guest comfort on the party runs. As well as the Captain, she carried an engineer, a steward and a deckhand. All experienced men.

"*Escorpião* had the supplies delivered. They finished provisioning yesterday. Food and drink for three weeks. The boys are on board by now with weapons. They arrived during the night. This morning they will be in shorts and flowery shirts, lounging about like a regular party."

"Tell me all the plans once more before the 'Vista' comes past the point."

"Once she passes *Touro Bravo* follows. We are aware of her course and where she is going so we need not be close until Porto de Moz. Then we need to find out exactly where on the *Xingu* they intend to stop, and we can anchor and let our canoes go exploring. We have the drone and it can spot them while we remain miles behind their vessel. This is good because we don't want to go around a bend in the river and see 'Vista' right in front of us!" The two of them smiled.

"Make sure you send a good communications man for the drone and the radios. We have to be sure of our connections to Fortaleza." Lorenzo made a note.

"Once we find out where their anchorage is, and their canoes have left, we wait for the rain. There are heavy downpours every night. When we are ready, we will use the storm with its thunder and lightning to hide our launch and pass into the tributary unseen. The electric auxiliary motor will be used, and the rain and thunder will cover any noise. Once past their boat, we proceed a few miles, get out of sight and anchor."

He drank more coffee and then put the cup on the table.

"The big, four-man canoes are ready. Each has an electric motor than can save the paddlers strength. The charging technology our own people developed will use a solar panel to re-charge a battery in six hours and then get four hours of power." Renatto nodded, and Lorenzo continued.

"We will tow a raft with six spare batteries, so we always have capacity available. There are four canoes, and four men to each. All heavily armed and supplied with enough canned food, sleeping bags and insect nets plus a few other necessities for two weeks. There's also a pair of binoculars. After that, if we have still not found what we are looking for, we live off the land and the river. We have a satellite phone aboard in case we need anything, but the boys are tough characters and they are to be well paid."

Renatto smiled. The Amazon, the biggest river in the world, had waters covering millions of hectares, however for all its size, gossip moved and down the waterway like a flash-flood. A whisper in Rio Branco at dawn became common knowledge in Manaus by the time workers arrived at their places of employment at eight o'clock. All of this information flowed to Renatto through *La Fortaleza*.

In mid-January, he heard through his intelligence sources that a CIGS instructor named Perez was seen in *Dantos* on the Xingu. He had gone to recruit guides and canoe-men for an expedition. By the end of the month he had found out a tributary of the Xingu would be the route. There was a nine-man team with two of the nine experienced security soldiers. They were seeking the final resting place of an Englishman called Fawcett. Benicio needed more news.

Knowledge was paramount on the Amazon. No one trusted anyone, and information equaled currency as valuable as gold. All very interesting but as even more news was forthcoming, his instincts told him that the large expense for such an adventure surely wouldn't be to look for someone's bones! He set his extensive network to work and had Lorenzo purchase equipment they would need to follow the expedition. Finally, he was told the previous evening, a catering employee delivering a large feijoada feast to a band of men on a military base, overheard talk of a lost City. They belonged to a group heading for a small river, the Olgo and would leave tomorrow. This news had reached Gustavo Lorenzo by midnight and he had advised the *Patrão* a few moments ago.

"Go make the final departure arrangements. Call me immediately all is ready. I want to watch *'Vista'* pass here. Then I will come down and we can finalize things. Be sure my special *Asombroso* Tequila is aboard and under lock and key."

Lorenzo left to make the last-minute changes.

Renatto thought for a moment and consulted a small notebook. Then he made a telephone call to the Mayor at a town they would stop at on the way. The Mayor heard what Benicio wanted and provided another number which he patiently dialed. He introduced himself, saying the Mayor had recommended he make the call. The answers he received satisfied him that he now had the right person and after a short conversation, he sat back to await the arrival of the expedition's launch which he expected to see in a short while heading east.

Benicio Renatto, had risen to his exulted position through a combination of oppression of competition, a head for finance and an utter disregard for conventional business methods. His 'Navy' as he jokingly called it, consisted of over a hundred fast launches and several river-boats acting as re-supply vessels along a 1,000 mile stretch of the river.

The river-boats carried gasoline, diesel fuel, food and supplies for the thirsty 'go-fasts' as they were commonly known. They registered and stored whatever loot the smaller boats bought to them, allowing them to continue their hijacking of vessels without having to return miles to a home base for refueling. They were also equipped with satellite communications and radios allowing contact with their headquarters south of Manaus. Periodically, the large boats would receive instructions as to where their cargoes should be unloaded and delivered to willing criminal buyers.

Renatto, if he had only realized it, had copied the method of the German U-Boats in WWII and their 'Milch Cows'. These big transport submarines, XIV's supported the type VII and type IX fighting boats.

The river-boats would hide out during the day at pre-arranged spots and receive their 'customers' after dark. When they themselves were low on fuel and supplies, they got radio instructions to sail to a rendezvous and unload whatever the 'go-fasts' had plundered.

The organization had its markets where the goods were sold, and the proceeds were remitted back to his operations center. A modern computer accounting system would instruct the river-boats how much to pay individual Captains based on their contributions to the common pool of merchandise and give them instructions on where they should head for next.

It turned out to be an excellent method of doing business, kept under control by a dozen special go-fasts controlled by Renatto's planning staff. These elite crews supervised the actual operations and made sure that everything the boats appropriated were sent to the river-boats. Woe to the Captain and crew that didn't play by the rules. The elites had no hesitation of killing everyone aboard and taking their boat. Before that however, they would amputate every finger and toe with a sharp knife. On the other hand, crews that were having a run of bad luck were able to obtain advances on future successful forays from the river-boats. It was an organization that any Fortune Five-Hundred company would envy!

A side effect resulted from the piracy business. After starting the hijacking, Renatto entered the legitimate Amazon freight trade. At first, he used it as a cover for owning so many vessels, but he soon found that the pickup and delivery of goods along the river happened to be a lucrative industry. But the Renatto River Freight Company did not want the publicity that accompanied a huge successful company and so the *Patrão* made sure it ran as an authentic business. It had a CEO and Treasurer plus all the departments of a genuine operation, unconnected in any way with piracy. The salesmen were not paid commissions and worked on a straight salary. They did not have to push for more business as they earned well without really exerting themselves. Thus, it was a prosperous but conservatively run operation, no bigger than many others and actually smaller than most.

A quarter of a mile from the high fence protecting the south-east corner of the vast complex, stood a nondescript, brick building. Its nickname was 'The Fortress'. There were no windows or doors, and it looked abandoned except for the dishes and aerials on its roof. However, beneath its walls a tunnel ran half a mile under the ground to a storage facility on the company grounds. Trusted employees entered there and took the electric rail car to their job sight. In the Fortress were the computers and all the other equipment that controlled Renatto's covert criminal operations and provided him with river gossip and intelligence. If it happened anywhere on the Amazon, the word arrived here fast.

Further along the shore an inlet was visible. Garbage floated everywhere. Plastic and paper, items of food, glass and plastic bottles. It did not invite exploration. A hundred yards inland the village of Mickeyland started. Of course, everyone realized the typical Brazilian play on words and by no stretch of the imagination could Mickeyland compare to the residence of the famous character who starred at attractions in Florida and California. Here, along the many streams and creeks fed by the inlet, stood wood and cardboard shacks. The inhabitants were families of the multitude of 'go-fasts' of Renatto's pirate operation. Some 'houses' were workshops for the boats, and most repairs might be carried out in them by skilled mechanics and workers in fiberglass. There was even a small clinic, funded by 'charitable support' from Renatto River Freight. The shanty town, for such it was, protected the eastern side of the company compound. Political contributions paid into the right hands, assured that Mickeyland was rarely searched and when it was, residents were advised in advance and little or nothing illicit was ever discovered. Another example of the Patrão's genius

On a hill at the rear of the immense property stood Benicio's mansion. From there he was able to keep an eye on his two empires, one legal, one not quite so. He visited his river kingdom frequently, checking on both businesses, using his own launch or the helicopter. It was important to watch everything.

It had been a hard journey to the top. Renatto was an orphan, a lucky one at that! He was fortunate to get a place when the ADCAM orphanage had started in 1985 in one of the poorest sections of Manaus. He was picked up off the streets at the age of five, taken to the orphanage, cleaned up and fed. Then they subjected him to the education system they had in place. Benicio thrived on the attention of the volunteer workers and the love they had for their charges, growing into a tall youth with dark hair and eyes with a hunger for books. At fifteen they found him a job as a baker's assistant and he moved from the orphanage to live over the bakery itself. Within a month he had impregnated the bakers fourteen-year-old daughter. The evening the baker found out, Renatto emptied the cash draw and fled with forty *reals**. He became one of thousands of kids living on the streets and doing whatever they could to survive. With the *Real's* he had stolen from the baker, he bought a stock of combs and brushes and started selling them on the busy City streets from a wooden tray that hung from his neck. After a month he realized there was far too much competition in the comb and brush business. He sold his stock to a would-be entrepreneur and walked down to the river. People said the docks might be a solution. After he had investigated possibilities, he paid a labor recruiter ten reals to get taken on with a company contracted to load and unload some of the many commercial river-boats that traveled up and down the Amazon. These boats would sell anything they could store on their decks at the small ports found everywhere along the waterway. He soon mastered the trick of stealing valuables from the cargo's he hefted up and down the boarding ramps and soon had enough money to rent a room in one of the infamous Manaus *'favelas***.

One morning he was using a dock hose to fill plastic tanks for a forty-foot vessel, a converted barge with a built-on deckhouse and an awning covering the rear deck. The Captain was eager to sail and kept looking at his watch and glancing along the pier. He eventually shook his head.

"No good '*Crespo's*', *** never on time! Well, he's history."

He noticed Benicio. "You, kid. Want a job? Pay is two '*reals*' a day."

Two *reals*? That was a lot of money and dropping the hose he jumped aboard the boat. The Captain navigated the launch out in to the river and they headed west. Two large 100HP outboard engines powered the boat and although they seemed to be traveling fast, Benicio could see by the throttle positions they were not being pushed hard at all.

"Start earning your money, kid. What's your name?"

"Benicio, Captain."

*Brazilian currency
**Slum residence.
***Name given to residents of a residential slum in Manaus

"OK Benicio. Gustavo, the engineer is below. He's from Altamira, a big den of thieves!" He laughed.

"I am Alfredo. I am of Iranduba."

Renatto was familiar with the town opposite Manaus on the river.

"You'll meet Gustavo soon. Get those water tanks stored. Can you cook at all?"

"I can learn, sir."

"Good. Gustavo will teach you how. We don't eat fancy, but we eat plenty."

He stored the containers below, surprised at the size of three plastic tanks in the bow of the vessel. Then he met Gustavo.

"The Captain says you will tell me how to cook."

"Right. Here's the stove." He pointed to a two burner in the deckhouse galley. "Turns on and off here." He indicated two dials. "Here are pans. Keep them clean at all times. We don't want no one sick. Food is simple. Fry meat on this pan here.

He held up a flat frying pan. "Rice here." He took out a small saucepan. "Two cups water, add salt, and boil. Put in one big cup of rice. When the water is almost absorbed, turn off the stove and put a top on the pan to let the rice cook with the steam. Easy! Open a can of those red beans and heat them then serve on the table here. Plates in that cupboard, along with spoons and knives. There's sodas or beer to drink in that little 'fridge underneath the sink. Soap powder to wash everything. That's it. Now *Senhor Cozinheiro*, it's time for lunch. Get moving!"

The engineer retired below, leaving Benicio to fend for himself.

He thought for a minute. How did all this come to pass? He hadn't even returned to the *favela* and his room. Not that there was much left there. A few clothes and toiletries, nothing else. Here he had a new life and was determined to make the most of it.

Little did he realize how different things would be for him in the future.

He made lunch with some fried meat and his first attempt at preparing rice produced an edible bowl, a little dry but not bad. The beans were easy. There were no complaints from Alfredo or Gustavo.

There wasn't much to do after eating. The Captain showed him how to drive the boat and keep out of the way of other shipping. The further south-west they sailed the less traffic they saw. Only near towns and offshoots of the main river, did things become busy.

That evening they tied up in a small river leading to the lagoon of Anori, about one hundred and fifty miles from Manaus. Benicio made dinner, fried meat, rice and beans. After, the three of them sat on the deck with beers and the Captain began to talk. Gustavo had obviously heard the speech before and closed his eyes.

"Benicio, this vessel is called *'Ana,'* that's this week, anyway. Next week she might be *Margarita* or *Sonia*. If you glance over the stern, you'll notice that the name is painted on plastic tiles. It can be changed at any time. Why you ask? Well our business is not looked upon with favor by the authorities, so we need to be invisible. Check the forward deck locker over there. You'll find a lot of spray paint cans of different colors and sheets of plastic. It's easy to change color and alter our appearance when we might run into trouble. We steal for a living my boy. Robbing gasoline mostly, but if we notice anything that might bring a profit and is not too risky, we can expand our choices. Now, Gustavo will tell you how it's done."

Gustavo, whose eyes were closed, had not been sleeping. He searched in his cabin and returned with two shotguns and an old Luger P08 handgun.

"We find a lonely floating gas station on the river. *Postos* they're called. Usually late evening. Pull up like a customer. Then when the hose is pumping we show the guns, hold up the crew and fill those three big containers in the hold. There's a funnel we put the hose in and it runs into the tanks. Take away three hundred gallons. We sell it for $3.00 a gallon. So we make $900 dollars. Gas sells here on the river for about $1.50 a liter or $4.00 a gallon. So, whoever buys from us gets a good profit." Benicio said nothing.

"Split is 45% for me, 35% Gustavo, and you start at 20%. We'll wait and see for a month and talk again. Now, get familiar with the pistol and shotguns. Tomorrow we work!"

The Captain had a trundle bed and Gustavo and Benicio, mattresses under the awning. They slept well.

The next day Benicio made $225 as a gasoline hijacker. They set out at first light finding a heavily loaded *Posto* making its way west. It was surprisingly easy. They pulled alongside asking for gas and as soon as they attached the hose they boarded the *Posto* and held up the two crewmen at gunpoint. Frightened, they put up no resistance. Gustavo cut a few of the inboard motor's wires, preventing the vessel from moving and confiscated the crew cellphones. That would allow them to get clean away. They tied the two men up, putting them in the small deckhouse with blindfolds. Opening up the twin motors the Captain gunned the *'Ana'* west, down-river. After half a mile he turned back and with the motors running quietly, passed the *Posto* and sailed east. It would fool the crew when they reported the getaway direction to the patrols.

They turned south into the Purus river where the Captain knew a gas station owner open to buying stolen cargo's. He paid them $900, and they unloaded 30 gallons of gas into his storage tanks. They continued on down the Purus until they reached the Paraná Sao Tomé, and a few miles in found a quiet bay behind a hook of land. They anchored there to share out the loot.

Benicio was impressed. When the Captain opened a bottle of rum and started to drink, he sat in the shade on the bow thinking.

An hour later, Alfredo lay snoring. Benicio now knew the answers to his questions. For a simple hold up two men, not three were needed. That would mean more money. He knew how to operate the vessel. They had an engineer to handle mechanical things, he might be persuaded to cooperate. If not, he could be eliminated along with the Captain. Benicio could get the boat back to Manaus after some repainting and with a new name. Crew would not be a problem. He would have the beginnings of an operation he wanted to expand and had plans on how to do it. He didn't hesitate any longer. Ignoring Gustavo, he slipped below and took the Luger from the drawer in the kitchen. He made sure it was loaded and then shot the Captain between his eyes as he slept. Gustavo sat up from where he was resting.

"Jesus Benicio, you've killed Alfredo!"

"Right. He's dead and there's two of us now. Take your choice. You get 40% and me 60% starting now. If you agree, fine. What do you want to do?"

Gustavo a quit wit, smiled at him. "That sounds like a trick question *Patrão.*"

Benicio knew he had a junior partner.

So started a profitable relationship for both. Benicio decided they didn't need to return to Manaus. This small, uninhabited bay appeared ideal for operations. They could leave an emergency stock of fuel and food here, returning when pickings were slim. Other boats engaged in thievery along the river that wanted to join them would be sent back here. They would select crew they wanted to keep, the others would be disposed of in the deep water.

Within four months there were six boats at the anchorage and a dozen bodies consigned to the currents of the river. Benicio, now *Patrão* to all, was ready to start his expanded business.

The coffee was now cool. He didn't want more, anyway. All he could think about was getting back on the Amazon. He narrowed his eyes. That looked like it! A large river-boat with a crowd on the deck, across the river sailing south. It had to be the '*Vista*'. He stood up and rubbed his hands together. Perhaps this trip might be like the old days!

CHAPTER IX

Journey to the Xingu

The 'Vista' chugged east. It wasn't too hot this early in the morning but the humidity mad things sticky. The men waited to get clear of the docks, shipyards, businesses and then residences, before unpacking and checking the pods again. They were now familiar with the contents and how they had been stored and spent the morning unpacking everything and then in the afternoon, putting it back together. It seemed repetitive, but it meant that every man knew exactly what they were taking with them. As usual, Sid took pictures.

Once past the heavily populated areas they became bored watching the riverbanks and took their activities below deck. Out of the sun, they found tasks easier to perform. They made their own sandwiches from chicken, lettuce, and sliced tomatoes, and later had a nap. They were at it again shortly after four o'clock, finally packing up at six. On deck it felt pleasant sitting with a beer and looking at the sun gradually slip downwards behind them. Dinner, a simple meal of stewed meat and rice, warmed in the microwave. A fresh salad of greens, carrots and celery with chopped fruit, all mixed in a large bowl, accompanied the food.

The boat didn't stop. The men watched television which came in through the satellite dish and at ten, Captain Thomas guided the vessel to a wooden pier at the Paraná da Trindade loop in the river. A deckhand called out to the gas station attendants and their tanks were topped off and the fuel paid. They bedded down and slept.

Next morning they awoke to the noise of the motors being started. Five-thirty and sunrise only minutes away. A large jug of coffee had been prepared and everyone took their mugs out on deck, some added milk and sugar. The boat sailed along the Amazon continuing east, the sun rising ahead of them, a red balloon in a cloudless sky. It seemed like it would be a hot day.

They took a break from packing and unpacking and sat around chatting until they came to Mocambo around noon. Here they docked and ate lunch at a small restaurant bordering the river. They found Tambaqui, a fish that eats fruits from low-hanging trees, on the menu. A large predator, it had huge bones and horse-like teeth. The crew and expedition members were happy to get off the boat for an hour or so and disposed of two of the monsters between them, along with the usual rice and beans.

Back on the Vista they moved below to the cool air and slept away the hot afternoon. They awoke at six as they passed the port of Juruti, known for its bauxite mines and the cloud of dust that always blanketed the surrounding area. By nine they were docking at Obidos and filling up with gas. Captain Thomas told them the story of the port. Óbidos was the scene of the sinking of the Sobral Santos II in September 1981, one of the worst maritime tragedies in the history of the Amazon. They said the river-boat, making its weekly trip between Santarém and Manaus, had been overloaded when it sank in Óbidos harbor, drowning over 300 people. Piranhas were the prime suspects for most of the deaths, but the Captain said locals believed several bigger predators had a hand in the fatalities.

The Brazilian men aboard made the sign of the cross as they glided to the pier where they would spend the night. Sandwiches were available, but most had had sufficient at lunch and slept shortly after ten.

Sunday the Vista sailed east again, passing Santorém at the head of the Tapajós river. They noticed its green waters mixing with brown Amazon for several miles. Then came Almeirim and the 'U' turn south into the Xingu and past Porto de Moz. They would not dock at any towns from now on, seeking instead a quiet, uninhabited area of the river to spend the night. Everyone had to stay below deck. No attention must be directed to a lonely freight-carrying river-boat.

Heavy rain came down passing Bello Monte. Here a new dam had been built but machinery had not been completely installed. The canoe-men and guides muttered amongst themselves and didn't look happy. There were protesters on the banks waving placards, but these were ignored by the men watching through the portholes in the cool hold. They continued south. Altamira came into view, and they gave it a wide berth. The Captain said this happened to be the most dangerous town in Brazil. A lunch of sandwiches and a nap as usual and then they practiced pitching the tents below deck for two hours.

Now the jungle around them became really thick and there were multiple options for navigation. The guides, Abilio and Dimas, stood on the bridge and were never wrong with the directions they passed to the Captain.

But there were no more towns. The further south they traveled, the less signs of habitation they saw. That evening there had a storm for half an hour and then miraculously it cleared. They came to the split of the Xingu and the Iriri, and continued on the former, stopping at nine after their longest run to date. Meat and rice went into the microwave to be heated, and beer distributed. They watched a soccer game on the satellite television channel and then retired to bed. At nightfall came an impressive electrical storm that woke everyone with its thunder and lightning. Fortunately, it lasted less than an hour and everyone returned to sleep.

Monday again they were underway early and after an unremarkable breakfast, had an uninterrupted run all the way past São Félix do Xingu. They were told that the approximate area of their search could be expected after dawn Tuesday.

So, it proved to be. With no inquisitive onlookers on the banks, the men were on deck at daylight and running over a last equipment check. The next time they manhandled the canoes it would be to put them in the water near the three-island opening to the Olgo river.

The usual sandwiches for lunch and they lay in the air conditioning to make the most of the coolness before the heat they could expect tomorrow.

Captain Thomas fired up a barbeque grill made from an old oil drum and they broiled steaks he had been saving in his freezer. They threw on sliced sweet potatoes and rustled up a green salad. Then they sat on deck enjoying the flavors of the meal as it grew dark. It was an early night for all.

By noon Tuesday, Lynn and Soames were using the sat-nav equipment to bring the vessel to the coordinates they had worked out back in Suffolk. They passed several waterways, but they told Thomas they still had a way to go. The guides stayed, searching the banks with the expeditions binoculars and examining the channels when the river became split by islands. Occasionally one would make a comment to the Captain, but they kept moving swiftly along, invariable pointing out the best channel to take. Finally, around two o'clock Tuesday, came a multiple choice of passages. Abilio nudged Dimas and pointed to the east bank. Soames and Lynn were called to the bridge, looking out to where three small islands defied the waters of a small river draining into the main channel. They checked their figures and confirmed this had to be what they were seeing.

They had found the entrance to the Olgo.

Captain Thomas steered the vessel around the islands and reversed course, finally anchoring inshore of the closest one. All three atolls were about a hundred yards long and perhaps fifty yards across the middle. When the Vista came to rest in the still waters, she could not be seen from the main channel, shielded by the tall trees and bushes on the islet which almost touched the riverbank. A bow and stern anchor were dropped and made secure, then unloading began.

The canoes were lowered into the water and the men passed down the equipment in the order practiced. One by one they loaded the small boats with supplies. Cannisters were carefully slid along the waiting runners and locked in tightly. The job took almost three hours. They manned the vessels and paddled them up and down the river. Adjustments for balance were made, and equipment swapped from one boat to another. Finally, Lynn felt satisfied, and they returned to the side of the Vista and tied up there. Gasoline was siphoned into the canoe storage tubes which were then sealed.

He called them all together on deck and stood in front of them.

"Well, we made it!" The men applauded.

"Tomorrow, at first light we will board the canoes and head east. We will be on our way to Kayapo territory. I have to tell you a little more about our mission at this time. Something that has not been mentioned yet. When Fawcett headed into the jungle from this spot he was looking for an ancient civilization somewhere to the east. Modern day research has suggested he might have been correct in his assumption as detailed satellite images show unexplained straight lines at various points. Perhaps these were towns or at least, buildings. Who knows? We may find out. Because of the heavy coverage of trees and other vegetation, nothing positive could be discerned. If and when we notice something, we will explore. In any case, it's certain that Fawcett disappeared within a maximum distance of 250 miles from here. We see the Olgo for the first one hundred and fifty miles on the images, but after that, because of the dense foliage, only isolated patches of water are visible. We carry supplies for two weeks. That should be enough to cover us. We will have satellite communications providing there are openings in the canopy. That's good enough for any emergency. No hurry, we will paddle slowly, take our time and watch the banks carefully. There's no reason to rush. Safety at all times must be our aim. There are rumors of unfriendly Indians. There are stories of a tribe that worship a huge pink Dolphin. These are, as I say, rumors. We should not worry too much about them. He scratched his head.

"With any luck we'll solve the mystery and return with all the answers that have been missing for nearly ninety years. Let's get some sleep now and be ready for the trip in the morning."

The group broke up, each three-man crew talking amongst themselves and hashing out last minute strategies before they finally decided to sleep. A storm hit in the night but it only lasted thirty minutes or so and passed to the north without waking anyone. Captain Thomas watched it go from the bridge, and then he also slept.

CHAPTER X

Uninvited visitors

Early Monday, Gustavo Lorenzo advised the *Patrão* the launch was an hour or so away from Porto de Moz and that the helicopter was standing by ready for his trip. He walked into his office with a small canvas bag and sat down while he opened the desk safe. From the interior he removed sixty gold coins. These British sovereigns had a value of $300 each in Brazil and were widely used along the Amazon. These were Renatto's 'go to' currency. Easy to carry and accepted anywhere in the country.

The coins were dropped into the bag and Renatto closed the safe. Closing the office door, he walked out. He now had his 'emergency money'

Five minutes later he boarded the Sikorsky S92 along with his bodyguards. There were two pilots aboard the large craft. Before purchasing the machine, Renatto had paid a considerable amount of money to reduce the number of seats from sixteen to eight and use the additional space for fuel tanks. Now the aircraft could fly 1,000 miles without refueling. They made it to Porto de Moz with plenty of gas to spare.

Renatto left the helicopter to be gassed up and carrying his canvas bag himself, walked down to the biggest wharf. His bodyguards hefted his luggage. *Touro Bravo* was in sight and ten minutes came to a halt where Renatto waited.

The Scorpion helped him aboard the boat. One bodyguard remained to return with the helicopter, one stayed with him.

"Everything is ready *Patrão.* Thank you for your trust in me!"

Renatto smiled at him.

"*Escorpião* you are my number one Captain. Who else would I have transport me? Now, we must get down to Altamira. Come with me to my cabin and I will give you the whole story. How long is it to the hell-hole?"

"It's ten now *Patrão.* Pushing a little, I'd say five o'clock."

"Push a lot. I need to be there at four!"

"Of course, *Patrão.* Four it will be."

"I haven't been there for two years. I suppose it's the same lousy place?"

"Yes *Patrão.* Since 2010 the population has increased by fifty thousand people. It's the dam of course. They say it will make cheap electricity and all will benefit. What we think is that it's the ugliest town in Brazil. Robbery, murder, corruption everywhere. Myself, I wouldn't walk on the street after dark. Come to think of it before dark either!"

"One hour we will be there. Take on a passenger I hope and then continue. Right now, I estimate that there's a day and a half between us and our quarry. That's fine. We are sure where they're going so we can push today and tomorrow. They will launch their canoes sometime Wednesday morning. That night we slip past their base, in a storm and sail into the Olgo anchoring a few miles upstream out of their view. Then we release our own men. Get the boys together and I'll talk to them.

They were sailing down the middle of the Xingu at a good speed. Renatto addressed them and told them where they were going. Then he passed out sixteen sovereigns, one to each man.

"There will be more when we return boys." They cheered. Nothing like a gold coin to make men enthusiastic.

"You need to become familiar with the canoes and the electric motors. *Escorpião* will explain everything and then you must make sure you know what you are doing. As we get closer, I'll talk to you again about things. Now, eat lunch and relax. There is a long way to go."

He walked to his cabin and called for *Escorpião* to join him.

"Who is steering?"

"Arturo, the deckhand. He's a good boy."

"No problem. I've a few things to explain and then you can get back to the bridge. First, watch these men carefully. You know who they are and what they are capable of, be careful. Secondly, give me names of four, the most reliable. They'll be the canoe Captains. Now, back to work."

The Captain returned to the bridge and Renatto went to his comfortable cabin to take a nap.

He ate a sandwich at one o'clock and then slept again. At three thirty, *Escorpião* knocked on the cabin door.

"Fifteen minutes to Altamira *Patrão.*"

"Thank you. Good speed you made! Tie up at the Porto da Balsa. I need to make a phone call and we will be met. I want my bodyguard to go with us. Take care of that."

The Captain left, and Renatto made his call.

The boat was tied up and Renatto was told a police car was parked on the dock. Before he left, he transferred the coins into a manila carrier bag along with a few articles of clothing, hopeful he might need these. A young Lieutenant saluted as they came across the gangplank and shook hands.

"*Patrão.* Welcome to Altamira. My officer is waiting. Please come with me."

The drove five minutes and arrived at a nondescript house in the center of town.

"It's better to meet here than at Headquarters. You understand? Quieter."

"I understand." Said Renatto as they walked through the door.

A man with the crests of a Major on his shoulders stood up from his chair and came forward.

"Benicio Renatto! I am happy to meet you. Unfortunately, I am unable say I am happy to see *O Patráo*. You represent a factor that the Military and the National Police are trying to suppress. However, in your capacity as the President of a large freight company, I welcome you." He smiled and extended his hand.

"I am Adolfo Sanchez."

After they shook, he offered refreshments and Renatto asked for a lemonade which was promptly bought to him by a police sergeant.

"You need information and a guide I understand?"

"Yes, I spoke to the Mayor before I called you. He said you were the person to have a conversation with. Thank you for receiving me."

"Fine. Now the information is that the vessel Vista passed here at Sunday at noon. She kept to the other side of the river and apart from the Captain and crew, no one was seen on the boat. That's usual, ships often bypass Altamira. We shamefully admit to the highest rate of homicides and violent deaths of all large Brazilian cities. Now that the dam contractors are finished with the structure, it's a little quieter.

However, the indigenous population still protests every week against the changes they say will destroy their lives. It makes things difficult for us on one hand but on the other, commerce thrives and every kind of business, legal and illegal is conducted in offices and on the streets." He lit a cigarette.

"You need a man to guide you on the Xingu. There is such a man here in the back room. He is a Kayapo. They distrust outsiders. They, like other indigenous tribes, were treated badly by the white men. Beginning in the 1960s, most, but not all, were moved from their homeland in Mato Grosso to southern Brazil and many died from disease, famine and warfare. In 2010 they started to re-locate back to their original lands. But, due to land-grabbing and squatters, much of their territory destroyed. Lush forest was burned to create sparse wasteland and pasture. Today, the remaining hundred or so live along the Olgo, east of the Xingu and stay away from outside contact. They are a handsome people and their women are particularly attractive. There is a legend the tribe once consisted of two groups, the Kayapo and the Keyepo. They separated when a huge Dolphin raised itself up from a river as the tribe crossed and prevented the two factions to continue together on their journey. From that day, the Kayapo have lived alone. They travel constantly, living off the land, fishing and eating birds and game. It is rare to find one in a City, but there is an example with us today. He is a savage. Nothing more, nothing less. However he is very smart. He learned Portuguese and some English while working for the sawmill. He knows the Xingu and its tributaries. Perhaps he will help you? You must ask him. I shall have him bought in now. Stay well back. He will be handcuffed, but he lashes out occasionally and we've had to take certain steps to keep him quiet. Teco is detained for stealing from his employer, *Maderas Altamira,* a big sawmill. The owners boast of their political influence and want him punished.

He asked the sergeant to bring the man in to talk with them.

"*Patrão,* here's Teco. He's a Kayapo. Do you wish to speak to him alone?

"Yes, please Major."

The officer left. He stepped into a room at the rear of the house and picking up a telephone, dialed a 92-prefix given to him previously.

It was answered almost immediately.

"Victor, the bait is on the hook." He put the receiver down and sat in a comfortable chair to wait. The man about to be interviewed was a deep undercover agent for Army Intelligence, and unknown to anyone in Major Sanchez's command. The day before, Sanchez had told him about Major Soames' call for help and he was now ready to provide whatever assistance he could. If anyone checked, a background story was in place for Teco. Sanchez was very thorough.

A handcuffed Indian stood in front of Renatto. He was of medium height with dark black hair cut in a fringe and had the darkest eyes that Renatto had ever seen. A large lump protruded over one of them and he noticed a bruise on one cheek. He wore a sack tied at the waist with a string.

"Olá Teco."

"Olá, Patrão."

The man smiled at him, showing brilliant white teeth.

"You know me Teco?"

"I know of you *Patrão*. They say you are the boss of all the great river.

"You stole money Teco?"

"I stole much money *Patrão*. This last time was over ten thousand *reales*! My boss was a fool with a big mouth. Stealing from him cost me no effort."

"It's not possible to steal and remain free Teco. There are too many policemen. Besides, look what your act has done. You are here and soon will be condemned in a court and sentenced to 5 years in prison."

"He was stupid and a cheat *Patrão*. If you disrespect someone in my tribe, then you can expect to be punished. Here, the white people have strange laws that do not allow killing, so I stole. A waste I say. But, the white men rule. In the forest things are different."

"You do not want to spend five years in prison Teco?"

"No *Patrão*. I do not. "

"I can arrange for you to leave today and come with me. You will not be mistreated again and once you perform a task, you will be free if you wish. Should you want to stay afterwards, I use men like you, and there would be work. What do you think?"

"Must I kill white men *Patrão?* "

"Probably yes, Teco. But only when I say."

Teco smiled. "Ah! I understand! The whites are like us when it's convenient eh? Good! I will come with you *Patrão*. How much gold you will pay this policeman I have no idea? but I am sure it's a good amount."

"Don't worry. There is gold. You will earn me more!" He held out his hand. Teco grasped it with his manacled fists.

"Now. I will ask the Major to let you clean yourself. He called the officer back and told him he wanted Teco and to get him ready. Renatto took the clothes he had in the carrier bag and gave them to Teco.

"Shoes you get on my boat."

They took the Indian out of the room and the Major sat in his chair.

"Well *senhor*. You want Teco? He's not cheap. There will be a lot a noise about him escaping as you can imagine."

"How much noise Major? Do you think ten sovereigns could silence everything?"

"Ah, Benicio! Sovereigns are like a muffler on an automobile. The thicker the muffler, the more noise it suppresses. Shall we say thirty?"

"We shall say twenty Major. That's going to give you enough to make the payments you must make. What do you say?"

"Very well. However, I will require a small favor."

"Speak."

"My wife has a sister who wishes to work in Manaus. I don't want to use my contacts for this. Therefore using your river name I ask. Will you help *Patrão*?"

"Take this card."

He removed his wallet and took out a business card. On it he wrote Gustavo Lorenzo's name. "In three weeks tell her to call this man at Renatto River Freight. He will help."

Thank you *Patrão*. Your Indian will be ready in a minute. I will leave now as this is merely a 'borrowed' house. I will arrange the escape of Teco and soon he will be forgotten. Tell me in advance before you make another visit and I will make sure you are suitable entertained and there will be no Indians!" He smiled.

They shook hands, and the officer left with his men.

On the way back to police headquarters, he made another call and when someone picked up he said, "Victor, the bait is set."

The 'phone was closed, and he put it away in his pocket.

Back at the house, Teco came into the room wearing the clothes he had been given.

"I am ready *Patrão*. Where do we go to now?"

"You are familiar with the Olgo?"

"Yes."

"That is our destination. I need a guide on a river trip I intend to take."

"Dangerous river the Olgo *Patrão.*"

"But you have sailed on it?"

"I have."

"Well then. That's all that is important for now. I will talk to you later about the money you will earn and what you will do for me. You will meet some men. Do not fight with them and you will not tell them who you are. You are a guide. Not one word more! Understood?"

"Yes *Patrão,*"

They returned to the boat. Renatto was pleased. He had proved to himself again that people did many things for money and also for assistance. The Major had proved he was one of the many. They reached the pier and slipped out of the port immediately. Renatto walked to the prow and used his satellite telephone to call Gustavo.

"I have a guide, his name is Teco. No problem. He was in jail for stealing from his boss at a politically connected company called *Maderas Altamira*. He will now 'escape'. The police will take care of the details. However, use your contacts to see if he is known. I will keep you informed. If you must call me, remember to be careful what you say. I will try to be in a secure place where we cannot be overheard, but in any case, we must watch out!"

It was five-thirty, and he wanted to be well away from Altamira before sunset. He told *Escorpião* to push past the point where the Xingu and the Iriri split and to keep going until it became too dark to navigate.

He called for Teco and started questioning him.

"Teco. Now you've got boots?"

"Yes. They fit good!"

"Right. We are going to the Olgo. I am following a group of men who are looking for a white explorer, an Englishman."

"Fawcett the *'poanjo'*, *Patrão?*"

"How do you know the name and what is a *poanjo*?"

"My tribe, the Kayapo, lives along the Olgo. Outsiders are *poanjos*. We have heard the legends of the English person. There were others who looked. No one found him. But there again no one went far enough up the Olgo. If they did, then the Dolphin could have stopped them."

"Tell me more."

"My tribe separated into two parts. The Kayapo and the Keyepo. A big Dolphin came from the river and separated them. Now we live alone in different areas without outside contact. The Dolphin raised itself up from a river as the tribe was crossing and prevented the two factions to continue together on their journey. Since that day, they remain apart. In the river where the Dolphin lives no one can pass. The Kayapo stayed near there to warn any travelers not to continue up the river or the Dolphin will stop them. Few people ever reach so far. The Kayapo live within two miles of the Olgo. The Keyepo much further south." He paused for a moment.

"It's possible to travel east, which is not recommended, perhaps fifty miles more and there the ferocious Piripkura live. These are called 'Butterfly people' because they move all the time. They are killers and allow no trespassing on their lands. He took the cigarette that Renatto offered him.

"Piripkura are wild and dangerous and make no contact with anyone. Men have been murdered when they enter their territory. They are said to protect the City that once existed many miles up the Olgo. I do not know about that, I have not seen it, but I met a Butterfly man once called Mande. He said a City exists, but no one can go there. Perhaps the English traveled there and was killed? Nobody is certain and it so far."

"Where is this Mande now?"

"*Patrão.* I am not sure. Perhaps he got away? He had been captured by the slave traders who supply men to chop down the trees. He said he was hunting, and they caught him and took him west to where they cut and burned the forest to get the logs. They treated him badly, and he was no more than a slave. He learned some *poanjo* languages while with them. There was nothing else to do. One of the other slaves was a man from over the seas that had been studying birds and was taken. He had strange words, but Mande said he talked often with the man and learned many of them. I gave him some food the one time I saw him. He knew I was a Kayapo. This was at first while I worked a month for the loggers and had no money. Not a good job and as soon as I was able, I ran. Mande said he wanted to go home but feared to run until he could be sure of getting free. Guards killed escapees at the logging center. He had already been there over a year." He shook his head.

"We are on our way to the Olgo and we will follow the Englishman seekers, and you will guide us. We've got men and guns. No tribe will try to stop us!"

"As you say *Patrão*. I am with you."

He gave him the pack of cigarettes and one gold sovereign 'on account'. Teco pocketed it, thanked him, and left to join the others. Renatto spoke to *Escorpião*.

"Where are we now?"

"We passed the Iriri and must stop as it will be dark. Tomorrow morning, we continue and by nightfall we can be close to São Félix do Xingu. Wednesday midday we pass São Félix and then be at the Olgo by the evening."

"Good. That night we bypass their launch and sail into the Olgo. This new guide, Teco, knows the river and can tell us where we can anchor out of sight. Thursday morning our canoes head out behind the expedition. We will find where they camp and watch them carefully from a distance. The drone will be out of range after ten miles, so we cannot use it."

"Yes *Patrão*. It will be done as you wish."

As the boat anchored, Renatto walked to his cabin and told the steward to bring him his Tequila and a sandwich. He had a drink and ate and then slept in his comfortable bunk.

Early Wednesday they were on their way south again. They saw a few settlements, but it was mostly jungle and more jungle. At midday they passed the ravaged forests near São Félix do Xingu. Huge tracts had been cut down before the Government finally stopped the logging in 2010, the devastation however, was still highly visible. They sailed by the town without slowing down, and half an hour later, the steward bought Renatto some soup for his lunch. He dozed for most of the afternoon and then watched the international news via the satellite link.

At four o'clock, *Escorpião* advised him they were within five miles of the Olgo and that from there on in, speed had to be reduced. In an hour the drone would be launched to find where the *Vista* had anchored. When the storms started, Teco had to show them a way round the other launch and take them into and along the river to hide. They would stop somewhere for the night and be ready to set out in the canoes at daybreak.

Renatto climbed up to the bridge and stood with *Escorpião* until the drone launched. Then Manuel, the communications operator sent up the Phantom IV PRO V2 and checked the monitor standing on a shelf close to where they stood. He could stand outside the bridge door and operate the V2 while he kept an eye on the screen. It was still light at five as the drone flew south over the river at over 1,000 feet. The operator adjusted the camera and video could be seen on the screen. After it had flown about two miles, they noted the three islands at the mouth of the Olgo. The *Vista* was tucked in behind the furthest north of these. No movement aboard was observed. Teco watched while the drone circled to provide a complete picture of the basin. Then it flew up-river for several miles until they observed a protected anchorage to use. Finally, he nodded.

"I know where we must stop and wait for the rains. They will not be able to see us as they are anchored on the east bank side of the island. When the rain starts the electric motor must be used and I will show you the way into the Olgo basin and up the river. I've seen a good spot to stop our boat. We wait there and then Thursday morning we go in the canoes."

The drone was recovered and the men fed. Then they waited for the storms which blew down the river every night.

At ten o'clock the first of them came roaring down on them passed north. *Escorpião* had the engineer rig the electric motor, and they started to move. The storm calmed down but immediately another one, this time with thunder and lightning, hit. Teco called instructions in a low voice and the *Touro Bravo* moved silently through the rain and across the river. A bolt of lightning illuminated the entrance to the Olgo and Teco instructed Dioneses, the engineer to increase to maximum speed on the motor. The launch entered the river and slowly sailed upstream. Here the banks were over a hundred yards apart and it was simple to keep to the middle of the waterway. Another storm blew through, but by this time they had rounded the first bend in the Olgo and were hidden from the Xingu and the three islands.

They reduced speed and kept going at for thirty minutes. Teco, in the bow, signaled 'slow' and the launch gradually slowed. Finally, he indicated they should steer towards the right bank and as they did so the moon revealed a point of land they had passed.

"Go back there, stop the boat behind that point. It will be out of the current and out of sight."

Ten minutes later they were anchored, and all aboard *Touro Bravo* took to their sleeping bags until the next morning.

CHAPTER XI

Along the Olgo

Dawn Thursday. The expedition had paddled for ten hours after leaving the Vista at six in the morning the previous day. When the air cleared, a satellite signal confirmed the canoes had covered fifty-four miles. They had stopped several times, and finally camped on the riverbank, fished for, and caught piranha, fried and eaten them, and gone to sleep, satisfied with their first day. A limited search of the area gave no indication anyone had been there before them.

Breakfast consisted of coffee and energy bars. Then they packed up the canoes and launched them again into the slow moving Olgo. It was very humid, but the sun did not bother them. The canopy of trees over the south bank where they paddled kept them shaded from its glare and they made good time without trying to push hard. It was a fairly easy pace, and they advanced steadily. In the first boat, Lynn lead the way with Abilio as the guide and Thiago as security. Then in the second, Soames, Erico and Gencio. Finally, in the third, Pullen Dimas and Marcelo. They would paddle a stretch and then Pullen's canoe changed places after speaking with Lynn, Abilio and Dimas.

Now they were well inland they noticed all kinds of bird life along the banks. These fed on the fruit hanging from branches almost down to the water of the river. Occasionally fish leaped to pull down berries, and monkeys were everywhere, chattering and making a noise. The brilliant blue hyacinth Macaws and crested oropendola with its jet-black body and startling white bill. Dimas told Pullen that the feathers of these birds were so colorful they were not dyed by the Kayapo who wore them ornamentally. As they paddled Pullen learned the names of more plants and animals that Dimas pointed out to him. He also showed Pullen where the Pacu, a great eating fish, could be seen beneath the surface under the rubber trees waiting for the seeds to fall.

By midday his head became full of strange and exotic names. The flowers were unbelievable. The cardinal flower was one of the most stunning with intense crimson-colored stalks rising above dark green foliage. There were cattails everywhere, providing nesting materials for the birds. The titi monkeys with their bright orange tails, hung from the Brazil nut trees lining the banks. Now and then spider, howler and squirrel monkeys came into view as they launched themselves from branch to branch with far more skill than any circus acrobat.

The canoes were easily paddled and navigated. The slow flow of the river west hardly bothered their progress and by noon they estimated they had covered a further twenty-five miles. Lynn signaled to pull over for a meal break.

A gap appeared in the tree-line where a small stream entered the Olgo and a tiny beach had formed. They paddled the canoes close and stepped into the water to dock them on the dirt. Immediately it started to rain but after a fifteen-minute downpour, the sun returned.

Thiago and Pullen used the last of the fresh bread to make canned chicken sandwiches. They washed these down with bottled water. The two of them then decided to explore the area while the others digested their food.

The trees were sparse and populated by blue morpho butterflies who seemed to appear and then vanish as their brown underwings hide the blue top-wings momentarily. They constantly returned to the small stream to drink and then the bigger males would chase the smaller females in and out of every bush in the area. They walked slowly, moving out of the way of the butterflies following the creek. Ahead the land rose, and they heard a waterfall. A few yards further on, the falls rushed down over some rocks twenty feet high. A perfect miniature cascade. To one side was a clearing. There were stumps where trees had been cut. A closer examination showed the cutting had taken place years previously. Dirt and weeds grew around the stumps but there could be no doubt this had been done by man. They split up and searched further. At the rear of the clearing Pullen saw trees chopped off about six feet from the ground, above where their first branches sprouted. When they investigated they noticed several straight poles laying on the earth. These were the remains of a shelter of some kind.

Thiago returned to get Lynn and Soames while Pullen continued to look around the area. He stood back and scanned the cleared space towards the tiny waterfall. It was rocky there, and he imagined the stones had been carried by the water and been washed haphazardly around the point where it flowed over the high ground to form a stream where it landed. In one corner of the clearing a circle of stones could be seen. Perhaps this had been their firepit?

Lynn and Soames arrived and started filming and taking pictures. They agreed, it had to be a camp-site. Could it have been one that Fawcett constructed? There seemed to be no way of knowing until Pullen remembered an old trick.

"Fawcett took canned goods with him. Being an experienced traveler, he buried any junk before leaving. Check carefully around the edges of the clearing for an indent in the ground. There's his garbage pit and where any cans that remain, can be discovered."

They spread out and walked around the camp-site. Pullen felt his left foot push down a little deeper than previous steps and looked at a depression in the earth. He called the others. Using his fingers he dug in the soft soil and found something solid. Excavating carefully he pulled out a large glass jar. The screw top was still on it and when he brushed the dirt from the sides, he saw a tin and some wrapping paper inside it. After all the years it had been buried, part of the label on the tin could still be read, 'John O'Hara, Scottish Corned Beef'' it proclaimed.

Lynn smiled "I believe that belonged to Percy. After all, who else ate Scottish Corned Beef out here along the Olgo?"

Pullen nodded.

"Let's keep looking around for the 'R' and arrow that Rimmell mentioned. It should be seen scraped on a rock or something?"

Again, they searched the area until Soames kicked a stone in the circle that may have been a firepit.

"Here. Over here! This is definitely the letter 'R' and a 'V' on its side!"

They agreed with him. This was the first trace of Fawcett's expedition from more than 90 years previously. They seemed to be on the right track. Lynn took photographs and filmed with the digital camera and they returned to the canoes and launched them again.

They informed the others of their find and the mood of the group took an upward leap. They felt more energetic as they headed east.

Finally, close to six, it was getting dark as the overhanging trees prevented the sunlight from reaching the river. Pullen's canoe was leading and Dimas, searching the banks ahead, saw an opening. He signaled the others and five minutes later they landed at another beach where a stream entered the Olgo.

Everyone worked as rehearsed and the tents were pitched on the flat piece of ground. Lynn complained of a headache and chills and went to lay on his mattress.

Gencio and Marcelo saw rubber trees along the Olgo banks and taking fishing gear, walked out to find a Pacu, well known for eating the fallen nuts from the tree. Five minutes later, after a few triumphant shouts, the pair returned with three large fish. These were quickly fried up and served with a dish of mac and cheese. The canoe-men, guides, and Thiago, liberally shook hot sauce on theirs but the remainder of the party ate the delicious fish with a little salt and pepper. Bottled water flavored with lemonade powder completed the meal.

The generator hummed, and the lights illuminated the clearing as they ate. Then, after cleaning up, all except Soames settled into their tents. Sir Paul worked on his laptop. Lynn, feeling better, updated his notes. An hour later he finished his report, closed the laptop, returned the satellite 'phone to its case, stopped the generator and lay down on his bed.

At three in the morning loud noises were heard and everyone awoke. Pullen and Thiago had their M4 Shotguns and torches beside their sleeping bags and immediately exited their tents and shone the lights around the clearing. Towards the river the beams picked up a dozen or so Capybara's digging in the mud where the Pacu bones were buried. They all returned to bed after ten minutes when the noise subsided.

"Well, John, now you know why we needed security on this trip," joked Lynn as he vanished into his tent. Pullen took some time to return to his dreams and slept through the night until the sun rising over the clearing, woke him. They searched thoroughly before leaving but found nothing to indicate that Fawcett and his party had ever been to this spot. A quick breakfast of coffee and energy bars and they got ready to launch the canoes shortly after dawn Friday.

CHAPTER XII

Following the leader

Dawn Thursday found the four large canoes with Renatto's men relaxing as the electric motors whirred and the boats made five miles an hour east on the Olgo. The Touro Bravo was miles behind them with Manuel, the communications man, Dioneses, the engineer, and the extra hands. A raft with the six spare batteries was towed behind the rear canoe. After five hours when electric motor batteries were low they were removed and swapped with fresh charged ones. They rigged the solar panels and immediately started to charge the depleted cells while the canoes carried on with the new power sources.

Soon Teco, in the lead canoe with Renatto, *Escorpião,* and one other man, pointed out where the Fawcett's, as they called the other expedition, had probably paused their journey for lunch. They stopped and looked quickly around but saw no visible clues. Lynn had insisted they take the garbage and the rock with them, leaving nothing to be found.

It was a brief stop, and that afternoon, they walked to the Fawcett expedition camp of the previous evening. There was not much there, but they noticed a disturbed patch of mud along the river bank which Teco rightfully identified as Capybara activity.

They continued for four more hours and then stopped at a lonely mudflat and slept. They didn't have the amenities of the Lynn and Soames people but cans of Spam and hard biscuits, washed down with beer, were sufficient, as were the cheap sleeping bags they used. All of them were hardened river pirates and had survived under much harsher conditions. There were no complaints.

Friday morning Renatto used his satellite phone and noted they had traveled one hundred and five miles from the Xingu. His calculations put him about thirty miles behind the Fawcett's. The electric motors were proving reliable and fast and his men remained fresh, not having to paddle. Then came a heavy rainstorm for an hour, and they waited until ten o'clock before moving out. This gave the bright sunlight plenty of time to charge the batteries in the boats and those towed in the raft.

After connecting the power, the canoes were launched, and they continued down the river. It was very hot and the canopy over the river kept the humidity high. Renatto felt thankful for the motors. The men hadn't complained about fatigue.

At two they stopped to eat lunch when Teco spotted a clear spot where lightning had downed a few trees. They paused for an hour and charged the batteries while they ate cold cans of soup. Shortly after three they started off again. Renatto spoke to him.

"We are perhaps twenty miles behind now and gaining all the time. We must be careful. It's 150 miles from the Xingu, meaning we could catch the others anytime if they make a long stop somewhere or tie up early for the night. What do you think?"

"*Patrão,* I believe if we push on until an hour before dark, then stop for the night, we will be all right. Tomorrow is Saturday and everything we have seen, points to the Fawcett's being in the area. It's over 200 miles from our start point. We can expect them to take frequent breaks to search for signs. Tomorrow we go slowly and have one of our canoes out front, perhaps half a mile. The first canoe must stay close to the east river bank under the tree canopy where it's shady and dark. At every bend they should wait and carefully get out in the shallow water, walk to the curve and scrutinize upriver. Even then we may not observe them stopped, however, we have ears! They suspect nothing and will talk in normal tones. Voices carry over water, so we stay alert."

At that moment a rainstorm came blowing down the river and the canoes sheltered as close as they were able to shore. The lightning came and shortly after, thunder. It was a large storm and hung around for half an hour. During that time, they did not dare move from the tree canopy shelter and even there, the men were forced to bail out the water that threatened to swamp the boats.

The noise diminished, and the clouds cleared a little. Suddenly they heard a rushing sound coming from upriver.

"It's a flash flood." Shouted Teco. "Out of the canoes and onto the bank at once before the wave comes. You must hold on to the canoe mooring ropes with everything you've got! It will be a fierce wall of water but should pass quickly. Now out!"

They stepped into the shallows and reached the bushes lining the river. The ropes fore and aft were held tightly as the wave rushed towards them.

Then it hit and only the closeness of the trees prevented them from being washed into the current as the flood surged along the bank. They held onto the canoes for dear life for a minute, then the surge slowed, and the river calmed.

Renatto knew the men were frightened and moved to negate the problem.

"*Escorpião*! That's the first bath you've had in days! It's a good thing the water washed the dirt off you!"

The Captain took the joke well, realizing Renatto's plan. He looked suitably chased and shook his head.

"I am much better after the shower *Patrão.*"

The men laughed, and the fear passed.

They emptied the water from the canoe's and repacked their contents taking care to dry the binoculars. Most of it was tinned goods and all the guns were wrapped in garbage bags and stayed dry. The sun came out, and they dried the solar panels and repositioned the batteries on the raft. When everything was connected, they launched the canoes, the river now brown with mud and carrying a lot of foliage downstream. The boats had to be steered carefully from the path of larger branches but after an hour, the water became clear again.

Renatto shouted to the men.

"Tonight, we will build a fire and catch Piranhas to fry! We cannot cook after that because we are close to the game we are chasing! So, it's warm beer and fish for us boys!" The electric motors drove the canoes further upstream until twilight and they stopped to make camp that Friday evening.

CHAPTER XIII

The Dolphin

Soames addressed the men before they launched.

"We are now near to the area where Fawcett is presumed to have gone missing. Today we must keep a very good lookout, all of us, from every canoe. First and last canoe's scan the left bank and the middle one, the right. If you notice anything, anything at all out of the ordinary, shout and we will stop and investigate. This is where we may meet unfriendly tribes, so our security will have their weapons hidden but ready. In addition, both Sid and I have the Glock 17's on hand. Naturally, firearms are a last resort. We do not want to use them unless lives are endangered. Now, let's move out.

They paddled across to the shade of the trees on the south bank, everyone with eyes wide open. After ten miles or so the river narrowed, and the current increased. Pullen, now in the lead canoe, realized the land was slowly rising as they traveled east. Soon the Olgo tapered to only fifty yards across, and then thirty. The water flow made it difficult to progress at more than a crawl. Larger trees were seen along the shore, taller, thicker to those they had encountered earlier.

It took a serious effort to advance as they made every effort with the paddles around a small bend, finally arriving at a narrow, but straight stretch. As they progressed the Olgo constricted until the banks were a mere fifty feet apart.

Then it happened!

A huge splash and a tidal wave rocked the canoes. Looking forward they saw an enormous pink Dolphin rise from the wave and settle back into the river. Every person aboard the boats was momentarily terrified. The vessels were thrust all over the place by the rush of water.

Then Pullen realized what had happened.

It was not a live Dolphin, but an enormous tree trunk carved in the shape of a fish with a long beak like the river dolphins of the Amazon and colored pink. It had been released from the north bank of the Olgo to fall in front of them and to check their progress.

Things gradually quietened down as the men got the boats under control and the wave washed down the river. The huge log, for it could be seen as such, floated around blocking their way. Pullen remembered the story Lynn has told him of the tribe that cared for such an animal.

He looked back and noticed Thiago talking with Abilio and Dimas the guides. He pushed his canoe alongside Thiago's.

"John. You've now met the famous pink Dolphin of the Kayapo's! What a fabulous description we had! It frightened the shit out of us three!" He indicated himself, Abilio and Dimas. "Probably didn't do the rest much good either!" They laughed.

Pullen looked along the river bank and saw movement. A few seconds later a group of Indians, armed with short bows, appeared. At their front stood a tall man with a magnificent orange feathered headdress. He walked over and beckoned to the canoes, no menace on his actions.

The crews looked at Lynn who nodded. The boats were beached, and the men alighted.

Thiago and the guides, approached the tribesman. They held up both their hands, palms outwards, and the Indian did the same. Then he spoke in dialect and the man seemed to understand as he nodded his head. He turned to Pullen. "John. Please bring a selection from the trinket box in canoe three. This man understands me, and I believe he's friendly. Tell Sid and Paul to relax and let me and the guides handle things."

Pullen returned to the third canoe. Being familiar with the containers, he located the trinket box and took out two machetes and three knives. Then came a reel of fishing line and hooks along with two mirrors, cigarettes and necklaces, broaches and earrings. These he handed to Thiago.

Dimas and Abilio were talking to the man with the headdress. They used many hand gestures, and the man did the same. They interacted for five minutes. When they stopped for a moment, Thiago placed the trinkets in front of the man. He picked up a machete and hefted it. Looking pleased he spoke with a rush of words to the guides and waved his companions forward to pick up the rest of the goods. They were all smiling as they realized these were gifts.

Thiago spoke. "This is Ado. He is the acting chief here. The village is a quarter mile north in a clearing, and eighty of them live there. Men are always here with the 'Dolphin'. They have a mission to warn any travelers that to venture further along the Olgo is to invade the territory of the Butterfly people and other unfriendly Indians who kill intruders. This is the sacred task of the Kayapo tribe, its only duty. Warn all travelers of what lies ahead! The Dolphin was to frighten them into believing the Kayapo's caution. Ado said it's the first time they have had to launch the Dolphin in fifteen years. No one in their right senses travels this far up the Olgo, anyway! The Dolphin is a huge carved log, dyed with an extract from the Achiote bush flowers. It's held upright on the bank there with its tail in a large hole. Vines keep it straight. When they want to scare a boat, they dig out the front of the hole and then cut the vines. The Dolphin falls into the water with that huge splash we witnessed. Ado said it's very effective! He has stories from his father and grandfather about it. Now the men will have to return to the tribe and bring more help. It takes about thirty people to put the Dolphin's tail back in the hole, pull it until it's vertical and pack the dirt back around the base to keep it from falling."

"Incredible." Said Lynn. "Absolutely marvelous. What do we do now Thiago?"

"He has agreed to take us to the village if we will bring more trinkets. The success of the Dolphin today has to be celebrated. There will be a feast tonight."

Lynn spoke. "Tell him we agree. Will the canoes be safe here?"

Thiago spoke to Ado.

"Ado said there should be no one within five days walk, so the canoes are secure. Tomorrow early they'll return and again guard the upper reaches of the river."

"Good. Let's decide what to take with us. Paul, please fill a sack with the trinkets. John, sort out food we can bring as gifts. Canned stuff will be fine and quite a novelty I would guess. I want the sat-phone, have Gencio carry it. Erico can handle a box of shells for the shotguns. Everyone should put on a pack and carry sleeping bags, biscuits, Spam, coffee and sugar for breakfast."

Ado and his men waited while the expedition packed their stuff and in a single file, they followed their hosts into the forest.

The biodiversity was amazing. A different tree and shrub every foot of the way. The plants developed defenses against insects. Because the constant rains destroy the natural nutrients in the soil, they evolved to be poisonous or bad tasting so that the tiny predators do not consume as many leaves as they otherwise might. Creepers and epiphytes grow up tree trunks. They eventually lose their ground routes and become exclusively climbers.

There were palms and vines, and a variety of fruits. Camu, soursop, passion fruit, avocado, acai and bacuri could all be seen on their route.

A giant green iguana moved slowly along the branch of a huge wimba tree, disturbing a pair of macaw's, who squeaked off into the treetops.

They saw Ado hold up his hand and signal them to stop. Then he left the barely visible path they were following and entered the jungle. As he did so, he touched Thiago's shoulder and pointed. He nodded and spoke to the man behind him and the message passed down the line as they moved off the trail. When Pullen got to the exit point, the man in front directed his gaze left. There, from a fork in a ficus tree on the path, hung a large green, black and yellow anaconda, about ten feet long. Pullen watched as he walked past the snake. It's only movement was the flickering tongue. The expedition avoided it and returned to the trail several yards further ahead.

They reached the village, a series of palm-thatched huts built up off the jungle floor. The clearing was large, about 1,000 yards square. To the north, they saw huge rocks. One especially big one had a painting of the pink Dolphin on it. Much of the cleared land seemed to be devoted to agriculture and the rows of sprouting plants appeared healthy. A score of small children ran forward to greet them but stopped and stared at them when they saw strangers. Women peeked out from the huts.

Ado walked to a larger hut and came out supporting an old man. They walked back to the paused group and motioned everyone to sit. He spoke for several minutes and then the elderly man greeted them, and they talked more. Finally, Thiago translated.

"We are welcomed. The other man is his father Ako, Head of the tribe. As he is so old, Ado performs most of his functions. The old man has all his senses about him though! He wants to find out what gifts we bought for him! We'll take them out in a minute. We are in luck says Ado, they caught two peccaries during the morning hunt and they are to be roasted for the feast. He said they've got red corn and platanos as well."

Gencio and Erico bought the trinket sack and Soames handed out more knives and reels of fishing line with hooks. Ako asked what the white sticks were, and they explained these were the cigarettes of the *poanjo*. They gave a lighted one to him which he took and started to smoke. He said they themselves had only green leaf wrappings for tobacco and that the white sticks were much better! Then he called the women over and they were given jewelry and cloth. There were cries of delight and laughter as they tried on the items. Pullen noticed that the younger females were light skinned and quite becoming.

Ado asked Thiago if he would translate as he and his father questioned Lynn and Sykes about the outside world.

They sat for several hours patiently answering questions about where they had come from and what foods they ate. How many children they had and other enquiries. In return they asked about the life of the Kayapo. Ado told them things were gradually changing and these days young men were restless and talked of abandoning the tribe and heading to the Xingu and north to work with the *poanjo*. Only one had gone however, the rest still complained but did not leave. It was his own son who departed five years ago, and he had not been in touch since he left.

By late afternoon they were getting hungry as they watched the women prepare the meal. They filled a fire pit with logs and ignited them. The peccaries were prepared and joints of meat spitted on green branches and hung over the flames, to be attended by the older children. In addition, two green iguanas were cut open and cleaned to cook. The platanos were wrapped in leaves and buried in the ashes along with red corn and sweet potatoes. The women placed wooden bowls loaded with mangoes, cocona, passion fruit and guanabana where the guests sat so they might help themselves.

One of the small children made everyone laugh as he ran from group to group of the meat roasters offering to help them. They all politely declined his assistance as he could hardly reach the green branches. He didn't give up though and made the rounds several times without success, finally returning to sit at the feet of Ako who sat chain smoking, lighting one cigarette after another.

Ado said the boy had been recently orphaned. A jaguar had killed his mother, a widow, some weeks ago. Efforts to find the big cat had not been successful. A party of women tending the corn had seen it several days earlier and had thrown stones at it, causing the animal to vanish into the brush. Perhaps, he suggested, the men who had fire sticks, as they called the shotguns that they carried, might help in the morning. They knew the jaguar was close and probably contemplating another easy kill. The tribe needed support. Lynn agreed to the request. When Thiago told Ado, he made an announcement to the tribe and said they would celebrate tonight because the white men with their fire sticks would hunt the predator. This was the signal for the women to bring out *chicha*, the beer of the jungle.

Ado explained, they cooked yucca root and mashed it. Added grated sweet potatoes, poured in water, and mixed it with the yucca. When it came to the right consistency, they left it for a week to ferment. At that point it became mildly alcoholic, and children were forbidden to drink it. The men though, had no such restrictions and consumed considerable amounts of the mash.

The roasted meat came to them on palm leaves and they agreed that the peccaries made good eating. Lynn and Soames were a little hesitant about the iguanas but changed their mind when they tried the chicken-like flesh. The chicha appealed to the canoe-men and guides but the others found it too thick and not at all like regular beer. Finally, at nine the men were shown to a large hut they were told was the community gathering hall. They stretched out the sleeping bags there and slept through the night. It rained twice, but the showers passed, and the leaf-thatched roof withstood all attempt of the rain to pass through it.

They were awake at dawn Saturday, Lynn complaining of chills and a headache. The women heated water to make the coffee the group had carried with them. Meanwhile Ado spoke to two of the villagers and the men walked over to the chicken pens that bordered the huts. There was a lot of noise and feathers flew as they captured two old hens. Ado explained that they would tether these about two hundred yards from the village to attract the jaguar.

The hunters ate the remains of the evening meal, but Thiago and Pullen swallowed dry biscuits with their coffee. Soames appeared saying he felt a little better and gave Pullen the Sony Coolpix.

"Take this John, keep it with you all the time. Get whatever you can on film." Pullen nodded and then followed Ado and others out of the camp and north into the jungle. They carried spears, but it seemed obvious to everyone that the Benelli M4's would be needed to finish the job if the predator could be found.

They walked along a faint trail and eventually became aware of the clucking of the chickens. Ado held up his hand for silence. The soldiers knew what to do. Ambushes were their business. The village men were told to stay back. Pullen and Thiago chose positions where they could observe the tethered birds in a small clearing forty yards further up the path. They lay flat on the ground and making no movement, listening and processing the early morning sounds of the jungle, waiting to hear something different, a sound out of the ordinary, that would signal the jaguars presence. Insects buzzed, and birds called. A lizard ventured too close to one chicken and vanished into its beak, a tasty meal for breakfast. Butterflies flew into the clearing but soon left when the chickens squawks disturbed their tranquil flight. A loud noise startled everyone. Then Thiago saw a noni tree had dropped some of its pungent smelling fruit. He pointed it out to Pullen who turned up his nose sniffing the bad odor. He nodded knowingly, falling fruit often caused alarm.

Suddenly the noises decreased. They were still there, but it was as if a dial had been switched to 'low'. The men were very vigilant now, their eyes searching the forest ahead. Then they saw movement and the chickens burst into a panicked chorus. Slowly Thiago and Pullen moved their shotguns forward and squinted along the Eotech 552 sights. They had checked the weapons before leaving the village. With five rounds in the magazine and one in the breach, the 12 gauge could bring down any animal to be found on the South American continent.

Like a magician's illusion, the jaguar suddenly appeared. One second it wasn't there and the next, it was. It didn't move, and its perfect camouflage made it hard to find again if one removed one's eyes from it for a moment. They waited, then it yawned, and the killing teeth were seen. The chickens were now frantic with fear as they pulled at their vine tethers. Unfortunately, they blocked a shot from either man as they moved back and forth. Then the animal moved closer and swiped with a paw. There came a high screech and an explosion of feathers and one bird fell dead. It gave Pullen the chance he needed, and he fired. The shell, a 2.75-inch buckshot, hit the big cat mostly in the side of the head and dropped it immediately. Some of the load apparently killed the other chicken as the clucking ceased. No one moved, everyone present realized the jaguar might only be wounded. They would wait a few minutes. After a short time, insects gathered and started feeding on the bloody wound. There seemed to be no movement at all and Pullen signaled Thiago they should move carefully ahead. Benelli's aimed at the jaguar, they walked the forty yards to where it lay. Pullen after walking all around it, prodded it with the shotgun barrel. It was finished. They waved Ado and his men forward, indicating the beautiful, but very dead, animal. The three villagers were smiling. They lashed the legs together with vines and cut a thick branch to hold their prize before hefting it up on their shoulders while Pullen filmed their efforts.

A triumphant procession returned to the settlement and everyone came out to see the now dead killer.

Ado spoke to Thiago, and he translated the words to Pullen.

"John. He said the skin is yours. It's valuable. They will prepare it and you can take it with you."

"Thanks Thiago. Tell him I am most appreciative of the offer, but the skin is for the young boy whose mother the beast killed. Can you do that, please?"

"Of course, John. A great gesture that will make everyone happy!" He talked to Ado who nodded, looking pleased.

Then he stood back and seemed to contemplate the group before continuing his conversation with Thiago. Lynn, Soames and the other members of the expedition waited. After a few moments of speech, the usually stoic faces of the guides showed animation and smiles. When Ado finished, Thiago told the others what he had said.

"Ado is saying you did him and his people a great service by killing the predator this morning. Even more, John's request that the skin be given to the orphan boy showed respect, a gesture very much appreciated by all the tribe. Because the white men had shown this esteem, he wanted to give something to them in return. He understood worldly goods were nothing to men who had food in magic cans that might be eaten weeks after being killed, who owned fire sticks and special bags to sleep in as well as many machete's and knives. But he had information and that could have a value. He is asking Ako to come and tell the story now."

The old man arrived and spoke with Ado. He nodded and indicated everyone should sit near the fire pit. When they were all comfortable he started to talk, pausing every so often to allow the translation.

"Many years ago, as a boy, I learned from my father, we the Kayapo, had a duty given to us years before. One day while we were all together and crossing the Olgo, a huge fish, a pink Dolphin rose from the river and separated us into two factors. We became the Kayapo and Keyepo. The Keyepo, as they now were, were unable to follow the Kayapo and traveled south. The Kayapo stayed north of the Olgo because the pink Dolphin said they were now obligated to stop any travelers from continuing up the river east where the Piripkura, the Butterfly people, live. It is a distance of perhaps thirty miles. They are a tribe that allows no one near their lands and kill trespassers. So, eventually like all things, the pink Dolphin died. Before he did so, he asked our tribe to make a Dolphin to replace him. You know now we carried out his wishes!"

The old man laughed and clapped his thighs as he remembered the story Ako had told him about the canoes nearly being swamped.

"Now, it's rare men reach this point. The last time was fifteen years ago, and these were 'big city' Indians searching for gold. We made it clear they should go back, and they believed the wisdom of the Dolphin. My father, who lived to be an old man, said that around a hundred years ago an expedition like yours arrived here and became frightened by our Dolphin as they walked by the river."

He sat back and smiled, taking a cigarette and lighting it from a branch in the fire.

"This expedition consisted of only three men. They carried everything they had on their backs in bags. They had followed the river they explained to one of the villagers. This man had worked for the *poanjos* and learned some of their words. We explained about the Butterfly people and how dangerous it was to proceed. To no avail, their chief, who we called 'Perfaw' as we could not pronounce his *poanjo* name, was older than the two boys with him. He said they had a mission to seek a hidden City near the Olgo. They did not know how far. They had been walking in the jungle, which is very difficult, covering about ten miles a day. One boy had bad feet, and they stayed several days while the women used herbs from the forest to cure him. They left on the third day. The boy's feet were not cured but looked much improved. The man said he would not delay further and that they might return when they found the City. My father told them the flat lands became rocks and hills and that it would be very slow walking. We waited, but they never came back. Every evening at dusk we looked and for four days saw smoke from their evening fires. Then no more smoke could be seen. They traveled no more than eight to ten miles a day, so they vanished less than forty miles from here. We did not see them again and think the Piripkura, the Butterfly people, killed them." He paused and lit another cigarette.

"I believe this will interest you. I think you seek the lost City. If this is so, then beware! The Butterfly people are invisible in the forest and use the skin of the poison frog to roll their arrows and darts in before shooting them. They make birds fall from the trees and then they are easy to kill. Other animals that are hit by an arrow or dart, act like they have drunk too much *chicha* and fall over to be killed by their knives. This is what I remember from my father. There are two more things. Go to the far side of the village, to the big rocks. On the biggest, with the painted Dolphin, one young man left a sign scraped with a knife. I do not know if it has a meaning. Certainly, we don't understand it. The other thing you will see now."

He called his son over and spoke softly to him. Ado walked to the old man's hut and returned a few minutes later carrying something wrapped in a skin which he handed to Ako.

"Here. Look at this." He opened the skin revealing a deer stalker hat.

Lynn reached out and took the skin, holding it so everyone was able to look at it. Obviously, it had been worn, but seemed in surprisingly good condition. He turned it inside out and bent his head forward.

"It has initials stitched here, look 'PHF'. That's Percy H. Fawcett. The hat's label says it's made by Lock & Co, St. James's Street, London. There's no doubt who owned this!" They all agreed with his analysis. "Let's go to the big rock. The men can pack up, I wish to leave here by noon."

At the Dolphin painted rock, Ado showed them the scratched sign of '$R >$', further confirming the presence of Rimmell. Lynn photographed it to take back to Halesworth.

They returned to where the group waited, and Ado spoke to Thiago who translated.

"From here on you will travel slowly. The flat land now turns into hills and the river narrows. There are many rapids where you must walk. We know the waters for two miles, but no one has been further, and we are unaware what lies after that point. We expect that the Butterfly people are there and will find you before you find them! Return to us and receive our welcome. May the spirits and the pink Dolphin protect you."

The women provided a basket of fruit and Ado raised his hand in something like a blessing. Shaking hands, he accompanied the men to the canoes. They paddled past the floating Dolphin tree and up the Olgo.

CHAPTER XIV

Leaping ahead

Early Saturday morning, they heard the gunshot.

"That was a shotgun blast!", said Renatto.

"Then they are much closer than we thought," replied Teco.

"We have to proceed with care, stopping at each bend. The shot didn't come from the riverside, it came from inland, not far away. Let's move now!"

The men started the electric motors, and the boats moved out. There were several small streams entering the river from either side. Within two hundred yards they came to the first turn. The current was fierce as they crept along the north shore of the narrowing Olgo. Teco climbed out with the binoculars. Walking in the rough shallows, the far side a mere fifty feet away, he peered ahead and, on his left, caught a glance at what looked like a huge floating Dolphin colored pink. He realized what it was. On the bank were three boats pulled up out of the water. He remembered the place, being a Kayapo, but had not been here for years.

He returned to the first of their canoes and waited, letting his eyes search the area. No one could be seen.

"I was born near here. The pink Dolphin floats in the water and the Fawcett people's canoes are on the bank. They are not present. No one is there. I suggest we take advantage of that. Paddle past and get further upstream while they are away. There's a bend in a hundred yards. I bet they are visiting the Kayapo village. If we go by now, we hide upriver and watch for them to come from one of the inlets and let them pass. There are many along here. It's getting higher, and there are hills. I'm sure there will be rapids. We go past, wait for them to get ahead, and learn exactly where they are intending to go,"

Renatto nodded. "I agree. Let me tell the men and we will start at once."

Five minutes later they passed the huge Dolphin and turned the next bend in the much narrower and faster flowing river. The electric motors were hard put to drive them forward and all the men paddled. After about a mile they heard the sound of rapids ahead. Sure enough, the white water appeared.

Renatto paused and looked carefully at the river.

"Teco, we need everyone out of the canoes and walking along the easiest bank. It seems calmer near to the shore and we can float the boats. Without the men in them we should be able to get past these rapids and find a quiet place to conceal ourselves."

"Right. It will be wet but it's the only way."

They paddled to the start of the cascades and exited the canoes. They attached a rope to the prow and stern and the lightened boats, now with very little draft, were easy to maneuver for the next two hundred yards. Then things became difficult.

Teco called to Renatto. "*Patrão,* the river is even narrower here and is running faster. We cannot all go on together. One canoe, with everyone holding it steady, can get past at a time. Then we return for the others, one by one. Finally, we take the raft with the batteries. It seems that this stretch is about a hundred yards and then the river widens again, and we should be through the rapids."

Renatto agreed and while three men held the three tethered vessels, the other dozen, six at the front and six behind, gradually manipulated the first boat through the cataracts. Teco waded ahead seeking the easiest route. It took thirty minutes to clear the rocks. They returned twice more and finally all four boats, and the raft were safely tied up at the far end of the cascades where the water was calm.

Renatto told them to rest and get some food for thirty minutes and then they would paddle until a suitable tributary could be found.

Half an hour later they started on their way again. The banks were rocky, with cliffs to the south, but the Olgo now widened, and there were no obstructions. A mile further on they noticed many small streams entering the river and realized that these caused the increase in the flow downstream. They navigated around several bends, confident that the expedition behind them would encounter the same difficulties and give them time to find concealment.

Finally, Teco pointed out a rock-strewn entrance to a narrow inlet which emerged from behind a point on the north bank. Immediately in front of the large rocks, the ground was covered with pebbles. It appeared they might be able to push their vessels into the creek and conceal them in the overhanging bushes and trees thirty yards from where it entered the river. The men climbed out of the boats and waded, pulling the four canoes and the raft. The small stones lining the stream bed made it easy to wade along the banks. Within twenty yards of the entrance, they became completely hidden from the Olgo. They cleared a space on the banks either side and made themselves comfortable after securing the vessels. Then it was a matter of waiting. Renatto walked in the waters towards the waterway and took a quick peek. He saw nothing. Suddenly his satellite telephone vibrated in his pocket. He looked around to make sure no one was listening before answering.

Gustavo spoke haltingly.

"*Patrão*. May I speak freely?"

"Go ahead."

"As you suggested I checked with friends in Altamira. I still have many contacts in my town. They are trying to find information about this man 'Teco'. There have been no escapes reported yet. They say the Major, Adolfo Sanchez, is not known as a bribe-taker. *Maderas Altamira* knows of this Teco. He stole from them, but their influence got him caught. He went to jail, but where he is now, I have not discovered. That is all *Patrão.*"

Renatto didn't speak for a moment, digesting this information.

"Gustavo. You are sure?"

"One informant works at the jail. He sees everything. Might Sanchez be hiding the escape? perhaps he needed money? We must wait for more information."

"So, it's possible I have a traitor. But why? Well, we will wait and find out what he wants. Good you told me Gustavo. There's a reward for this, it's very important!"

"The reward will be when you return with gold *Patrão.*" He laughed.

"Might your contact find out more do you think?"

"I'll investigate *Patrão.* If I find information I'll call."

"Good. Take care."

Renatto closed the call, confident he had not been overheard. So, this Teco was a thief but no one in Altamira knows where he is. Not so unusual in the Brazilian criminal system where not every town has computerized files. Teco had not betrayed himself in any way up until now, of this Renatto was sure. Perhaps he was innocent of anything and Major Sanchez was supporting a pregnant girl-friend who wanted an abortion? But what if there was something else?

Benicio's devious mind raced. He had not survived this long by being trusting. Far from it. He had faith in no one. So, Teco if he was a spy:

1. He was a spy for the Fawcett's
2. Perhaps for a *favela* chief?
3. Or his own people planted Teco?

It wouldn't be #3. He had set up the meeting with Major Suarez. Gustavo had not known in advance. After being bought into the plot, he immediately told Benicio of the possible problem.

When he had originally dissected the intelligence, he had ruled out the Rio and Paulista *Mafiosos*. He recalled thinking '*Being too distant for any action from them.*' That took care of that.

Only one option remained. He had been planted as a spy for the Fawcett's. But why? Gustavo said he was unable to get all the information on Teco. There was no confirmed escape. Perhaps the story was arranged by the 'honest' Major, Adolfo Sanchez. Hadn't Sanchez asked for a job for a relative? Perhaps, as a bonus, he thought he might slip a person into Renatto River Freight as well. But enough of that. He probably came to spy on them and find out what they wanted from the Fawcett expedition. Did Sanchez act alone? No! Someone may have contacted Sanchez, and he made the arrangements. But who, and why?

It was still quiet; the men had stayed with the canoes. He looked around, and seeing it was clear, called Gustavo back and quickly explained the situation.

"Was Teco a plant?"

"I do not know *Patrão*. Part of his story checks out at least."

"Advise me when you get news."

Benicio disconnected the call and returned to the men.

"Teco. There will be nothing in sight yet. But go down to the entrance and let me know as soon as you notice anything at all."

Teco left and everyone sat down to wait.

Benicio called *Escorpião* to him.

"My friend, there might be a traitor in our group."

"A traitor *Patrão?*"

"Yes. The one that calls himself Teco."

"The Indian guide we picked up in Altamira?"

"That's the one."

"I have not seen anything unusual about him. He has taken us this far without arousing any suspicions. Why do you think that, *Patrão?*"

"I spoke with Gustavo earlier. He has information from his contacts in Altamira. Not everything we learned can be checked out."

Gustavo was the one who originally contracted *Escorpião*. He saved him from a jail sentence and the man was forever in his dept. Whatever Gustavo said was good enough for Cezar 'the scorpion' Costa."

"Shall I fix him *Patrão?*"

"No. we have no clear evidence. We may be barking up the wrong tree, wait a bit longer. He can do nothing against us without hurting himself. We are all out here and must depend on each other. Watch him with great care and keep me advised of anything out of the ordinary."

"It will be done *Patrão.*"

At one o'clock Teco splashed his way back along the stream to where the group waited. The men sat around the beached canoes.

"*Patrão,* they passed and are headed up-river."

"Good. Let them go. We will wait. It's not so bad here. We leave at four, paddle two hours and stop for the night. They will be only a few miles ahead and we can expect them to find whatever they are looking for tomorrow, perhaps. Now let's eat. They others have gone so we can cook some fish. The breeze is coming from the east, so they will not get the stink of our cooking. Have a couple of the men go to the main river. Anything we catch in here will taste of mud!" He grimaced.

"Get a fire going. There will be ray's around in the shallow water, there always are in places like this that have rocky bottoms. The Xingu river ray is not usually eaten but I've eaten them a few times and their wings are sweet and the bones large enough not to bother a careful eater! We will perhaps catch a few and enjoy them. Make sure the beer is put in the river to cool!

Renatto felt happy. At last separated from all his legitimate and illegitimate businesses, he was able to relax. There were no big decisions to be made. He was on the water, something he enjoyed.

There would be a fish fry and beer, two of his favorites. Ah! Sometime life was good!

Two of the crew took hooks and hand lines and walked down to the Olgo. The rays were not difficult to find when they left the eddies of the river. Polka dot backs showed up against the gray pebbles and the men trailed the bait downriver to them and were immediately successful, pulling in a pair of ten-pounders. Twenty minutes later, the rays and a dozen piranha had been cleaned and sat broiling over a wood fire. They used palm leaves as plates and laughed as they ate the sweet, hot flesh. The beer wasn't ice cold, but the river had lowered its temperature to where it was drinkable. When they finished, they took a nap and swapped the batteries from the raft to the canoe's. At four o'clock they pulled their four boats and the raft out to the Olgo and started to paddle.

CHAPTER XV

Finding a friend

They pushed the three canoes into the torrent, finding the going difficult due to the strong current running between the narrow river banks. On either side the terrain seemed to be rising. The first bend appeared, and they heard the sound of rushing water and rapids ahead. Pullen, in the first canoe, held up a hand and all three boats converged.

"We'll have to walk and tow the boats. We get out and stick to the left, close to the bank. It should be deep enough to float the vessels without passengers. Tie ropes to the prow and as soon as we get to the start of the rough water we start the tow."

A few minutes later they hauled the now lighter canoes, over the submerged rocks. It was easy going for a couple of hundred yards but then the river narrowed, and the water became deeper, moving the canoes around and threatening to break them loose from the prow ropes. Stopping to rest for ten minutes they were surprises how the Olgo, so calm until this moment, had suddenly turned into a dangerous torrent.

"We go one canoe at a time. Six men in front with a tow rope and two to the rear with another line to hold the canoes straight. If they get sideways, we will lose control. Thiago will go first and watch for any problems."

They attached a stern rope to the first canoe. It was difficult walking in the flood, especially with rogue rocks underfoot. Finally, after two hours, all three vessels were in the calmer waters of the river and away from the cataracts. They rested and ate hard crackers and spam on a tiny beach. After digging a hole for the garbage, they entered the canoes and started to paddle again.

The river became both wider and calmer now. To the north there were steep hills covered with greenery. The other bank was flatter. There were often small streams draining into the main watercourse from both banks. Pullen checked his watch, almost one thirty, and he felt tired what with all the effort they had expended earlier. Lynn and

Soames were obviously under pressure, and when Pullen noticed this, he called for them to pull out of the current on the north bank and disembark for an hour's rest. There they sat, walking around or stretching out on the narrow beach.

Pullen, carrying his Benelli walked in the shallows and around the next bend. A hundred feet ahead he noticed a rocky point to his left. There, a small stream flowed into the waterway, no different to fifty others they had passed previously. He continued to wade past it.

Now there were cliffs rising from the south bank. He estimated that they were over three hundred feet high at the start of the upcoming stretch. Narrowing his eyes, he deduced that they got even higher further along their route. The river widened more ahead but remained calm and would be easier for the paddlers.

He turned to walk back around the bend, passing the outcrop he had noticed earlier. As he did so, there was a flash of sunlight directly into his eyes. Stopping, he raised the M4 but saw nothing. The flash came again as he peered ahead, shading his eyes. A dark-skinned man, dressed in shorts and a sleeveless shirt, stepped out from behind the rocky point. He had a finger to his lips. Beckoning Pullen forward he held both hands high to show he was unarmed.

He spoke quietly in heavily accented English.

"I am Teco. A friend. This reflected the sun to you." He showed Pullen a gold sovereign he held in one hand. He returned the coin to a pocket.

"I must talk quickly. There are men following your group and they are in this stream with their boats and guns." He pointed behind him. Pullen waited, shotgun ready.

"We have little time. I work for Major Adolfo Sanchez of ABIN, the Brazilian Intelligence Agency. Major Soames, the son of your leader, is also from ABIN. He asked Major Sanchez in Altamira, for his help and I was inserted into this rogue group. They believe you seek a lost City and are sure there is some kind of treasure involved. No action will be taken by them until you find the City. If you find something they will find out and you will be killed. Before that happens, I will try to assist you."

He spoke in such a matter-of-fact manner that Pullen felt sure he was telling the truth. "My name is Pullen. I believe you Teco."

"Good Pullen. I must go immediately and report your boats are passing. Right now, I can do nothing, there's sixteen heavily armed men here. Remember I will do what I can. It may be information I get, or something else. Be ready for any signal I provide. After your group passes, we will follow. Do you understand?"

He nodded. The man disappeared into the stream and Pullen, mystified, made his way back to the group. He beckoned to Lynn and Soames and took them to one side.

"A Kayapo called Teco approached me up the river from here. He said he had been planted in a rogue group of thieves that is following us. Paul, he said your son Victor is an intelligence agent, and he arranged to have this done to see if Teco might help in some way. These men want to find out about the 'lost City' and if we find riches, they intend to kill everyone and steal them. Right now, they are very close and will let us pass and then come in their canoes, out of sight, behind us. Teco said he would do his best to keep us informed and that we should be on the lookout for any signal."

Soames looked confused. "I know Victor is with ABIN, the intelligence group. I didn't know he had become involved in this matter." He shook his head.

"Where are they now?"

"About two hundred yards up-river, hidden in a stream that drains into the Olgo. They will wait until we pass and follow us at a distance until we find the lost City."

"What do you think Sid? Do we keep going or go back to the village and call for help?"

"We might call Victor but what do we say? That we 'think' these men will rob or kill us? That's hardly evidence to arrest them! In any case, he knows this and has probably drawn the same conclusion. No. We must keep going. We are close, and I believe tomorrow we will find something."

They floated the canoes and paddled off again. On the broad waterway there wasn't as much current, and they made good progress. By five, the bluffs shaded the south side of the Olgo and once out of the sun, the men increased their speed. Now cliffs started to appear to the north, boxing the watercourse on both sides. It remained very wide and calm, but the overhanging cliffs were reducing the light.

Half an hour later, Sykes called across to Pullen.

"John. I figure we have come about ten miles from the village. It's going to be dark in twenty minutes, so we need to make camp. Take the lead and pick out the first decent place we can land. You know what we will need for safety now we are in range of those Butterfly people that Ako talked of, not to mention our 'friends' behind us!"

Pullen's canoe moved forward and in ten minutes they found a suitable camp-sight. It turned out to be a dirt beach protected by a reef-like formation of rocks pushing the water towards the center of the river and left a small strand of land at the bottom of the high cliffs.

Very soon the generator started, the tents were pitched, and food prepared. Lynn and Soames turned on the laptop and worked out their position. They estimated that the spot they were in was twenty-six miles from the Kayapo village. This meant that Fawcett had disappeared somewhere in the vicinity.

Dimas and Marcelo volunteered to catch red-bellied piranha and threw lines baited with cracked water snails into the torrent. Within ten minutes a dozen fish were landed and prepared for the pan. They ate the piranha with the Kayapo women's gift of fresh fruit. The guides and canoe men using a lot of the hot sauce as usual. When they finished they cleaned up and lay in their tents to sleep. A guard roster had been set. Pullen and Thiago were to take two-hour shifts followed by Gencio and then Marcelo. It turned out to be a quiet night. During Gencio's shift, the Piripkura, following the odor of the roasting fish, gazed down on them from the cliff-tops. They didn't see any movement and returned to their camp to discuss what to do with these *poanjos* the next day.

CHAPTER XVI

Ambush

The four canoes of Benito's group paddled through the steep gorges. Whenever a break appeared in the cliffs, they saw the hills to the north and the thick jungle covering them. The sun hung low in the west and much of the time the river was in shadow. The men were content. After all, a few days ago they had all been on bandit boats, stealing along the Amazon. Any minute patrols from the Brazilian Navy might find them and there would be no mercy from the military in their 'Marlin' and LPR fast patrol vessels. These heavily armed boats had no set schedule and were therefore a menace to the river pirates, shooting first and asking questions afterwards.

With their stomach's full of fish and beer they happily allowed the electric motors to do most of the work, paddling as little as possible to keep the canoes in line. They traveled slowly, not wanting to get within a couple of miles of the 'Fawcett's'. It wouldn't be long now before something happened.

They would have to take care not to catch up too quickly. The ideal scenario would be to find the other group's canoes beached, with them ashore. Then they could wait until something developed. Should they return loaded to their canoes then they might be attacked, and their prizes stolen. If they came back with nothing, and continued on, that would mean that they had not encountered anything valuable and Benito's group would continue to shadow them. It was a waiting game.

Progressing slowly, they paused before each bend while one canoe moved forward and cautiously investigated before proceeding. Finally, around six o'clock Teco, in the lead boat, held up his hand.

"*Patrão.* I detect the scent of a fire and cooking."

The boats stopped immediately and sought the trees overhanging the north bank. All electric motors were stopped. Men clung to the branches with all their strength and pulled the vessels in as close as possible to the shore.

111

"How far ahead are they Teco? asked Benicio.

"A mile at the most *Patrão.*"

"Look around the next bend for a place to stop. If you don't find anything we may have to go back a little." Teco waded close to the edge of the north bank and carefully looked forward. It was now twilight, but there was nothing to be seen of the Fawcett's camp ahead. He walked a little further and the next stretch seemed clear. There had been a rockfall about twenty yards past the curve and he felt sure the canoes could be pulled up onto it. Turning, he splashed back to his group.

"Nothing ahead. There has been a rockfall and we can pull our boats up on it for the night. It must be cold food. We cannot chance a fire, the flames will reflect off the water and if they are looking behind them, they may investigate. Better we leave the fire until morning for coffee. The early breeze comes from the north and they won't notice anything."

Benicio nodded. "Very well. Let's move."

They paddled ahead and came up to the place where rocks had tumbled down from the heights. It looked steep at the riverside but when they climbed over the stones, there was a narrow strip between them and the cliff-face. It was not perfect, but it would be safe the next twelve hours.

Benicio warned all of them about noise and said they would eat cold canned tuna fish and soda biscuits tonight because they must not show any fires. In the morning when it the sun came up, they could make coffee. The men weren't happy, but they had no choice. They ate, drank a beer apiece and settle down to sleep.

Overnight, the Piripkura investigation of intruders on what they considered their lands, had taken a new development. Observing scouts had reported two groups of canoeists, not one. The second group was bigger than the first with four canoes. They were not as disciplined and did not have as much equipment.

The Piripkura council met at the top of the cliff before dawn on Sunday. There were twenty warriors. They listened to any man who had an idea as was there custom. Finally, the eldest member asked one of the Sub-Chiefs, Mande, to speak.

"There are more than three handfuls of *poanjo's* in this new lot we found. They are closer to us than the other, smaller one. We should attack them first and then move on and strike the others. As I have said before, I got captured some years ago. I escaped. Now I know their ways. They have no respect for weakness and will capture us and make us work in the wood cutting camps or kill us, whatever is easiest for them. We have to be careful. The scouts say these new people have many guns. These are hollow sticks like our blowpipes but are made of metal and launch their darts they call bullets that kill from far off and give bad wounds. Without the fire sticks however, they can be killed easily. The other smaller group has only two firesticks. The big group have four boats. They do not sleep under the cloth covers the others have. They rest in sacks. Now they are at the rockfall. All are sleep. There are no look-out's. We know the stones and that they are broken and loose. We are twenty warriors. The *poanjo's* are down there." He pointed to the cliff edge.

"As soon as light comes, we push the large rocks we know are on the trail down below, on to them and their canoes. If the rocks don't kill them, they will jump out of their sacks. There's no protection from our arrows. But, if they get their firesticks will be beaten. So, we kill as many as we can quickly while they are not able to shoot the firesticks and then we run. We know the land and where to hide. Like all *poanjo's* they will come after us, they always do. But not right away. We'll kill the other people first and then ambush this group again, once, twice, three times until they all die or go back to their own lands. When we finish here, we should run to the other camp and find out if it's possible to attack them before they are prepared. Those *poanjo's* are very near to the revered City, and that's not good!"

The elders agreed to Mande's plan and after cutting thick staves, they carried their bows and quivers of poisoned arrows on their backs and moved out. Slowly they filed into a crack in the cliff. It had partially collapsed and had sent boulders and stones down to form the small beach beneath them. After thirty feet the crevice widened, and there rested four big round rocks that had not fallen. They looked down and saw a sheer drop for another fifty feet to the strip of earth before the stony shoreline. Lining up behind the boulders they worked their poles under them. As the sun came up over the Olgo, they readied themselves. At the elders signal they put all their weight on the poles and the stones tumbled downwards.

There was panic amongst Benicio's group. Two men were killed outright, hit by a pair of rocks as they lay in their sleeping bags. The other two smashed down on Benicio's canoe and pushed it into the water. The Piripkura prepared to fire their arrows downward as the group threw off their bags and scrambled to the cliff-face. In the half-light, the arrows missed, the Piripkura being unaware that when shooting any weapon downhill, one should aim below the target. The consequence of that lack of knowledge was that no one got hit.

"Don't move!" shouted Benicio. "Stay and those arrows cannot possibly touch us."

The Piripkura fired another volley as two men foolishly left the shelter of the wall in an attempt to get their weapons from a canoe. Not stopping to observe the results, the Indians climbed to the cliff top and ran east, up-river to where the other group were camped.

Two of Benicio's men were struck by the second volley. The fast-acting poison disorienting them and causing them to stagger about in circles and finally collapse. Darting out from cover as the second fall of arrows ceased, *Escorpião* was able to grab their AK47's they dropped and make it back to the cliff-face without being hit.

They pressed as close as possible to the rocks, but no more arrows came. After five minutes Benicio took a chance and stepped forward from cover. It was now light but looking up, he saw no one. The Piripkura had gone. Benicio's group had not fired a shot but had lost four men. Today had started very badly.

The corpses were deposited in the river and as they drifted with the current, piranhas attacked them, pushing the bodies from one side of the waterway to the other. From the bank, blood was seen staining the surface of the water. Benicio's canoe, crushed at the rear, continued to drift in the current westwards and vanished around a bend. He called Teco and *Escorpião* over to him and told them to light a fire for coffee, then they would discuss what was to be done.

CHAPTER XVII

Cat and mouse

As the two river pirates were breathing their last after being hit by the falling rocks that Sunday morning, Lynn sat talking to his group.

"Today perhaps, will be the day. We must be vigilant. We'll eat some breakfast and leave."

They drank their coffee and ate energy bars. Then they packed everything into the canoes and made ready to move out into the waterway.

The group was unaware they were being watched from the top of the cliffs. The Piripkura looked down on them from the cover of the trees overhanging the rock race. Not a suitable location for an ambush and they wanted to take no chances. They had plenty of time. Mande suggested they return to their camp, eat, and search again for a decent spot in the afternoon. His idea was accepted, and the group slipped back into the jungle.

Round the next bend the cliffs disappeared, and the land flattened on both banks of the river. The banks were still covered in trees and brush, but they could see for miles northwards where eventually, hills appeared again. They slowed down and looked back. The rockface where the cliffs stopped seemed to be primarily shale and sandstone. Veins were visible where these had been cut. They probably contained pyrite and quartz.

Both river banks, especially to the north were tree-covered, and sloped gently down to the water. Then came another bend, and they halted immediately. Ahead on the left, visible under the multitude of trees, draining out into the waterway, they could see a wide stream. Bordered on its north bank by a double wall that started well inland, it then projected out into the watercourse, diverting the torrent. The construction consisted of huge cut rocks, perhaps from the quarry they had passed. It seemed to protect the stream, allowing it to flow without impediment into the Olgo. As they looked inland they noticed the water flowed towards the river from under a rock arch.

They paddled past it and two hundred yards further on was another even bigger triple wall. As they came level with it they realized it had been built to divert a great deal of the Olgo's water that flowed downstream, inland to a canal built and lined with well-fitting rocks. A lot of water rushed into the opening and through the rock-lined channel, vanishing after fifty yards into what appeared to be an arched tunnel.

Paddling back, they beached the canoes below where the water drained from the City and about fifty feet from where the tree-line started. After dismounting, Lynn, Soames, Thiago, and Pullen, sat down on the stones to discuss the new development. It was ten in the morning.

"It seems we have come upon the irrigation system of what may be the lost City. Behind those rocks the river runs into the channel we noticed, and here, further downstream it drains out from where ever it has been and back into the Olgo. Perhaps in days past that channel carried sewage as well as waste water. In any case we have found something important and I suggest we start inland to find out what else is there."

They all agreed with the assessment and laid out the plans to move forward.

The canoes would be pulled further up the beach and made secure. Five of the group, including Thiago with his Benelli would remain as guards. A Glock 17 would also be left along with ammunition for protection. Soames, of course, would bring his camera. The remaining four, Lynn, Soames, Pullen, and Abilio, the guide, would take light backpacks containing food and water, and head inland. They would go as far as possible, making sure to return by six that evening. Tonight, they would meet back here and discuss what they found and how they would proceed.

They beached the canoes, and everyone helped build a protective wall. It wound around the boats and continued for forty feet before making a right turn and going back to them. They had plenty of room to pitch the tents in its confines. The rocks they were using for the wall were not that large and turned out to be easy to handle. In an hour, a three-foot barrier had been erected. In one corner they built the walls higher, to almost six feet, cutting brush and palm leaves and positioning these on top of thin branches so there would be shade during the day.

Pullen told them what to put in the backpacks. Two cans of canned meat. Four bottles of water, dry biscuits and a small medical kit along with a fire-starter and dry tinder was all they would require. They put on belts with water bottle pouches and sheaths for the machete's and Lynn pocketed his camera and a digital tape measure. Pullen pushed a portable shovel into the backpack webbing and strapped on a wrist compass. They were all wearing hats and sun glasses and had sprayed themselves liberally with insect repellent and 65 block sun-tan lotion.

At eleven thirty in the morning they started off inland, entering the tree-line and brush as they headed north. They could see no trail to follow, so they plunged ahead taking the easiest path. There was plenty of space between the trees, and the brush rarely grew over waist length for the first quarter mile. Then the ferns and bushes became higher and harder to pass. They slashed with their machetes but were still able to continue without worries.

Then the distance between the trees and brush diminished slightly, but they still found it difficult to see very far ahead. Finally, twenty yards in front of them stood a crumbling wall with a rampart. It ran east and west in a straight line and closer inspection showed it had been constructed from stone blocks and mortar. It was about eight feet tall at its undamaged parts, however occasional falls were frequent. Some parts of the wall had lost their battlements, but the remainder was still intact.

"We might climb it but perhaps it would be better to seek a gate further along the wall. If we do that at least we'll enter onto a roadway that leads somewhere. Jumping over here it will be impossible to know where we are, the outskirts or even the City dump! No wonder it's never been found. Everything is hidden under the tree canopy."

They followed the wall, impressed that the construction had held it together despite the ravages of time. After half a mile they could see an entrance ahead. Here it stood firm and its crinoline battlements were intact. The opening had no gates but the pillars that had supported the original posterns were still partially standing. They surmised that the doors had been of wood, long rotted away. A closer view showed that a paved roadway ran back into the jungle where it vanished under the maze of brush and trees. On the interior though the boulevard, for its width proclaimed it to be much wider than a mere road, the slabs stretched twenty feet from side to side. Then ahead, they noticed the first of the structures under the trees.

Lynn took a lot of pictures and film. It would be impossible to recall everything they came across and the camera would provide a record. The building ahead was constructed with large quarried rocks, joined by mortar. In parts, where it still stood undamaged, its height was recorded with the laser measure as eighteen feet. Ferns, palms, and brush, grew from every cavity providing perfect camouflage from any satellite sweep. The structure was dissected by the thoroughfare which ran through it under a huge, intact arch. There were several openings along its measured four hundred-foot length. As with the main gate, no wood remained. They walked through the closest door, into the structure's interior. There they found a long passageway which stretched all the way down to the next entrance. Spaces, probably for doors, were to be seen all along confining wall. Staircases to an upper level, most in a collapsed condition, dotted the rooms. They talked among themselves and agreed this had to be some kind of administrative center. Its position beyond a major gateway, made it probable that it might have contained offices for officials who governed the City. There were creepers all over the stones and lizards, snakes, frogs and other small creatures obviously had made their homes there. Then an even larger snake appeared, and they halted as it vanished into an opening.

"Probably looking for prey", suggested Pullen as they started forward again.

The height of the doorways, under six feet, baffled them for a few minutes and then Soames suggested that back four hundred years or so, people were smaller than today. Hence the lower construction.

They stopped to eat and drink water for twenty minutes while they talked and then decided to explore a little more before their return.

Walking right through the building, and following the boulevard, they exited out the other side. Here there were large square buildings, all constructed as bases for various governing ministries, perhaps? A closer inspection of the walls showed carvings concealed under the vines growing there. They scraped the surface beside the doorway of a large structure and found a mosaic made up of colored stones. It was a symbol that none recognized. Its borders were blue green rocks and within rested a hand, palm held forward beneath a pile of coins and a simple scale. Could this be the customs house?

They stopped. Ahead every building was in ruins. They noticed a large crack in the ground running north to south. Coming closer they saw no bottom to the deep fissure. It seemed that an earthquake had occurred around this spot previously. Perhaps this had persuaded the population to abandon the City?

Pullen looked at his watch, it showed four o'clock. Time had flown by and they would now have to return. Not wishing to chance getting lost, they returned the way they had come and arrived at the small stronghold shortly before six. Soames told Thiago to tell the men what they had seen. It was always a good idea to let troops know what was happening. It gave them confidence and eliminated worries.

The generator started up and references were checked and checked again on Lynn's Laptop and data uploaded to Soames PC as a backup.

Pullen made up a guard roster which would go into effect immediately.

Gencio and Marcelo were the cooks, and they decided to try their luck fishing for peacock bass with live minnows they had caught using a mosquito net in the shallows earlier. Their efforts had the whole crew cheering as the feisty peacocks fought against the lines. Five were landed and the canoe-men were roundly congratulated. They boiled water for spaghetti which they mixed with a canned sauce and grilled the cleaned fish. Marcelo had found a mango tree and combined the fruit with wild watercress from the river banks. A bottle of dressing completed the dish.

It turned out to be a spectacular meal. The group, minus the two guards on watch, sat with their plates, close to the water, enjoying the calm night. They drank beer that had been cooling in the river and Soames came up with a box of cigars that had been slipped into the supplies.

Looking out of the water, they watched a family of river otters catching fish and playing in the brilliant light of a full moon. They were tireless as they climbed the banks to chew on their catch. The bones were swallowed down with the remainder of the flesh and they leaped back into the water to chase the young pups and look for additional food. Finally, the otters decided to call it a day and vanished into burrows above the waterline on the far bank.

To the north there were flashes of lightening and they heard thunder, but the rains didn't come. Soames tried to use the satellite 'phone, but the atmospherics were bad, and he could get no connection and eventually put it back in its case.

Cleaning up, they buried their trash. The main generator lights were not needed and were switched off for the night. Everyone returned to their tents, tomorrow would be a hard day. The guards, carrying the Glock 17's, and experienced in their jobs, walked different routes. There was only a spotlight that one guard used to sweep the tree-line. They never patrolled the same route twice and occasionally dropped from an upright positions and lay prone, peering out from behind the retaining wall for minutes on end. There would be no way they could be surprised.

CHAPTER XVIII

Watching and waiting

Benicio sipped his coffee as Mateo, one of his crew, attended to the cuts on both elbows sustained when he scrambled to cover under the cliff-face. He winced as the iodine was painted onto the abrasions. Gustavo, thankfully had told *Escorpião* to make sure he put a first-aid kit aboard the canoe's. Now, with band-aid's almost invisible below the short sleeves of his shirt, he felt a little better. Thanking Mateo, he stood and addressed the group.

"Listen to me carefully, all of you. From this moment forward, you must carry your AK's with you at all times. 'All times' means when you are walking, sitting, eating and shitting! It must be in or close to, your hands. This morning the rifles were in the boat and you lot were in your goddam sleeping bags! No more! The guns go with you everywhere. We lost a canoe and the satellite 'phone, food water and beer as well." He stared down at the men.

"Now. Four comrades are dead, and these Butterfly Indians have made us look stupid. The next time it will be different I assure you. You get a sovereign for every man or woman you kill. So, aim carefully and remember, those arrow tips are coated with poison. I've seen them in other parts. They use the poison for killing birds, monkeys and even fish. However, it doesn't differentiate between animal and human flesh! It's venom from poisonous frogs. Some of them are tiny, under an inch long. Doesn't matter, they are all covered with poison slime. By the way, they also use the sap of the curare plant, it's deadly! The good thing is that the accurate range is short, under fifty feet. Don't let that lead you to think they can't hit you. A volley from twenty men can land in an area ten feet square and if you are in that area, you can die! So, take care. Now get ready, we leave right away!"

The men stood up, but before they moved, he called out to them.

"Stop! There are arrows around everywhere. Don't touch them, the poison is still very potent, even hours after they fire them. Get the canoes ready. We will not launch until this afternoon. Rest but keep your eyes open.

They sat for a long time in the shade of the cliff, waiting for Benicio's order to move out. Finally, at three o'clock, with a great deal of care, and after looking up, down and around, they launched the three remaining boats. Once afloat Benicio called to Teco.

"Stop before every bend and walk forward. It won't be long now. Here, take these binoculars. He handed over the glasses and they paddled forward.

An hour later a tiny dirt beach appeared, sheltered by a rock formation that pushed the water outwards leaving a small strand of dry land. A closer inspection revealed that a fire had been built recently and Benicio realized this was the previous day's camp of the other group and they were now very close.

Thirty minutes afterwards came a bend. Teco got out and waded forward. He walked carefully and searched ahead every few steps. Finally, he sheltered behind a large bush and looked over the water.

The view north was uninterrupted. The hills had flattened, and he looked out at what seemed a plain covered with trees. East, these stretched to within fifty feet of the banks of the river. Through the binoculars he observed a rough fort built from rocks about four hundred yards downriver. There were men inside it.

Three canoes were almost hidden in the enclave. A short distance further on was a tall wall that bordered a fast running body of water flowing out from the jungle and into the Olgo.

He raised the glasses higher. Two hundred yards further back, east along the river, a massive rock wall was built into the waterway. It seemed to be diverting water inland while the main flow continued downriver. This was obviously a base camp.

Teco returned to Benicio.

"*Patrão*, they are staked out round the next bend less than a quarter of a mile away. They have built a small rock fort and their canoes are inside it. There are several men inside the enclave but not all of them were there."

"I'll go with you. This I have to see."

Benicio accompanied by Teco and *Escorpião*, walked to the bend and sheltered behind the bush that Teco indicated.

He handed the glasses to Benicio and stood back while he raised them and scanned downriver.

Sure enough, he picked out the rock fort and noticed men inside it. The two walls diverting the river were huge, and he realized one bought water inland and the other expelled it to the Olgo. Was this the City? Surely it must be.

He handed the binoculars to *Escorpião*.

"Examine carefully and then tell me afterwards, everything you see. We will compare notes before we decide what to do. Teco, is there a place for us to camp before this bend? We want to be able to have two men here with glasses all the time to see what the Fawcett's do."

"Where we are beached now is fine *Patrão*. The cliffs are very high and there's no way down from the top. They overhang so we will be dry and safe. We can brief the men after our discussion and then send them, two at a time to keep watch. If they see anything, one can return while the other stays."

"Good. Let's return and talk, then have men back here right away."

They returned to the canoe's and raft, pulling them further up the rocky shoreline.

"Sit around here." Said Benicio. "I will tell you what we are to do next."

He had Teco and *Escorpião* explain what they had observed. Then he laid out what he believed was happening. Mentioning the City had the men asking questions, but he told them to wait until he finished and then he would try to answer them.

"I think this must be what they seek and that they are already exploring. Not all the men were in the rock fort. I need to know when the others return and if they are carrying anything. We do not want to make a move until we are sure they have valuables with them. You must keep your eyes open all the time, no dropping off for a nap!"

After half an hour everyone seemed to understand what was required and the first two men were sent the hundred yards around the bend to observe and report.

Benicio lay down on a flat slab of rock and put his hands under his head. He racked his brains. What should the next move be? If his men noticed the Fawcett's carrying any objects, then it would be reasonable to assume they would be valuable. Should he wait until they were asleep and then attack the fort? No. They would have guards. Better hold on and when they started back, ambush their boats. If they did find something would it be small enough to carry? Suppose it happened to be a hoard of valuables and they could only take a few? What then? Hold on until they left, then go and search for their find in the City? What about the Butterfly people? Would they attack the Fawcett's? Might they attack his group again? One thing for sure, they did not know his group had been tracking them! That was good news. What of Teco? Could he be trusted? He had been fine so far. There were so many questions! His brain raced, and he closed his eyes. Soon, he dozed off to sleep.

A hand shook his shoulder.

"Patrão. Are you awake?"

He opened his eyes and saw Mateo.

"Yes, Mateo. I am awake."

"I have come from watching *Patrão.* "

"Speak then!"

"It is after six. Four men returned to the rock fort. Two had long guns. They were not carrying packages. Now some are starting to fish and make a fire. Probably to cook their evening meal. Another thing *Patrão,* the Butterfly people are observing them! We were not seen but the Indians are in the trees not far from the Fawcett's camp and are looking at them."

"Get Teco and the Scorpion. We will go to the bend and I want you to show me where the Indians are. Hurry, it's getting dark!"

They waded to the observation bush and Mateo pointed out to Benicio where the Indians were hiding. They were nowhere to be seen but Mateo said he had noticed them earlier. It was three hundred yards from where they were hidden and about a hundred yards from the fort. Suddenly the slight noise of a generator starting could be heard and lights appeared inside the enclave. As they watched, a spotlight came on and swung in an arc along the tree-line to the north of the fort.

Benicio gestured to the others, and they walked back around the bend.

"They have guns. The Butterfly people are quite a way from the enclave and I don't think they can make an attack if that spotlight is shining. Anyone trying to approach would be shot. There are no rocks to roll down on people either. The only way they could get the Fawcett's would be to ambush them when they go back tomorrow."

The Scorpion spoke.

"*Patrão.* Perhaps when it's dark, we might go ashore round the bend, get into the trees and catch the Butterfly's by surprise?"

"No. They are in their own territory. It would be difficult. We know they are in the trees now but not where they will be tonight. No, we wait. In the morning before it is light, we will go through to the jungle. When the sun comes up, and it's certain the group has left, we walk east to cross their trail. If the Indians are after them they will depart before we get there. Then we will be behind both groups. We are twelve men with AK47's. There should not be a problem killing everyone ahead of us if necessary. There cannot be more than a dozen of them and bows and arrows are not automatic rifles!"

Returning to the boats, they opened tins of tuna, and ate it with hard biscuits and beer. In the moonlight they took out their sleeping bags and arranged them as comfortably as possible on the rocks. There seemed to be no need for everyone to stay awake tonight. Two men would have the watch for two hours each. The cliffs would keep them safe and they felt sure the Butterfly people were occupied elsewhere.

CHAPTER XIX

Preparing an ambush

Mande and the other warriors were awake at dawn Monday. They had not seen Benicio's men an hour earlier as they crept around the bend using the trees as cover. These came right down to the river bordering the rock quarry. The Piripkura had not seen them because they had abandoned the forest the night before and made their way to the tribe's ancient home in the south-west corner of the City.

It was a big camp. The wall that bordered the Xingu measured several thousand feet from end to end, and the sides probably twice that length. Piripkura occupied only a tiny corner where the west wall met the south.

This happened to be a sacred place for them because it contained a temple where their tribe had always worshipped. This pre-Colombian structure, built around 1450 and finally finished some ten years later, was strange in the fact that people were allowed to choose their own gods to worship and build their own temples.

It was not until after the 1602 earthquake that the Piripkura were given the name 'Butterfly people'. It came about because other tribes that made contact with them during the two hundred years when they were wandering in the region, realized they lived in no permanent homes. They were like butterflies, flitting from one place to another.

They eventually returned to the ruined City, but the name stuck. True, they still rove wide and far on their hunts and ensured no one came close to the revered place. They had escaped the terrible damage from the 'quake because as poor itinerants they lived in palm huts outside the walls and were not crushed by the falling masonry.

There the City sat for centuries, covered after a few months with plants, trees and vines making it all but invisible under its canopy. Occasionally a hunting party or a lone traveler from another tribe, would find it, but these visits were unusual. Most of the time any attempted incursion on the lands claimed by the Piripkura would result in death. The Butterfly people jealously protected their territory, and that included the revered City.

When they finally did return to their ancient home after two hundred years, things had changed, not only with the structure but with the Piripkura themselves. There were now no artisans whatsoever. No longer were they a race of workmen and builders. The returning survivors were the same poor people, who always lived near to the edge of the town. They were the only ones to survive. Most came back but had no idea how to re-build their magnificent structures or repair their roads.

Now they became a tribe of indigenous forest dwellers, suspicious of the outside world and determined to remain exactly how they were. However, they understood the infrastructure of the City and encountered no problem navigating through it, usually though, they stuck to their small enclave and its unique temple.

Not far from their village stood one of the twelve huge cisterns, fifty feet deep and rock lined, situated throughout the metropolis. These were disguised as lakes and lagoons and many were bridged. Water would come in, diverted from the Olgo by the huge wall. It ran through one of the underground channels, and would fill the reservoirs, and overflow into a main pipeline. This eventually surfaced from under an arch near river bank and then flowed back into the Olgo along the wall. Unlike the majority of the cisterns, theirs had not been damaged by the earthquake and still functioned as designed. The women got their water from it and were thankful, as their ancestors had been, that they did not have to walk to the river. The engineering planners, all those years ago, would have been pleased with their praises.

There lived the Chief, cared for by women of the tribe. The man had survived for nearly ninety years and although he could still walk, he was not as mobile as he had been years earlier. His mind however remained sharp, and he was a formidable disciplinarian. His laws were the laws of his ancestors and he saw no reason the change them. One day he would die, and then the tribe would select a new leader, until then, he was Jafa, supreme Chief of the Piripkura, the Butterfly people. An impressive title for a man that now ruled less than fifty tribesmen and their women.

Tall for a Piripkura, He towered over most of his subjects. His eyes were dark brown rather than black and his hair, unlike the jet color of most Indians appeared finer with a reddish tint. His skin was tattooed with black markings from head to foot. He wore only a loincloth and a headdress of bird feathers, but what a headdress! It consisted of the feathers of the crimson rosella, the most colorful of the parrot family. The plumage started with a leopard-skin pattern of yellow and black and then blended with two blues, a bright royal color and a more subdued sky shade. Jafa didn't seem to be nearly ninety. The sun had been kind to his body. It had wrinkles, but these smoothed out when he stood up and walked. His face was not round like most of the men but longer and his nose was not flat. He was not an unhandsome man!

Jafa walked outside his abode that Monday after Mande called him early. The house, constructed from the stone walls of the original residence, had a palm-thatched roof, replaced many, many times over the years. The other warriors were seated in a semi-circle waiting. He motioned Mande to sit. He held out a hand and immediately a woman gave him a gourd of water which he drank down. This was followed by a piece of roasted breadfruit which his toothless mouth mangled slowly. Finished, he looked up and nodded to each of the men, one after another.

Taking his time, he finally spoke.

"Well Mande? You have been away three days. Tell me what you did? It appears to be important, all these men." He indicated the warriors seated in front of him. "First though, what game did you bring back?"

Mande understood the Chief of old. He never rushed anything. He had an answer ready to recite.

"We hunted west and north. There saw no game the first day except two monkeys which we ate in the evening. Yesterday morning after our battle, we killed three aguti's and two peccary. The women cleaned them last night. They are all being smoked now. This morning I learned that the women took six turtles from the water traps. Those will be eaten later today." He smiled at the Chief.

"Good. Now tell me about this 'battle' you mentioned. Don't tell me that the monkeys attacked you for killing their brothers!"

All of the men laughed. The Chief and his humor must be recognized.

"No. Not monkeys. *Poanjo's!*

"*Poanjo's?* Who were they? Where were they from? Tell the whole tale Mande!"

The warrior settled back on his heels and spoke.

"Saturday evening, we caught the odor of fish cooking. We followed the smell, it lingered for hours, and finally we came to the river and from a cliff, could see nine *Poanjo's* sleeping in a camp. They had a sentry on guard and seemed to be very careful. Their beds were inside cloth enclosures. Later that night our scouts reported, so we decided that we would attack this group at dawn Sunday. Before light we rolled rocks down on them. These crushed two men, and sent one of their four canoes, into the waterway. It broke and would soon sink. Our arrows killed two more but then they retrieved fire sticks and we ran before they used them. Perhaps they will go back to their own lands? We do not know what they are seeking, but anyone approaching the revered temple must be stopped. They have not been seen since yesterday afternoon over there," He pointed to the river.

"We found the other group. They went into the City and we saw them returning. They built a rock fort and they possess a flame that illuminates the night without a fire. The sentries are alert and very careful. They can be ambushed perhaps later today if they go out and if you agree. That is everything. We left the forest this morning at dawn and came here to tell what happened."

"I understand. Double the guards at the temple. We must take no chances. It's not likely they'll find this corner any time soon. These men will go through the big building and out to the ministries, parks, fountains, and monuments. They are *poanjo's* and think everything is fascinating. That is good. Of course, we should kill them all, or they will take their information back to where they came from and tell others. They will be looking for gold because they are fools. Only we, the Piripkura know where the treasures of our City are hidden. So how do we kill these men? There are many of them and we must bring in the other hunting party's immediately. Send scouts out now Mande please. Two must go north, two east."

Mande designated four men, and they walked off to speak with the women before leaving to search for the huntsmen. Before any group started a hunt, they would explain where they would seek game. This would make them easier to find if needed.

"There will not be enough men until morning. Watch the *Poanjo's* today, assign the men. Take care and return at dusk. I will visit the temple when we finish here. I need to ask for guidance and help there."

The men stood and Jafa returned to his hut.

The scouts set off at an easy run. They were aware of the fastest way to the hunting areas and harbored no doubt they would encounter their fellow warriors later today.

They took hardly anything with them, quenching their thirst from accumulated water held in the many bromeliads growing in the rain forest. Some chewed on meat jerky the women had provided. An excellent nutrient, light to carry and eaten without stopping. The remainder left to seek out the *Poanjo's*.

Mande returned to the forest and saw the group in the fortress readying for an excursion. He spoke a few words and half a dozen of his warriors set out to follow them while he and his men walked east to seek the others. These nine men headed towards the river, the going would be easier there. Little did they know that they would come upon their prey very soon, and not under the circumstances they had expected.

CHAPTER XX

A clash of warriors

Benicio and his men had successfully left their camp, walked around the bend and quietly vanished into the forest. It had been dark, and they were obliged to go slowly, crouching over to make the smallest of silhouettes. They were unaware the Butterfly men had returned to their village, but it made no difference. The important thing was that no one could guess where they were. The Piripkura had last seen them sheltering under the cliff-face on Sunday morning. Now, twenty-four hours later that's where they would head to start their search. They carried food, water, and spare magazines, for the AK's. Benicio had said this had to be a fighting patrol!

Escorpião found the trail. They had stayed quiet in the trees until light, then strolled in a line north-east.

"Here *Patrão*", he called.

Benicio and Teco walked across to a small clearing. There he noticed feces beside a bush. Human feces.

"They were here earlier."

He stood back and scanned the terrain ahead. From this angle he saw where people had walked through the brush after crossing the clearing. Benicio smiled. He turned around, and now he was able to make out the way they had come. The traces were very faint but once you had a clue, it became easy.

"Let's wait for a little. I think they will come back. They are used to having everything their own way and won't expect anyone to be waiting for them." He rubbed his hands together in anticipation.

"Into the brush here and keep quiet. We'll wait and watch what comes. Check the weapons. No smoking, eating or drinking until I say so. Stay quiet until I fire. When I do, give it everything. Put the safety on full automatic. That's the middle setting. Stop when I say stop. Now get on the ground."

The group of twelve spread out and sat on the ground, pointing their weapons at where they expected the Piripkura to appear. Benicio made sure they were all under cover and hid himself. They waited.

An hour passed, and then sounds were heard. Voices speaking in normal tones but in an unknown language. The first Indian entered the clearing. He saw the feces and pointed, calling to the eight men behind him who started to laugh as they walked forward. Benicio waited no longer. Pointing the rifle at the emerging group, he squeezed the trigger. Thirty rounds of 7.62 ammunition from his gun and another 300 bullets from the other eleven men, decimated the Piripkura. The magazine from Teco's AK fired way above the heads of the attackers who fell in bloody heaps, arms, legs and even heads, almost severed.

"Stop. Stop!" shouted Benicio, but the men emptied their magazines, anyway. Finally the noise ceased.

"*Escorpião.* Go and check."

He walked over and stared at the mess, poking with the rifle barrel at a few corpses, moving them off each other.

"*Patrão,* eight dead here. One grazing shot to the skull but he fell to the bottom, the others took all the fire. He's unconscious but alive. Do I kill him?"

"Wait! Is he conscious?"

"No *Patrão,* He's sleeping like a baby!"

The men roared with laughter.

"Teco, could you understand the dialect should he speak?"

"Probably *Patrão,* my tribe's language is similar I believe."

"OK, let's go back to our boats and wait until he recovers. Then we can find out if he knows anything. Teco, he's wearing a headdress, the others wear nothing except a woven band. Might he be a Chief or something?"

"I'll see *Patrão.*"

Teco walked over and gazed down at the blood-covered man. His only wound was a crease that bled profusely where a bullet had grazed his temple. Teco looked again. He steadied himself so not to give away his surprise. This was Mande, the Butterfly person he had given food to at the logging camp some years ago. He wore a head piece of black and white feathers probably from an anteater bird. He called out to Renatto.

"Yes *Patrão*. It means he is probably a Sub-Chief, a little more than a simple tribesman."

"He might know something. Tie his hands and legs, but not so much he can't walk. We don't want to carry anyone. Get him awake, throw water on him."

It took five minutes but after two bottles of water had been poured over his head and Teco had wiped the blood away, Mande returned to consciousness. Teco walked over to where Benicio sat cleaning his AK.

"He's awake *Patrão*. There is a rope around his waist, he will not run. His hands are tied tightly behind his back and the leg ropes will let him walk slowly."

"Bring him along then." He looked at the men. "Back to the canoes. Be careful at the tree line, there's not much cover so go one at a time." He didn't bother to check the prisoner's bonds.

Turning, Benicio lead the way, Teco and Mande bringing up their rear.

Teco walked slowly. He told the men near to him that his prisoner was still recovering from his head wound and could not walk fast. They shouldn't worry, everything was under control.

As soon as there was space between him and the group, Teco looked directly at Mande. He said nothing. Mande's eyes cleared, and his mouth opened to say something, but Teco shook his head. He waited until there until even more distance opened up between the men and himself and then spoke to Mande.

"I am Teco. I will explain quickly. and you must listen. Trust me! You are Mande. I gave you food at the logging camp when you were a slave there. Do you remember?"

Mande blinked in acknowledgement.

"I did not shoot my gun at your men, I shot over their heads. Their blood is not on my hands but on the hands of those in front of us. They are bad men. Now they want to question you. I'll say you speak a little of my own tribal language but not a lot. I will tell them your answers reveal nothing. They will probably beat you, asking for information. You stay silent. I'll explain you are not very intelligent. They will not kill you, not yet anyway. You may be a hostage. Tonight, when it's dark, I'll cut you free and we will escape. There is another group of *Poanjo's* close, as you probably have realized. They can help us.

Believe me when I say this. In return, you must tell your men we wish them no harm. Are you willing to help?"

Mande replied.

"I will. I remember you Teco. Don't worry, I will say nothing and trust you to help me. The Piripkura remember our friends."

Teco nodded and then shouted, "Get moving you lazy savage, walk faster."

He prodded him with his rifle and the men, looking back, laughed.

In fifteen minutes they were all safely at the canoes.

"Right, let's find out how many of them there are first. Teco, ask him that."

"Yes *Patrão.*" He walked over to Mande who sat tied in front of the group.

"Now my boss is asking how many men are in your tribe?"

"Shall I tell him?

"Say what you wish. I will tell him there's over a hundred of you and that they are very annoyed right now and will be even further upset when they find what happened today!"

"I understand. However, our tribe is small, only fifty warriors, women and children remain. Who are these *Poanjo's?* What do they want? Why should these others help? Are they different in some way?"

"I must reply now. As for your questions, I'll give you answers when I am able. Just wait!"

He turned to Benicio.

"He says over a hundred tribesmen are now coming here and that they intend to kill us all. Tomorrow they will arrive. Perhaps we could negotiate using him as a hostage?"

"Hold on a minute! First find out about the valuables, is there gold? If there's money here, then we must decide if it's worth fighting these Indians to take it. First, we must find out. Ask him."

"I'll trick him into giving us the truth *Patrão.* It may take a while, but I'll try now. Please be patient."

"Go ahead Teco. I'm going for a drink." Walking to his canoe he retrieved the *Asombroso* Tequila and drank directly from the bottle while Teco started his questioning.

"The *Patrão* is not sure what to do. Negotiate a retreat or fight? First, he wants to know if the Piripkura possess valuables?"

134

Mande laughed. "You expect me to tell you of our wealth? What kind of fool do you believe I am?"

"I am asking you because he wishes to know. Say whatever you want to but take care! What will allow you to continue living? If you tell him are hiding gold, he will shoot you here and now. Then he will fight your people for it. If you insist there's nothing, then you are of no use to him. Now, should you tell him there may be valuables, but you're only a Sub-Chief and not authorized to see them, perhaps he will have enough interest to use you to get to the truth. This would be the easiest way. I'll tell him you will speak to your people and negotiate."

"Teco. I would not tell you of the Piripkura valuables even if I did know something. Say I will talk to our Chief and see how a settlement can be reached. Perhaps you can suggest that they may be willing to pay us to leave?"

"Well, let's see what he says." Teco stood and walked to Benicio.

"*Patrão*. He says he is only a Sub-Chief and knows nothing of the tribe's wealth. I'm sure they own something of value though if only by his denials! He said he could speak to his Chief and see if the tribe might pay us a tribute and we could go in peace."

Benicio smiled. "He's smart for an Indian! What the hell! Let's find out if he can do that. Can he get the Chief here? I doubt it! Ask, but be willing to say we can talk at a distance. Out of the range of their arrows but in range of our AK's. That second option would probably be best. This Sub-Chief is our hostage after all. Make him think we are not sure. If things don't go well, we shoot as many as possible. That should scare the shit out of the rest of them! We must find out about what they actually own that we can use. Go ahead."

Teco turned back to Mande.

"He says to ask if you can bring your Chief to talk. He really doesn't imagine it's possible, so he said if not, let's talk at a distance. What he wants is for your tribe to pay him to leave. If they agree he might do that. However, these river pirates are very dangerous, and their word should never be believed completely. If he thought the other *poanjos* had something of value, he would say yes to taking your payment and kill you first and then go for the others. Anyway, I'll say we will go around the bend, stay under cover and show you as our prisoner on the end of a rope. Perhaps we build a smoky fire with green branches to call their attention. When your men appear, you will shout to them and negotiations can start. Let's see if he buys that. Tonight, we will run when the time comes."

"I agree to your plan Teco. By now, the bodies will be found, and the men will be talking about what to do. No hasty decisions, and they will probably wait for morning to do anything."

Again, Teco walked to where Benicio sat with his bottle, quietly watching them.

"Patrão. He says that when his tribe realizes he is a hostage, they will want him back. He will agree to see if we can be paid to leave. Tomorrow, early we can take him around the bend. He stays ties up and we remain vigilant all night here. In the morning we make a smoke fire ready to show when we get to the corner. We shove him out on a rope and he calls his people. Good! Tell him we will kill him if he tries to run or does anything to betray us. We possess the guns and we can cut down everyone in a very short time!"

"Yes. I'll tell him. We need guards tonight. Three all the time. Two watching up river and one keeping an eye downstream and on the prisoner. I don't expect trouble from there, the cliffs reach down to the river and the water is deep. Nothing can come down there. Change the guards after two hours of duty. I ask the men to get food and we can eat. It's early but we can't do anything until dawn."

They settled in for their long wait.

CHAPTER XXI

Negotiations

Monday, shortly after dawn, Pullen awoke. He peered outside his tent and watched the two guards at different corners of the fort. They were looking outwards as they should be. He stepped out, and as he did so there came the noise of automatic gunfire that lasted about twenty seconds. Then it became quiet. The others left their tents at the sound.

"That's AK47 fire for sure," said Pullen to Thiago who stood beside him.

"Right. It came from over there." He pointed down-river to the bend.

Pullen replied "Down-river and inland I would say."

Thiago shrugged. "The other group you were told of John, they are here. That sound wasn't one gun, it was a dozen at least. Had to be an ambush, right?"

Pullen nodded. "Right. Big volley and silence. The others were either wiped out or didn't own modern weapons. We heard nothing beside that barrage. My bet is that they were Indians and got caught somewhere over there in an ambush by the sixteen following us. They have no firearms, hence the silence. There's nothing we can do."

Lynn had been listening carefully.

"It must be the Piripkura, they are the only tribe that live in this area. How come, if they are jungle dwellers and very tuned to these conditions, did they get caught? How many were killed? Why was there an ambush? Had the Butterfly people already attacked this group?"

Soames nodded. "They showed their hand. They must know we are here and surely heard the shots. We must bide our time and find out if your Indian friend contacts us. Today should be quiet. These river pirates will be celebrating their victory, and the Indians mourning their dead. I can't call Victor and tell him all these things because we are unsure as yet. Let's go to the City and take another look around over there. Perhaps this evening we can decide how to proceed."

They all agreed to continue exploring and for the men remaining, to keep a good lookout. The Indian, Teco had said he would contact them in some way. They would have to wait.

They made breakfast and drank their coffee. Shortly after nine, Abilio, one of the guides, made his way over to the group and spoke to Thiago.

"I saw at least two men in the trees as the river bends. They crouched down while crossing a clearing where the forest thins a little. Perhaps others, but two for sure. They were heading down-river. It's hard to see much."

"Thanks, Abilio." He turned to the others and explained what had been said.

"They are returning to their camp then. Abilio observed two making themselves inconspicuous, but we can be sure there were more, and they were probably going back to where they are camped. As Paul said, they might be celebrating. They will not come here today. In any case, as the Indian told John, they will wait until they are sure we found something valuable before attacking us."

Lynn paused for a moment. "We are looking for Fawcett, not valuables. Let's continue to follow our original mission. It's what we came to discover. Of course, finding the City is a tremendous achievement and we must report this to the Brazilian authorities. When we do that the bureaucracy will take over immediately. In all likelihood we will be restricted, or even stopped completely for exploring further until they conduct a thorough examination. Therefore we must carry on for a day or so and then report our find. Today we can go north and east and tomorrow north and west. Investigate everything, compare notes and come to a decision. Frankly, the Piripkura must be contacted. They may have news. Getting that information is something else! Our last hope is the Indian, Teco. God willing, he'll get to us and we can learn what's happening. Now, same as yesterday, let's move out."

Lynn, Soames, Pullen, and Abilio moved from the fort and into the City following their footsteps from the previous days. Pullen had taken a flashlight, binoculars, and a coil of rope from one of the canoes. The light rested in his pocket and the nylon knitted line over one shoulder. The glasses were in their case, over the other. This time they passed through the big building and north-east. They noticed the structure that had the mosaic besides its front doorway and headed to the right. Turning a corner, they came upon a domed edifice with steps leading up to a wide entrance. They climbed up and entered. The dome was intact.

Soames scratched his head. "Incredible! This type of structure didn't exist until after the first world war, or so we thought. It looks like a geodesic dome. A lattice-shell based on a geodesic polyhedron. The triangular elements of the dome are structurally rigid and distribute the structural stress throughout the structure, making geodesic domes able to withstand very heavy loads for their size. How did these people know about that?"

It appeared to be a temple. Directly beneath the dome was a huge square block, perhaps an altar. Soames stopped suddenly.

"John, there's a snake! It moved behind the altar, be careful!"

Pullen looked but didn't notice anything. Channels dug in a circular pattern all around the building. It was easy to guess people could put their feet in the channel or well and sit on the bank. The estimated it would hold about five hundred worshipers. Walking past the altar they came across another crack in the ground, smaller than those of the previous day but still significant enough to cause the far wall to collapse. The fissure ran north west and when they peered through the gap in the wall, they saw that it had cleaved a path through the City in a straight line. It looked like a highway cut by engineers using a theodolite for accuracy. Houses bordered the split and large buildings were not common.

Soames held up a hand, and they all stopped where they were.

"Exploring residences will not further our cause. If Fawcett was here, then he would probably have searched for treasure. Perhaps a bank structure, a clearing house, money changing business, anything where valuables might be found. That means a big building and close to the administrative center, not amongst houses. Churches, temples, shrines are another source of wealth. Altar decorations, chalices, their own religious symbols. So we had better stick to the bigger structures. Before we leave let's take a good look here. It's obviously an important church and we may find something."

They did! Behind the altar, hidden under a small slate table-like structure, was a hole in the ground with broken steps leading downwards into the darkness.

"I've a flashlight here." Said Pullen.

"I'll tie the rope round my waist and go down to the bottom. Get ready to haul me up if needs be!"

He walked gingerly down the crumbling stairs, pieces of rock falling ahead of him. The flashlight illuminated the hole, and he realized the staircase ceased about five feet further under the altar. Descending carefully, he reached what turned out to be a sizable room. Slate benches lined three of the walls and other was filled with different sized pigeonholes. Over these, engraved into the rock wall in large letters he made out the word *'MACHAY'*. Pullen used the flashlight to peer into one of the larger apertures. Nothing more than dust. He took a handful and rubbed it between his fingers. It was small pieces of an unburned material. It felt like ashes and left black marks on his palms. He continued his search and was rewarded in the second row when he saw something inside the slate lined hole. Holding the torch with his teeth he gingerly used both hands to remove the item. It was an octagonal tablet with hieroglyphics engraved on it.

"Got an unknown item here," he called to Soames.

"Hand it up, I'll step down a few stairs."

The exchange was made, and Pullen continued his search. He found a lot more tablets, one in every hole. Pullen left them alone, but an idea began to form in his head. He climbed the staircase to speak with the others.

"I don't really know but those holes might be sepulchers for cremated bodies. From the second row down they all have a lot of dust or ash in them. By the way, over the top of these, engraved in big letters was the word *'Machay'*, if that means anything?"

Soames nodded. They called mummy's *malqui* in the Americas. Perhaps they burned them and put the ashes here, but it's up to the museums to decide. *Machay* is a Peruvian dialect word used by the Quechua. It means 'final resting place' and is a very old expression. Why it's here who knows? This is one mystery after another! The clay tablets are similar to a *turbah*. Unusual because they're a Muslim item. So perhaps it's made the same way and has nothing to do with Allah. The octagon shape is the same though. I guess the scholars will tell us one day. We'll take it with us in any case.

Lynn took multiple pictures and videos before they left the dome and walked south, back towards the big building. Once there they headed west, but their way was impeded by the deep fissure they had seen yesterday. It had ended suddenly a few hundred yards before the big structure and they circled around it to the west side, following its path as it meandered north. Here were hills with little or nothing in view on their jungle covered land, however, on the other side a new area of structures came into view.

The first of these was shaped like an inverted cone. They walked up to it and then all around the whole building. It was almost twenty feet high. At the top they estimated its circumference to be about a hundred feet. Inside was a ring of bricks. Walking over they recoiled in horror. It encircled a pit filled with snakes. The sunlight reflected directly onto them as they wriggled and crisscrossed each other. The lip of rocks prevented them from getting out but when Soames looked down, he noticed openings below and imagined the holes allowed the reptiles to enter and depart through other vents.

"What kind are they John?"

"A few different kinds. Fer de Lance. A pit viper. They aren't usually called that in the countries where they are found. In Panama it's a Bushmaster, in Belize they are known as 'yellow jaw'. Doesn't matter what they name them though, these are nasty reptiles and won't back down from an encounter. They can grow up to twelve feet in some cases. I see corals, they're the ringed brightly colored ones. The third kind are rattlesnakes, another nasty customer. Perhaps they worshipped snakes here? There's a bunch of them and surely, another exit exists through those holes. We should to be careful when we leave!"

The open top allowed plenty of light to enter, to what ends they had no idea. Lynn suggested it might be some kind of observatory, but they couldn't really tell. They left the mystery and walked forward.

On each side were residences. They entered a few of the double storied abodes and found very little except that they all had hearths which were recognizable because of the openings above the blackened walls where they were located. Decorative surfaces were observed on many houses, but not on all. Soames speculated that the owner's wealth might have had something to do with that.

Finally, they took a break and ate hard biscuits and canned chicken, washing it down with water from their bottles. Once finished they cleaned everything, buried the trash and started out again. It was two o'clock.

As the residences ended a crossroads appeared. What seemed to be a fort was visible ahead. It was built from enormous blocks of stone and seemed to guard the junction of the multiple streets or avenues that came together at that spot. It stood three stories high with crenelated battlements around its top. The entranceway gaped on the southern side and they wandered through it. The walls had arrow slits cut into them and all sides, there were fallen rocks and brush littering the floor and a firepit could be seen built onto the eastern wall. A stone stair case lead to the upper floors. Above was what had probably been sleeping quarters for a garrison. Spaces were marked out with bricks that looked like grave markers, but were in all probability, soldier's beds. Another staircase reached the roof. From there was a good view all around the area. In one corner they discovered a cache of stone swords. A pile of rounded rocks stood in another corner, projectiles for a catapult or similar weapon. They stared over the battlements and back the way they had come. The fissure continued north until it vanished amongst the small hills. Pullen climbed on top of the tallest battlement and looked west. There was an area clear of vegetation which was strange. After that, a building, far higher than any encountered in the City so far. It was standing on flat ground. Taking the glasses from their case, he adjusted them to suit his eyesight and focused carefully, pulling the structure into closer view.

There was light smoke issuing from a tower at the top. It hadn't been noticeable without the binoculars but now he could see it clearly. Lowering his focus he saw that it was a stone structure. A single floor and then a tall tower. If was from the tower that the smoke came. As he watched a procession of some forty figures made their way from the tree-line towards the building. Those at the fore were all carrying stretchers on which were piles flowers. Behind them another twenty or so walked. Even at this distance he noticed the figures were dressed in finery. At the end of the line a dozen women followed. Pullen realized immediately this had something to do with the gunfire that morning. Was this the Indian funeral for those who were killed if indeed that is what had happened? They entered the edifice and vanished from sight. He climbed down and called the others.

"To the west is a big building, perhaps a church. I've watched a procession with forty plus Indians carrying what seemed to be bodies, into the structure. Then there was nothing else. I suppose this is a funeral and those on the stretchers were killed in that gunfire we heard this morning. I don't know how much of this is accurate, but it appears to me to be the case."

Lynn rubbed his chin. "John, you're probably right." He looked at his watch. "It's almost three thirty and will take us an hour to get back. We had better use the time to contemplate what we should do. Everyone should think this situation over. Then, if we decide to call Victor, we'll do it. Let's wait a little, perhaps a bright thought might jump into someone's mind!"

They took their time and at four, were approaching the fort. The guards were alert and welcomed them back. They were all soaked in sweat and decided to walk to the river and wash off, telling Thiago to come with them. As they sat in the shallows letting the cool Olgo flow over their bodies, each spoke in turn after Pullen had explained what he had seen.

"That's what I saw. It probably means that we won't hear from the Piripkura for a day or so when they finish with the burials. After that I imagine they'll be extremely annoyed and looking for blood. Perhaps from the other group, perhaps us. We should wait until midday tomorrow Tuesday, and if Teco has not made contact, call Major Soames."

One by one they expressed similar views. The matter had been decided, and they were in agreement. Now they were all hungry and by mutual concurrence wanted the excellent piranha for dinner. Tonight with spaghetti they declared! Thiago volunteered to fish and returned to a canoe to get lines and hooks. Gencio offered to find bait and started to scrape river snails off the rocks, smashing them to get to the meaty part inside the shell. Hooks ready, they had a dozen fish waiting to be cleaned in fifteen minutes. The generator was started, and Lynn and Soames transcribed their notes from the trip. The spaghetti boiled and in a few minutes the fish had been grilled and a jar of sauce added to the pasta It turned out to be an excellent meal.

Later they sat around talking about what they had observed that day, however, by nine o'clock everyone felt tired and after posting sentries, they climbed into their tents and sleeping bags. After two hours the guards changed. The new pickets started their constantly changing routine, never halting at the same spot and crossing and re-crossing the fort as they took turns in peering through the binoculars towards the tree-line.

Shortly after five in the morning Pullen, on duty, noticed a slight noise. He signaled to Abilio on the other side of the fort and he crawled across to Pullen. They pointed their Benelli's outwards to the bend in the river but saw nothing.

Taking the glasses he scanned the beach. No movement. He waited, lowering the glasses and then raising them again. Now he saw something as two figures raised up from the ground and crept forward. He touched Abilio's shoulder and pointed. The guide nodded as he picked up the crawling men. Pullen searched the area but nothing else moved. By now the figures were fairly close. He spoke in a normal voice. "Teco, is that you? This is Pullen."

"It's me with a man from the Piripkura. May we come into your fort?"

"Of course. Move to your left and enter on the side facing the river."

The two men moved along, and Pullen sent Abilio to wake the others. Fifteen minutes later, after Mande's wound had been cleaned, and a sticky bandaged applied. Most of the group was seated inside the fort holding coffee mugs in their hands. Erico and Marcelo with the shotguns, watched the perimeter. Suddenly there came the sound of rifle fire from down-river.

Pullen pointed west. "I believe our friends have found out you didn't like their company. That might have been punishment being doled out!"

Mande nodded. "I think you are right."

Pullen shook his head and then made the introductions. "This is Sid Lynn, Paul Soames, and Thiago Perez. Our guides and canoe-men are Abilio, Dimas. Erico, Gencio, and Marcelo. I'm John."

Teco nodded. "I am Teco of the Kayapo, and this man is Mande of the Piripkura. I can speak a little English, but Mande can only talk his own tribal language and some Portuguese he learned while with the *poanjos,* the foreigners, or outsiders, as they are called. He is the only one alive from the ambush this morning. I will explain. We need to understand each other, and this will be the start. He spread his hands, palms facing upwards.

"First, I am a Kayapo. You probably met my father earlier. He is called Ado and is the son of the Chief. I left the tribe about five years ago and traveled to the Xingu." They understood and nodded, they remembered Ado had mentioned this.

"I worked there doing odd jobs in a sawmill at Altamira. One day Major Sanchez came to pick up some chairs. We talked in Portuguese and he asked about my tribe. I told him Kayapo. Our tribe is not known for leaving our ancient hunting grounds and the Major appeared interested in talking more. He spoke to the mill owner, a friend, and asked him if he could allow me to work with his own organization. Of course, he agreed. The military and police were good friends to know in Altamira. I went with Sanchez, he is from ABIN who you probably know of. He started to train me to pick up information and pass it back to him. Altamira is a bad town and there are dozens of crimes being committed every day. I infiltrated several gangs over the past four years and provided evidence of the worst schemes these people had been guilty of. It paid well, and I learned to speak not only our own national language but the English of the *poanjos*. Two weeks ago he called me for this job. Sanchez said that another ABIN officer, Major Soames, who I now know is the son of this man Paul wanted information."

He pointed at Soames.

"He needed to put a man into a group planning something big on the Olgo. I told my cover story when he took me to see them and was hired. Until now they will not have known anything. This group is made up of very bad men. The leader is Benicio Renatto, the *Patrão,* or boss of the Amazon pirates. He's also the President of a legal Amazon transport operation, one of the biggest. A very bad man backed by a large organization that makes money by stealing cargoes on the big river. He runs a lot of other illegal activities. Major Soames would love to capture his scalp! He paused and drank more of his coffee.

"I am told you are looking for news as to the fate of Fawcett, the explorer. You spoke to my father and grandfather, perhaps they gave you information. Mande could know more, I have not talked to him of that. What will happen now? The Piripkura will be terribly angry and want revenge. I'm sure you can help them, and in return they may reveal the Fawcett secret. I will translate what I told you first. Remember, he was badly treated by the *poanjos*. Now the pirates hurt his tribe. They are round the bend on a small rocky beach that has an overhanging cliff, untouchable from the west down-river. The bend in the river is sharp, and the water protects their rear. The cliffs are high, with no loose rocks. They also overhang the beach so cannot be fired on from above. The *Patrão* wanted to talk with the Indians and bargain. He said they would leave if they were paid. I doubt that, but it's what Benicio said. He would tie Mande with a rope and take him to the bend, light a green leaf smoke fire to attract the tribesmen. When he got a response, they could start to talk using him to interpret with his little Portuguese." He looked at Lynn and Soames.

"What he really wants is the riches he is sure you will find in the City, he doesn't think much of the lost explorer story and is convinced you are here only for money. That's the way his mind works. So, how we can fix this problem?"

He sat back on his heels and waited for a reply.

Soames shook his head. This seemed unbelievable!

"Wait for a moment please Teco, I must speak to Sid Lynn."

"Sid, I'm sure Teco is being truthful, and he's talking sense. What about you?"

Lynn smiled. "No doubt about it Paul. It's the only way." Looking at Pullen he raised his eyebrows and Pullen nodded.

Soames pointed to Teco. "Speak to him. Tell him everything and ask if he will help. Then see what he says."

Teco turned around, addressed Mande, and started to talk.

They watched the two speaking and once or twice, Mande interrupted to ask a question. At one point he became animated and beat his knees with his hands before he finally regained his composure.

Teco turned to them.

"Mande says he wants revenge for the deaths of the men who were with him. He has no love for *poanjos* but says you have not done him harm. The other group has more men and guns than you do. Mande asks how can you defeat them if what you say is true? If you can tell him that he said he may assist you. I understand the Piripkura's have less than fifty persons now, including women and children."

"John. You and Thiago can answer this."

Pullen pointed to Teco.

Teco nodded and spoke with Mande for a few moments. The Indian replied at length, obviously there were questions.

"He said he is sure you are special warriors, but he wants to know how two can kill twelve? You own only two guns, they have a dozen. What will you do to defeat them?"

Pullen nodded. "We will start with snakes! Do the Piripkura women use woven baskets in their camp? About the size of an oil drum?"

Teco looked at Mande.

"There are baskets Pullen. Why?"

"I need at least one. Also, I suppose vine ropes are available? We want them about a hundred feet or more long. Two if possible. When we have everything we will go to the cone-shaped building in the City. In a pit there we found a number of poisonous snakes. These will go in a basket. After that we take them to the cliff top that overlooks their beach. We lower the basket with one rope and when it reaches ground, pull off the top with the other one which will be attached to the lid. Those snakes will have nowhere to go. They will be very unhappy and ready to relieve their frustrations on any human in their path. That means the pirates!"

Thiago grinned, but said nothing.

Teco shook his head in amazement.

"Pullen! That is a very bad thing to do. How many will the snakes kill?"

"Half a dozen or so before they all get shot probably."

"Mande is sure to like that! Let me tell him and if he agrees, I'll ask him to relate his story." He glanced at Mande and spent a few minutes speaking with him. Suddenly Mande let out a diabolical laugh and nodded his head vigorously!

"He likes the plan and will tell his tale. I'll translate as he talks."

Mande spoke and Teco put his words into English.

"Mande says he was born here in the City. There is no name for it. Some say it is called 'Kupic' but they refer to it only as 'the revered City'. The Piripkura's story was handed down, generation to generation. They were the workers; masons and such many years ago and then came the earthquake that devastated everything. It knocked

147

down buildings and killed most of the population. His group were poor men and lived outside the west wall in huts. The huts crumbled but as they were made of lightweight materials people survived. Not like the stone buildings which collapsed on the citizens working in them, and those who lived in the City residences. The tribe moved away and became jungle dwellers for many, many years. One day, their leader had a vision and said they must protect the City. So, they returned." He paused and spoke to Mande who answered him and continued talking.

"This was over a hundred years ago that they moved back. They found a lot of snakes now lived in the City but otherwise it remained as their ancestors left it. They have been there since, living by hunting and preventing the very occasional visitor from entering the City. He says it is a quiet life really, and for some years no intruders appeared. Whenever they found trespassers in the past, they were killed with the poison bows and spears. He assures me they are very potent. He was hunting to the north alone one day. Men came out of the jungle. They had guns and nets and took him. There are gangs that live from this. They capture Indians and sell them to the loggers. I met him when I worked for them. This was near to Altamira; the gangs did not operate so close to the City, so I felt safe. I gave him food once, and we talked. He explained he wanted to escape but must wait because should he be caught they would kill him. It rained very hard one afternoon and he made a run for it. He got to the Olgo and floated on a log raft for two days. At a set of rapids, he took to the jungle and penetrated inland. It took him about six weeks go get back here and he says he would never leave again."

Teco looked at Mande but he now sat silently.

"Can you mention Fawcett?" said Lynn.

"I will ask but he seems to have said all he intends to say."

He spoke to Mande for a moment, but his words were met with a terse reply and an emphatic shaking of the head.

"He assures me the Piripkura do not speak of that and only the headman would be able to answer the question. I'm certain he knows something but will not say anything until we comply with our part of the bargain."

"I understand. Well, I suppose John and Thiago must make their arrangements. How about it John?"

Pullen looked at his watch.

"It's after six. Mande needs to go to his people and ask for help. Perhaps Teco and Thiago should also go. Mande can go in first and then tell them it's safe. I'm sure the story must be told again. I can go to get the snakes and take Abilio with me. We can put them in the empty sacks we bought with us. If and when we get the baskets, they can be transferred. First though, let's get breakfast!

CHAPTER XXII

Change of plans

Shortly after dawn Tuesday the pirates awoke to the shouts of Calixto, one of the guards.

"Teco and the prisoner escaped!" he shouted. Everyone came awake.

Benicio was furious. "Is there anything to be seen around the bend?"

Two men ran to check but returned immediately and reported negatively.

Benicio called to *Escorpião.*

"Who had the watch with Teco this morning?"

"Calixto and *El Cojo.* They had the four to six turn."

"Bring them over here to me. Get your AK ready. Stand to one side. Everyone needs to be taught a lesson!"

The two pirates shuffled over to the end of the beach where Benicio sat smoking a cigarette.

"Well, what happened between four and six this morning you two?"

He glared at them and they cringed. Then Calixto spoke.

"*Patrão.* About five o'clock the Indian, Teco came to me and said the prisoner had cramps and he was going to walk him up, down and around the camp. I told him that he could go ahead. He helped the man up and held his arm as he stumbled a bit. After all, he had been sitting all the time and probably the circulation had been interrupted."

"I don't want your medical opinion you asshole. I want you to tell me what happened!"

"Sorry *Patrão.* He paraded him up and down and up and down and I saw everything seemed all right, so I checked *El Cojo* was awake. I kept my eye on Teco and he walked the Indian around and then down the beach. I stopped where *El Cojo* stood and told him what was happening. He said he had seen them already so not to worry. Then, when I turned to go back, they had vanished. I think they got to the end and kept going around the bend. I guess they ran away."

"Ran away? Ran away? They buggered off while you and the other idiot had a little chat! You probably cost me a fortune because you cannot perform a simple task!"

He stared over at *Escorpião* and nodded. There was a short burst of fire and the two guards fell to the ground. He shouted to the others.

"See what happens when you don't pay attention you fools! Now we have ten instead of twelve men. That's what happens when you cost me money! Get coffee, I need to relax. *Escorpião,* have those bodies pushed into the water. Check their pockets, you can keep their sovereigns for yourself."

"Thank you *Patrão."*

He moved over and started to search the corpses clothing before pulling them one by one to the Olgo and consigning them to a watery grave.

Benicio took the coffee mug that Mateo handed him. Now what should he do? His hostage had gone, along with the traitor, Teco who had turned out to be a plant. They must have planned this when Teco was supposed to be negotiating. He hadn't understood what they were saying and had to take Teco's word for the translation. Now they were gone. Where he wondered? Had they run to the Piripkura, or had they sought out the Fawcett group? Probably the second. Mande would not know where the Indians were for sure. However, the other camp was visible from the bend in the river and easy to get to once they convinced the guards to let them enter the stronghold.

He called *Escorpião* over and told him to take the binoculars, go to the bend, stay under cover and reconnoiter the fort. Report if the two turned up there.

Should they be over there it would narrow his choice of action. He might kill the remaining Piripkura or alternatively, attack the other group. There were ten pirates with automatic weapons, but Mande had said there were many tribesman, over a hundred but perhaps he was lying, who knows? He would be unable to kill all of them. They would not bunch up into one group for him. Could he get rid of a few and scare the others away? No, that would never work. He didn't know for about treasure. If it existed, the Piripkura were the ones that had it. The other group didn't seem to have discovered anything yet.

He scratched his head. Money was the important thing. He had to get information from the Indians and steal what he might find. That meant attacking them. They might be at their village early in the morning now it was light. Perhaps it would be better to wait though until later in the day. Yes, when everything settled down, he would head there and see what could be done. Leave the other group alone, they had nothing as far as he knew. Get to the village and terrify the occupants into revealing their riches. The language problem wouldn't stop them. He would show the captives his sovereigns and there would be no doubt what he wanted. Good idea! He called *Escorpião* to his side and explained what they would do.

The men would first of all clean their weapons and make sure they had plenty of spare magazines available. The canoe's and the raft must be ready for a fast getaway if required. They would have to be unloaded and then turned around on the beach and made ready for a quick launch. A plan of attack had to be agreed on and how they would approach the Indian camp.

Then, at midday they would eat a meal and relax. After sleeping they would leave around four in the morning. The trees would cover them as they walked around the bend and headed into the jungle. Based on where they had ambushed the Piripkura the last time they could be fairly sure the camp would be to the north west. They would then skirt the ambush sight, staying west of it and then make a left turn east and walk while having scouts out to the south to find the first signs of the camp. Once they were aware of the layout, they could stay on the outskirts and pick off any guards. When the time was ripe they would attack, making sure that they kept out of range of the arrows and spears that they were sure would be utilized against them. That would be the difficult part, avoiding the Indian's weapons.

His men would have to cover as much of their bodies as possible, using long-sleeved shirts and long pants. It seemed like a good plan and there he had leeway for change at any time.

He reached for the tequila bottle and took a huge swig.

CHAPTER XXIII

The revenge of the Piripkura

Wednesday morning, Pullen and the men ate energy bars before their departure. Teco and Mande, with his European 'skin, colored' bandage, not really matching his bronze pigment, would head west towards the village and Pullen and Abilio with their sacks, would look for the inverted cone structure to get the snakes. When they separated, they walked north west, through the long 'administration' building as they now called it. They noticed the fissure and kept left until the residences appeared and the cone edifice became visible.

Pullen walked to one of the canoes and took cigarettes and a mirror from the trinket box. He felt he might need these. Finally he pocketed a roll of twine.

"We will cut poles first and attach the bags. Then we need thin branches that we can weave through the top of the sack and double around to keep them open."

Abilio nodded and in a few minutes, they had everything they needed for the job. The poles were about eight-foot long and the sacks were held open with the bent branches. With the twine, Pullen tightly fixed them to the staves, and they were ready to go snake hunting. There was no need for either of them to say anything, Abilio had been raised in the jungle and would have a natural caution of the reptiles. Pullen had seen enough snakes to ensure he would make no beginners mistakes when handling them.

They walked into the building and over to the ring of rocks. The collection seemed quieter today without much movement, but all the big players were visible, the bushmasters, corals and rattlesnakes tranquil for the moment. Pullen realized that when the bags were put down into the hole, all that would change.

"We'll fish for the snakes. Lower down the sack and let their curiosity get the better of them. Wait until we get two or three inside and we pull it out, twisting the pole make sure it's closed. When we get them up here, we get another bag and transfer what we have, into it. We'll take off the top part with the branch and insert the closed neck into the next bag and release the contents. Then we turn that bag and close it up and start again."

Abilio stood waiting as Pullen leaned over and dropped the sack down the cliff. It provoked a frantic response as the reptiles struck at the material before realizing it was not alive. Finally their instincts told them to explore this new item, and they wriggled around in the sack. This was Pullen's signal, and he twisted it closed with a quick wrist movement. A couple slid out, but he felt sure there were half a dozen trapped securely.

The pole was lifted with Abilio's help, the load very heavy. Placed on the floor it moved violently this way and that as its contents sought to escape. After a few minutes things quietened down, and they started the transfer process. Abilio opened the other bag and Pullen took of the branch that served to hold the other sack open. Carefully the empty sack was held up and the top of the occupied one, put inside of it. With a couple of shakes, Pullen emptied it and Abilio secured the neck of the other receptacle with a prepared loop of twine which he pulled tight and closed. The first transfer was complete, and they smiled at each other.

"Two more should do it." Said Pullen, as he attached the bent branch to the sack and readied to snake-fish again.

Twice more they repeated the operation safely. Then with around twenty snakes in three bulging bags, they exited the cone and made their way carefully back to the fortress. The bags hanging from the middle of a long pole supported by their shoulders.

Meanwhile Teco and Mande left the fort and headed towards the Piripkura village. Mande took them along the inside of the wall.

"We will not be bothered for the first twenty minutes but after that we have to be very careful. My tribe will be very upset about the killings and out for blood of any *poanjo*. The fact you are wearing *poanjo* clothes may make you a target."

"In that case We will have to be doubly careful! I will remove the shirt though if that will help?"

"Yes. It will. There's no time to weave a headband but as you are barefoot, and your skin is dark, we must hope it will be sufficient."

They walked along the wall, detouring where it had collapsed and then finding it again. Gradually they moved westwards until Mande held up a hand.

"There will be a sentry in a hundred yards. That will be the first test. Walk behind me and lower your head in respect that will let the guard see our intentions are not warlike. Do not speak. I will do all the talking. If I ask you a question, then answer and I will translate your words."

"I understand," said Teco.

Ahead the wall was solid without falls. They walked slowly now and as expected, they were stopped. Two Indian's had appeared from behind a tree holding bow's and spears which were pointed at them.

"Is that you Mande? I thought you were killed with the *poanjo* firesticks with the others or that they took you again to cut their wood? He lowered his bow.

"Who is the man with you?"

"Greetings to you Kadu. And you Nodo. This is Mande, he is a Kayapo from the west. He helped me once and I am bringing him here because he must meet with Jafa and the elders about the problems that are here now. I need safe conduct for him to continue to the camp please."

"You are sure it is right to take him to our village Mande?"

"I am sure."

"Then take the safe wood. It is here so make sure you display it as you walk. You would not like an accident to occur to your friend no?"

He held out a stick to Mande. It was split at one end and the division held the black and gold feathers of the black crowned robin, used by the Piripkura to show the bearer came in peace.

"Thank you Kadu. I will take the stick and leave now for the village. There will be other *poanjo's* as well as those who ambushed us. We have met them, and I must tell Jafa of the talks." He took Mande's arm and walked him past the guard and along the wall. It was hot and humid, the sun penetrating the overhanging trees which grew some feet away.

"There will be another watcher outside the village. We will be there shortly. We will identify ourselves and then go to meet Jafa. I will beg for him to receive us. Please remember, he only understands tribal life and his always lived here. He was a warrior before becoming our

155

leader. He has no knowledge of *poanjo* life and probably little of the Kayapo. Please be respectful, he is old, but he is very wise."

"I understand Mande. I will take care with my words."

Again they were stopped as they turned inland from the wall. They were making their way through what were obviously ruined residences. At first these were seen to be substantial homes but the further west they walked, they became smaller and their inferior construction became noticeable. Then, the houses ceased, and a stretch of uncultivated land was seen. Where the jungle started again Teco noticed a large building with a tower.

"That is the revered temple and the place where the Piripkura live. When we get close to the trees, we will be met.

They walked across the plain for about a hundred yards and then from the brush, appeared four warriors armed with spears and bows. They stopped as Mande and Teco went closer.

One man held up a hand. "Mande. You have returned! You were hurt?"

"I got injured a little, but it is better now. We lost our friends though. I need to take this man to Jafa. Will you send someone to ask him please to accept?"

"I will send someone Mande." He dispatched a man after speaking quickly with him. "What happened? There was the sound of fire sticks for the first time in many years. These were continuous noises not separate ones like we know of from hearing such sounds in the past."

"Yes, they have these sticks that shoot stones one after the other without having to insert another stone into the stick. They give bad wounds and we must take care to avoid these in future. I don't know what is happening to our world with these *poanjo's* trying to change our life? I will tell Jafa and he might have some knowledge of things. He has lived a long time and perhaps understands."

"Here comes the messenger now!" The warrior was beckoning from the trees and Mande and Teco took their leave.

They followed the man along a path that bordered the temple and turned a corner. There were old stone dwellings with thatch roofs there and women and children stood waiting. A group of warriors were at the opening to the sepulcher on guard. One called out.

"Mande! We are happy you are here. We thought the *poanjos* had taken you for a slave!"

"No. I escaped and have a Kayapo man here to tell a very interesting story. Is Jafa coming?"

The old Chief, resplendent in his finery, emerged and nodded to Mande. His brilliant blue headdress bordered by iridescent purple gold plumage, gave him a commanding presence.

"Mande, come close and bring the Kayapo man with you. We will talk now so please sit here." He indicated the ground in front of him.

"Jafa. This is Teco the Kayapo."

"You are welcome Teco. I am interested in why you visit the Piripkura? We do not have visitors and therefore nothing to eat or drink has been prepared. While we talk, I will have the women bring chicha and corn cakes, but it may take a little time. Let us listen first to Mande so he can explain things."

The two visitors and a dozen warriors that were in the village when they arrived, sat in a circle and Jafa had a stool fetched for himself. "Please begin Mande," he said.

"You recall I was taken by the *poanjo* who sold me to the woodcutters. I told you They beat me and made me work as a slave. I also said a Kayapo man gave me food. This is that man!" He pointed to Teco, and the men gasped in surprise.

"Yes, this is he who helped me when all were against me. He saved my life. Yesterday he saved it again when the *poanjo's* killed our comrades and I was hurt. He pulled me from the pile of dead and told the *poanjo* leader he would get information from me. Remember, I learned to speak a little of several languages while a prisoner." The men nodded and murmured for a moment.

"Early this morning he distracted the guards, and we fled."

There was a gasp from the sitting warriors.

"There is more. Wait! We spoke to another group of *poanjo's* who helped us. "

Several men jumped to their feet shaking their heads.

"How is this Mande? Who are these others? How do you know them? Did they not try to kill you?"

"Wait. All of you. Allow me to finish my story."

The men quietened down and resumed their seating positions.

"This other group is not like those who attacked us. They are here seeking the story of the Fawcett."

Everyone, including Jafa, stood up shouting now and for a minute complete confusion reigned. Then Jafa held up his hands and everyone relaxed.

"Speak more Mande. We must be told everything that is known."

"I do not understand it all. Only what they told me. They are explorers and not seeking to enslave or kill us. All I know is that they will help us kill the bad *poanjo's* and ask in return that we give information. They say they want nothing else."

No one spoke for a moment and then one warrior stood up and spoke.

"Mande, how can they kill all of these men with firesticks? Surely, they will be slaughtered themselves, please explain?"

"They will do it with snakes."

Again the men shook their heads and muttered amongst themselves. Jafa spoke, halting the noise from the warriors.

"I will not ask how they can do this but is it possible Mande?"

"I am sure it is Jafa. They have two special warriors who live in the jungle and do nothing but fight in *poanjo* wars and protect the animals. I believed them when they say they can assist, they are serious men."

"So, they want information first?"

"They will help with whatever we say. It seems that they are telling the truth."

"Very well. You will tell them that we accept the help and perhaps we can give them information about the Fawcett. Do not promise anything yet. Tell them to use their snakes."

"I can take them to the top of the cliffs where the bad men are camped. They will send the snakes from there. I will not bring them here but take them north first of all and then west and after, south to the cliffs. That way they will not realize you are here. One last request, they need two wicker baskets and long, woven vine strings."

"Good." He called out instructions to one of them women and she hurried off to carry out his wishes. "May this man Teco stay with us. In case we have a mistake with what is to be done, we will at least have a hostage. Can you return alone?"

"I could return alone. However I must have Teco to translate. He cannot stay here but should travel with me."

"I am not pleased with that, but if you must use him to help and it is the only way, do it."

The women asked permission to bring the corn cakes and chicha and set them down on palm leaves within the circle of men. They helped themselves while Mande told them of the power of the *poanjo* firesticks.

"I should return now Jafa. I do not know when the jungle men will use the snakes, but it will be sometime today I am sure. Perhaps you can send a warrior with us and when we start back to the cliffs, he can help carry the baskets and, on the return, leave us and tell you we are going to do what we said."

"I agree. Go now and take Baska with you," he indicated one of the men. "Here is the woman with the baskets and vines. We will await word from Baska later. You should take Nadu also from the guard post. I wish you good fortune." He held up a hand in blessing and the three Indians left the compound and began their journey back to the fort.

They were stopped by both sentries on their return and to each, Mande had to explain what was happening. Both men seemed happy with the plans and said they hoped they would succeed. It took almost an hour to get back to the fortress and when they arrived, Abilio and Pullen had already returned. They walked in and immediately a conference was convened.

Teco explained what happened with the Piripkura.

"So if we help they may speak to us of Fawcett in return. By the way, they refer to him as 'The Fawcett' which means they definitely have information about him. Almost like a special person."

"Will they help us?" asked Lynn.

"If we succeed with those snakes, I am sure of it."

"John, are you and Abilio ready?"

"Yes, but I want to take Gencio. Those snakes are heavy, and we have a way to travel."

"All right, when do you leave?"

"It's almost noon. I'll have Teco ask Mande how long to get to the cliffs."

Mande and Teco spoke and Pullen learned it would be about two hours for the journey.

"Right. We leave at two. By four we will arrive and do the job. I have one more idea for when we arrive. That can wait for now. Let's make sure we have everything we need and then rest before we go."

They talked over how to transport the snakes safely and what would be required for the journey. Shortly after two in the afternoon they filed out of the camp, Pullen with a Benelli over one shoulder, Teco and Mande carrying on their shoulders a stave from which hung a basket with snake contained in a sack. Abilio and Gencio carried another. Baska would provide relief. Mande also had the 'safe wood' safely stuffed in his loincloth. They had run stout poles through the weaved material and the basket hung between the two carriers swinging back and forth but well away from the carriers themselves. Mande directed them along the route. Pullen asked what the buildings were used for but when Teco mentioned it to Mande, he said that only the Chief was aware of these answers, and these had been passed on from the Chief before him.

Once again, they cut through what Pullen thought of as the 'Administration building' and Mande had them turn east. After a few hundred yards the sides of the fissure came together for a short distance and they crossed over it westwards. As he looked north, the gap soon opened up again.

They walked easily along a road bordered by opulent houses, interspersed with larger structures which offered no clue as to what they had housed. Ahead there was the sound of water running and around the next corner a plaza and a lake appeared, bordered by well-cut rocks around its perimeter. In one corner stood a brick-faced tunnel which seemingly had supported a bridge over the lagoon. Part remained, but crumpled arched supports were installed at regular intervals all the way across the lake. From the tunnel flowed a steady stream of water. When they circumvented the lake, they watched the waters rushing into another tunnel on the other side that vanished underground. It was obviously part of the city water system and Pullen wondered how many of these lakes existed?

They rested after forty-five minutes and then continued north for twenty minutes. Mande stopped them again and told them to wait. He told Teco he would check if an outpost happened to be manned close to where they had halted as he wanted no problems with the guards should one be there. A few minutes later he returned with Nadu and said the sentries wished them good fortune.

He spoke to Teco who then translated to the group.

"Mande says that we meet the wall at the back of the city in ten minutes. There we turn west and follow it for a mile. At that point we enter the jungle and it will take about half an hour to reach the top of the cliffs where the pirates are sheltering. He'll send Baska back now to report we will soon be in position. Nadu comes with us. Should we ask Baska to say anything else to Jafa?"

Pullen answered.

"Yes. Tell his friends that in less than two hours the snakes start their work. Perhaps the pirates might panic and try to make their way east, around the bend. Ask him to make sure his warriors will be waiting for them!" Teco translated and Baska smiled, running off into the trees and vanishing immediately.

Sure enough, the wall appeared, and they walked through a gap and followed its meandering course west. Ahead they saw a plain and after that, the jungle started. They realized they had been slowly climbing for the past ten minutes and stopped to rest for a while. It would not be long now, but they had the route through the trees to navigate before they reached their destination. Finally, tired and soaked with sweat, Mande held up his hand and called Teco over to him. They spoke in low voices and then Teco walked back.

Quietly he explained to Pullen that five minutes ahead they would come to the clearings that marked the cliff edge. It would be wise not to speak in normal voices as they might be heard. They should whisper anytime they wanted to communicate.

The clearing appeared, bare ground covered with shells perhaps from times when the river actually ran over these clifftops. When they ventured into the open, the clearings allowed them to look up and down the river, east and west. The water, where it could be seen between the high cliffs, looked calm. The skies remained blue, and no clouds could be seen. Then the sun beat down on them and they retreated into the tree-line to talk.

"We have arrived. I will ask Mande to show me the position of the pirates and the parameters of the beach where they are resting. Meanwhile I want everyone to collect pebbles and shells. These go into the two sacks after we empty the snakes directly into the baskets.

Use small ones only. Once we have released the reptiles at the western end of the pirate refuge, we launch these shells down behind them assuring they are frightened by the noise. They will head east to where the group will be sitting resting. Start now and get them ready while I go to the cliff edge. Take care with what you are doing, you all know these snakes and their danger. No one must take a chance and if one escapes, let it slide into the jungle, don't make a noise trying to capture it!"

Mande understood what Pullen wanted and led him to within ten feet of the cliff edge. He signaled that they should lay flat and then pulled himself forward followed by Pullen. The dirt they lay on was only a thin layer with solid rock directly below them.

Looking over the cliff, Pullen watched his adversaries on the beach. He did not know them individually, but he assumed the tall man sitting alone, was their leader. Eight others sprawled about three canoes. East, they saw where the cliff edge rounded the bend. Based on his observations at the fortress he looked for the trees and brush that skirted the corner and noticed another man there facing east. A lookout watching the fort! Had he watched them leave earlier and did he have any idea of the cargo they carried? Of course not! He worried, breaking the soldiers cardinal rule 'It's not worth thinking about things that might never happen' He smiled at his self-doubts. This was to be a type of ambush, nothing less, nothing more. He had set hundreds during his career as a soldier. This happened to be one more. He relaxed and motioned to Mande to take him to the other end of the cliff where they would lower the snakes.

They carefully looked down and Pullen realized what a perfect position they occupied. There was no way back down-river for the pirates. The bend to the west offered no escape by land as the water came well up the cliff-face on the turn. Their only alternatives were to rush around the corner where hopefully Baska had arranged for the armed tribesmen with bows and spears to be waiting. Perhaps the pirates would try launching a canoe or two, which would not be easy if they panicked as he expected them too.

He crawled back a few feet and then stood and walked back to where the others were grinning as they pointed to the baskets rocking back and forth with the movement of their contents. Teco looked up at him.

"Ready for delivery!" he said smothering a laugh.

Pullen noticed that the vine ropes had been tied to the sides, and the tops were held on by a wooden peg, also attached to a vine.

The sacks on one side bulged with what Pullen surmised were shells. A vine rope was attached to the open top of each.

"Right. We're ready. You did all the work, so you will be in charge of the release!" Smiles radiated from the faces of the group members who had wrangled the snakes into the hampers.

The baskets were pulled to the western end of the cliff and Pullen looked over to make sure they waited in the correct position.

"Go ahead. Slowly and no noise. They won't be noticed if we are quiet about things!"

Nadu and Mande were accustomed to working in silence. Slowly they lowered the two baskets and at last they came to rest. There were no alarms. Pullen risked a look down to the shoreline. The baskets now rested behind some boulders, out of sight of the men on the beach.

"Good work!" he whispered. "Now the sacks. Not all the way down, stop them about five feet from the bottom."

The sacks went down, their nondescript color blending with the cliff-face and not attracting attention with the slow descent.

"Now pull the basket tops off!" Pullen looked down and watched snakes spilling out and wriggling around everywhere.

"That's it! Now move the sacks until they are behind the snakes and release one of them. The pebbles will frighten the reptiles and make them move forward towards the pirates."

One sack was emptied as it slid behind the boulders. Nothing could be seen.

"Now release the second sack!"

He watched the shells spilling out and the visible snakes moved eastwards towards their prey. The first scream came two minutes later.

"*Culebras, Culebras**!" Mateo saw the advancing reptiles first. By the time the pirates reacted the first man was bitten. A loud scream rang out as the sleeping and resting men jumped up in panic. Another man was struck and then one more. *Escorpião* opened fire with his AK and several rounds ricocheted back and hit two more men. Terror ensued as Benicio fired his weapon, killing a group of the reptiles and frightening the others towards the water.

*Snakes

163

Another pair of pirates made for the bend in the river and into the brush, trying to escape to the east. Their arrow-pierced bodies were found the next day.

It was now dusk. Benicio called the three remaining members close to him under the cliff. Mateo, the Scorpion and Joachim, AK's at the ready, retreated to the space where he waited.

"We need to get out now! Four of us, one canoe, and we launch it before these reptiles kill everyone. Quickly! load as much as you can from the other canoes into mine. Bring the raft. Take an extra motor." They hurried to carry out his orders. At five in the afternoon Wednesday, a solitary canoe towing a raft carrying three batteries, slid into the river.

CHAPTER XXIV

Mysteries solved

Pullen and the others watched the mayhem below for a moment, but then even these hardened men became disgusted with the slaughter. They saw two pirates flee around the bend, then walked back to the tree-line and took shelter as the sun started to set over the river. When the screams subsided they returned. The four remaining men were in the process of loading one canoe from the contents of the others. Once this was done they pushed the boat and a raft into the watercourse and headed downstream in the twilight. Pullen hoped that that would be the last of them, however, *'the best laid plans of mice and men....**'

He turned to Teco.

"I hope that's the end of it. What's that raft?"

"They have electric motors that make it easier for the paddlers. The raft carries extra batteries with a solar charger. When the working ones run low, they swap with the extra power unit. Very efficient!"

"Smart idea," said Pullen ruefully. "We might have used something like that! It would have saved a lot of effort!"

They retrieved the now empty baskets and sacks and in the gathering darkness, led by Mande, returned to the Piripkura village.

Strolling slowly and talking amongst themselves they headed back. They talked all the way, possibly because of the dark, possibly because they valued the companionship. It was a long journey, taking almost two hours. Finally, walking south inside the wall, they were challenged by a sentry. Mande produced the 'safe wood' and they were allowed to pass. Soon they saw the glow of a fire and exiting the brush, found the village waiting for them. As they appeared the warriors stood and waved their spears and bows. They shouted to the group that they had killed two *poanjo's* as they had attempted to escape around the bend of the river. Jafa appeared, and the crowd became silent.

*From Robert Burns' poem 'To a Mouse'. 1786.

"Mande. Come forth. Tell me who you bought to our village?"

Mande walked forward and saluted Jafa by bowing his head.

"Jafa. I bought these strangers as it is night and they cannot return to their own camp. There is Pullen the jungle warrior who knows snakes. The two Indians are Gencio and Abilio who helped him and who arrived in the canoes and live in the fort. We killed six of the pirates and I am told our warriors disposed of two more. We saw four escape in a canoe and head down the river westwards. Pullen did what he said he would do and has rid us of the bad men. May I bring him forward to greet you?"

"Yes, indeed. I want to meet this *poanjo* who speaks with snakes and knows the jungle. You will translate Mande."

Pullen walked forward and stood before the Chief. He bowed deeply and held the bow for several seconds before coming upright. Reaching in his pocket he took two out two packs of cigarettes and a mirror and offered them to the Chief.

They were taken and Jafa looked at the cigarettes in a thoughtful way.

"He is respectful Mande. That is good. What are these packets he has given me?"

He managed to remove the cellophane with a horny thumbnail and pulled out a single white stick.

"The reflecting circle shows what we see in still water but in the back of my mind I have a memory of the sticks here." He pointed at the cigarette.

Mande of course understood what they were and taking a small branch from the fire, showed Jafa how to smoke.

The old man seemed delighted and puffed away.

"Much better than the dry herbs we have. I like these! Tell him that we welcome him because he helped when we were in pain for our losses. Also, because he kept his word as you told us. He killed many of the pirates and drove two more onto our arrows and spears."

Mande translated, and Pullen bowed again.

"Now I wish to hear everything about the attack. Have Pullen start at the beginning and to miss nothing. We are all anxious to know what happened."

Again Mande spoke with Pullen. "He said he wants the whole story, leave nothing out. It does not matter how long it takes but tell it all."

"Please tell him I am happy to help the Piripkura who have shown great bravery facing pirates with firesticks when they have none. It is a mark of courage to stand up to these people and I am deeply appreciative of their deeds. Now I will tell the story."

He related everything, step by step and the tribe, with Jafa at their fore, gasped in amazement as Pullen told how they captured, and released the snakes at the bottom of the cliff from their baskets. They were told how the snakes were sent on their way by showering them with small shells. He was as dramatic as possible with the narration, knowing that was the way that they wanted to hear it. Finally he finished with the walk back and Mande's bravery in the dark leading them. It became obvious that Jafa reveled in the participation of Nadu and Mande in the ambush. It gave the tribe much face and Jafa showed it by his huge smile.

"Bring food and chicha! Mande called to the women who were sat to one side enjoying the tale. They immediately left and small fires appeared around the seated warriors. Jafa looked at Pullen who stared back into his eyes. There was something there. Something familiar. What could it be? He respectfully lowered his gaze and motioned to Mande.

"I would like to speak with Jafa if he can listen for a moment. There are things I must be told about before I ask our questions about Fawcett."

"I will ask him. The women should have corn cakes and meat soon. Let us wait until these are served and the men start to talk about the fight. When they are distracted, you may ask your questions, and none will pay attention."

Minutes later the women bought gourds of chicha and corn and yucca cakes on a large palm leaf. There were small, roasted birds which Mande said were pigeons and also piranha roasted and opened ready to eat. Soon everyone was talking, and Mande signaled to him to come over to Jafa.

"Ask your questions soldier and I will translate. I hope I am able to do your words justice."

Pullen began.

"Please ask who gave him his name?"

Mande spoke to the Chief who nodded and looked knowingly at Pullen.

"He says why you ask a question that you already have the answer to?"

"Tell him I am not sure, but I'll say what I believe. That the name was given by his father."

Again there were words between the two Piripkura.

"He says yes and asks how you were aware of this."

"Tell him Jack Fawcett. Jafa." He spelled out the letters.

Mande, showing no emotion, passed on his words.

Jafa smiled and spoke.

"He said you are a very observant person soldier. He asks what else do you know about him?"

Now Pullen smiled.

"He is tall. His eyes are brown and not black, and his hair is finer than most tribesmen. I believe he is the son of Jack Fawcett, Percy Fawcett's son. I am sure his mother is from this tribe. If I am wrong I sincerely apologize."

Mande talked at length with Jafa and answered several questions. Then he turned back to Pullen.

"Well, you are much favored soldier! He first told me that I translated and merely passed words, none of which I should recall later. I told him that I understood. Then he said he hopes you are not tired because he has many things to speak of with you. I am to remain to tell him what you say as best I can. He said to tell you my story also so that you would start to understand the Piripkura. I do not know all of your words. The ones I can remember were taught by the science man at the logging camp. He studied birds in the forest and became caught by the loggers as he listed bird species. They didn't care who you were, they wanted men and anyone careless got taken and enslaved. I spent over a year before escaping and would sooner die than go back. We were chained all the time and only released once weekly to bathe in the nearest river. That's when I eventually escaped. I ran and ran. Then I made a raft on the Olgo and sailed it using my shirt as a sail to fight against the current. I abandoned the raft at some rapids and walked north and then east and finally returned. That is my story. Every day I thank the gods for my luck. I do not want to leave here again. I am not to ask how you learned of Jafa and I am forbidden to mention anything to the rest of the tribe. That is good because I will listen to your tale for myself even though the secret must remain in here." He touched his heart and smiled at Pullen.

"He wants you to say how you came by your information. Speak in short sentences and will tell him what you said."

"Very well." Pullen spoke, but paused often so that Mande could translate his words to Jafa.

"I'm a soldier lent to this expedition by my country to help them with security for the group, along with Thiago, a Brazilian Special Forces man. You have looked at my firestick, he has the same kind. These are not similar to the guns of the pirates. They shoot a very short distance, but they are deadly. We came to the Olgo in a large boat and then took to the canoes. We have food, water, a generator for light and fuel. It's a very well- equipped expedition. Before I left, I read much about Fawcett and found him difficult to understand. What was his intention? To find the City or to find riches, perhaps both? He paused for Mane's translation.

"I had plenty of time to think and question his decisions. Why did he take Jack and Raleigh Rimmel with him? Many experienced explorers wanted to go, but he took Jack who had some experience and Rimmell who had none at all. I found several books on Fawcett and from what I read I believe he may have been heavily in debt and needed funds desperately. The City of 'Z' as he called it, would be his salvation. They did not know that Z existed so close to the Olgo otherwise I am sure they would have used boats as we did. Instead they walked inland with horses and mules as well as porters, a very strenuous undertaking. Eventually they left the other men and pushed on alone. They found the Kayapo, and the tribe helped them. Why? Fawcett had an aura about him that encouraged belief in his cause. People sensed a special person and saw him as a true explorer. Ako, the Chief of the Kayapo said that his father told him of Fawcett's visit. He left a hat he owned, and they still kept it safe. I suppose it served as a token of his regard for them. Then they came here and strangely, the Piripkura accepted their arrival. What happened then I do not know, and that's why the expedition has traveled all this way to find out about their fate. We are recording as much as we can on film to take back with us. I have not asked about Fawcett at all as yet. First, I would like to hear Jafa's answers to my questions."

Mande finished translating Pullen's words and readied for Jafa's words. He started with the first enquiry.

"What did the Fawcett intend? I was not born when he came here. However, my father of course was alive then. It became part of our history, a very important part. Warriors out hunting found him and two others dying to the east of the City. They carried them here on two poles. These had cross sticks tied with vines to support the body. A man pulled it from the front, standing where the sticks met and used as handles." Pullen recognized the description of a travois.

"Our men had never encountered white skins and blonde hair before and therefore did not kill these intruders. Our Chief, Zabe, said he wanted to find out more and ordered the women to care for them until they might talk. The oldest one stayed sick for two weeks before he could sit and speak in sign language. Another, his son, the Jack was recovering. Finally the third man, not family, did not get better. He caught the flesh-eating sickness and died. All he left was a sign that he scratched on the stone wall where he lay dying. It was a letter 'R' and an arrow. It is still there, and you may see it when you leave. The old man told Zabe his name was Percy Fawcett. Zabe, and everyone called him 'Perfaw' because we were unable to pronounce that name. He liked that, and they say he laughed often with the tribe. They had never known anything like these men and Zabe, being a wise man wanted to learn everything about them. They sat every day and evening, making conversation with their hands and drawing pictures on the floor. Perfaw showed Zabe all the things he had in his pack. There were combs for the hair and scissors which were gifted to Zabe. He said it would not be wise to gift the firesticks because these possessed a mysterious powder that enabled them to kill men from a long distance. He showed Zabe one day by shooting a mango from a tree two hundred paces from where they stood. Zabe was very impressed. He drew pictures in the dust showing buildings in his own country and machines that carried people in them! Wonderful things that seemed magic. We have never heard of these again and wonder if this soldier has knowledge of them?"

Mande replied without asking Pullen.

"He knows much Jafa and I am sure he is telling the truth. In the canoe they came in there's a machine that makes light from darkness. I recall something similar to this when I became captured, but they have a very small one, not like the big ones at the logging camp that drive the sawmills."

Jafa nodded.

"When the young man Rim, died, Zabe showed the other two what they did to the bodies of important tribesmen. They honored the boy by making a *malqui,* a mummy of him. This is usually only for Chiefs of the tribe. It is a sacred ceremony and first they took him to the temple and Zabe himself opened the body and removed the entrails. The heart he put to one side. His guts were burned as they were no further use. After, the insides of the head were taken out with a hook inserted in the nose." He took a deep breath and continued.

"All cavities were filled with rock dust that we get from the quarry. It is very dry and does not swell or shrink. Then they were sewn tightly with the heart put back in the corpse. The cadaver is wrapped in the skins of capybaras and closed with thread. One last operation fills the eye sockets. Then the corpse goes to the temple. It is put into a special room where a white smoke fire always burns. It is hung in the smoke for one year and removed. The capybara skin is cut off, and the cured body is stood in a specially cut opening in a sandstone wall and secured with a hook at the back. This is done on a feast day with a solemn ceremony the whole tribe attends." He stopped to allow Mande to update the translation.

"Perfaw could not wander far from the hut where he slept. Zabe did not want him to know everything about the tribe which was very wise. Finally Perfaw told Zabe he had come to find a lost City that had been built many years ago. Would Zabe tell him more? All excuses were made not to say anything that would give away the secrets and Perfaw had to stay put without walking too far. Of course, he felt unhappy, but what could he do? He was sure this was the fabulous City 'Z' but he had no permission to explore it. Perhaps sooner or later, Zabe would allow him freedom? In a few weeks even!" He shook his head.

"Jak, as they called his son, was young and had been cared for during his sickness by a widow whose husband had been killed by a falling tree in a storm. They admired each other and became lovers. She, against all orders from Zabe, took him to explore the City several times before they were caught. They had no punishment, widows are greatly respected, but

171

they were now obliged to live together and from this union, I was born. I not remember my father, he died along with Perfaw killed by the slave traders almost ninety years ago." Zabe paused and tears came into his eyes. He coughed and dried his face.

"The slavers were found by our warriors to the east one day. Because Perfaw was a good man, he and Jak for once were allowed to go on the hunt away from the City. Perfaw thought the men might be good and he, Jak, and Zabe, walked forward to meet them. The men were friendly and said they were seeking precious stones that might be found here. Drinks from bottles were offered and all the warriors, Zabe, Perfaw and Jak sipped from them in friendship. Two of the warriors and Jak died that night. Zabe and Perfaw were made very sick. Zabe told the unhurt man to bring more warriors as they had been poisoned. The next morning they arrived and killed the six men. After, Perfaw said he thought the drink was probably water with sugar and had arsenic in it. Everyone was pissing black urine which indicated that kind of poison. Zabe lived for two years after that but Perfaw died two days later, Zabe was never the same. Because of his respect for Perfaw and what he had taught him, he asked the elders to make Perfaw's grandson, myself, Chief. I received the honor even although I was only two years old. The elders made all the decisions until I became fifteen and then I became the Chief in my own right. I have lived now for ninety summers and I am old. But I am the Chief and the tribe obeys me. That is why you are here and made welcome." Pausing, he held up a hand.

"We made Perfaw and Jak *Malqui* and they are here in the temple. I will take you there when it gets light and you can may observe how we revere them as friends. I hope they stay there always and we will continue to honor them."

He stopped talking and took a big breath. Turning to Mande he spoke a few sentences.

"He says you and your men sleep here and tomorrow he will take you to the temple. Then he wants to speak to your Chief's that are in the fort. You bring them here. He asks you not to say anything about Perfaw until he gives his permission."

"I understand."

"Good. I'll take you to where you sleep."

The three walked back to where the fire still blazed.

CHAPTER XXV

Finding Fawcett

It was dusk Wednesday when the solitary canoe sailed west into the darkness of the Olgo. After ten minutes the four men, Benicio, Mateo, the Scorpion, and Joachim, were calm enough to think clearly.

"Stop the electric motors and pull to the south bank over there." He pointed to a smooth stretch of sand. They grounded the canoe and raft waiting for orders.

"Here, take a drink." Benicio offered the tequila bottle and everyone had a swallow. "What a disaster! We lost six men. There's only four of us now. Climb out. Let's find out what we have here in the canoes."

They took inventory and much of the canoe's contents were unloaded in the moonlight onto the sand.

"Make a fire Mateo. We will re-organize here before we do anything else."

Mateo walked away to cut brush, and they soon had a bonfire blazing.

"Open some tins and we can eat and drink a beer. Then I'll decide what we do next."

They ate and re-loaded the canoe. There were plenty of provisions plus sleeping bags, five AK's, and ammunition, beer, and water.

Benicio surveyed everything. He swallowed his can of beer.

"The Indians and the Fawcett's have not beaten us! I want revenge for the deaths of our men! This is what we will do."

The next ten minutes he outlined a plan of action that bought smiles to the faces of his companions. Now they would show the Piripkura how satisfactory revenge made up for everything. Twenty minutes later the lone canoe, towing its raft, headed east and in the blackness, passed the fort, eventually beaching on the north bank of the river about half a mile past the huge blocks of stone that diverted part of the Olgo current, inland. They found a beach and pulled the canoe and raft to safety. After posting a guard, they settled in to sleep until first light.

At the Piripkura village Pullen, and his men slept soundly until dawn on Thursday. They were awakened by the sound of people moving about and voices of the women as they prepared the first meal. After eating corn cakes and drinking water they waited for Jafa to appear. He came out shortly with Mande and beckoned to Pullen.

They walked past the ruined huts and along a trail until in the half light, they saw the temple, a large building with a tower in one corner pointing to the sky. From vents in the side of the tall structure, they saw a very light smoke emerging and vanishing into the slight morning breeze.

Jafa smiled. He spoke to Mande.

"He says to come with him soldier. Come and meet the revered Perfaw, Jak, his father and Rim. I will walk inside and then I'll wait there. Only Jafa can enter the inner rooms. Inviting you to do so is a great honor. I have never been there and neither have most of the tribe. Only a handful of elders who placed the *malqui* in their recesses. I envy you Pullen, but you have earned the honor I have to admit. Do nothing to break the old man's trust I ask you, please!"

"You have my word," said Pullen as he followed Jafa through the entrance.

The first room had window-like openings in the walls. As in an auditorium, stone benches were positioned in rows from the back and continued on to within twenty feet of the end of the chamber. There he noticed a block of square stones resembling an altar. To one side stood an archway and when they passed it, Pullen saw piles of stacked dry wood beside a fireplace in which boughs crackled and small flames sprung. The light smoke generated vanished into a chimney near the top of the structure. An Indian stood there occasionally stirring the fire with a long branch.

"This is the fire that burns always. Men in turns are here all day and all night the cut wood and feed the fire. The flames never go out, and smoke is always entering the chimney. Now I will leave you. Go with Jafa and he will show you the secrets. He said you killed six men for the tribe and that brings you honor and a reward."

Mande stood back, and they passed through a doorway and into a smaller room. Pullen searched for his camera. On one side there were stone shelves, and it was to these that Jafa led him. There were several headdresses, all made from the same jungle bird, the paradise tanager.

The feathers were lime green and light blue all mounted on a band designed to be worn around the forehead and tied in a knot at the rear. Next to the headdresses there were small capybara pelts that Pullen realized had been dyed with urucum, extracted from the seeds of a fruit similar to the horse chestnut. The result made them a bright scarlet.

Jafa removed his large rosella headdress, put on one of the tanager bird headbands and tied a scarlet cloak around his shoulders, motioning Pullen to do the same. When they were dressed Jafa took the lead and walked to a very narrow entranceway. Above, carved into the wall, he noticed the same word seen earlier over the vault when exploring the City, '*Malchay*'. He passed through and into a magnificent hall. Pullen gasped as he saw figures upright in the many wall alcoves. He counted seventeen all told. From small angled openings in the roof of the chamber, beams of light shone through, catching the eyes of the *malqui,* and throwing green rays across the sepulcher. Looking closely he noticed the eye sockets contained large emeralds, and these provided the stunning crisscrossing of green beams.

Jafa smiled pushing him forward so that he could observe these notables up close. The features were still recognizable, but the skin appeared dark brown and stretched tautly over the bones. The bodies were the same, dark tanned skin and covered below by loin cloths. So these were the Piripkura leaders who had died during the past two hundred years.

Jafa beckoned to him and pointed at three additional alcoves, bigger and with decorated sides, floors, and roofs. He looked up and realized that these were the three members of the Fawcett expedition of 1925.

From above came the smell of smoke, and from a vent in a side wall, he saw a very light cloud emerging, circulating, and then being drawn through a flu in the roof. Now he understood how the mummies were preserved.

The three were dressed in western clothing. The one in the center had to be Percy Fawcett. He wore a check shooting jacket and what appeared to be plus-fours and boots. Unlike the Chiefs in the shrine, his skin appeared slightly lighter, and the lips upturned in a smile. Jack Fawcett, Jafa's father, stood on the right in a shirt and trousers and he assumed the other body had to be that of Raleigh Rimmell, Jack's friend, in similar dress. For a moment he stood transfixed. These three had been here for over ninety years, visited only by Jafa. The mystery of Fawcett's death had finally been solved but how many other questions would this discovery now bring. He shook his head, not knowing what to think next. By his side, Jafa nodded, as if he understood what was going through Pullen's mind. Jafa stretched out a hand and took his arm. He allowed himself to be guided forward, past where the Fawcett's hung in death and into yet another small room. There was the sound of water running and at the end of the chamber, a small stream spouted from a stone spigot in the wall, landing in a deep slate tray. Jafa urged him forward towards the receptacle. The water ran in from the stone pipe protruding from the wall but before it overflowed the tray, it ran out through a drain on the other side. The old man pushed him against the tray and pointed downwards. Pullen looked and stepped back involuntarily. The bottom of the tray shone bright green as he realized it was filled with emeralds. The flowing water enhanced their beauty as it skipped and flowed over the tumble of stones. He couldn't believe what he was seeing! Right in front of his eyes a king's ransom sat bathing in clear, cold water which he surmised had been diverted from the City supply to provide this spectacle. The hoard must be worth millions, but how had it arrived here? He looked at Jafa who smiled and nodded. He indicated that Pullen should put his hands in the water and touch the stones. They were icy from their soaking. All seemed to have been polished and many had been cut into shapes. The most beautiful were the step-cut oblong ones. These had rectangular facets ascending to the crown and descended in steps. They showed off their color and gleam to perfection. Pullen held up one of them to the light, amazed at the beauty of the jewel. Over three inches long, it had a circumference of over half an inch. He was not an expert but even an amateur could tell these and the others, were prime gems with a deep unflawed appearance. A five-carrot stone, extra fine, this size would be worth perhaps twenty thousand dollars. So, a quick calculation of the total value of the stones in the font would be in the millions. He let the stone fall back into the water. Jafa stepped forward shaking his head. He held up five fingers on one hand and one, on the other, pointed to Pullen and down to the stones. It seemed obvious he wanted him to take six of the emeralds. Pullen understood and sorted through the treasure. He picked half a dozen step-cut's and Jafa nodded his approval indicating he should put them in a pocket. As they turned to walk out, Jafa again caught his arm. He made a very clear gesture by putting a finger to his lips. Pullen understood, this could never to be spoken of to anyone.

They removed the cloaks and headdresses and Jafa signaled him to leave and pointing to himself and at the ground to indicate he would be staying. Pullen made his way back to Mande, and they waited half an hour until the Chief returned. Not a word was spoken when he finally exited the temple. Slowly, in respect for Jafa's age, they walked back to his hut.

Gencio, Teco, and Abilio sat talking but stood when he arrived.

Before he retired into the hut Jafa spoke to Mande.

"He said he will go to your camp with you and your men. I'll guide the group. There he wants to speak with your Chiefs and learn what they know. He will be ready very soon."

Jafa appeared twenty minutes later. He wore a magnificent headdress of macaw and crimson topaz feathers. Around his neck hung a leather collar supporting a large square-faceted emerald that had been pierced to allow it to hang on a string. He carried a ceremonial spear, six feet long and of this, a full two feet was a sharpened slate blade which fitted into the notched wood, held in place with leather strips. The shaft was decorated with crude designs in multicolored inks.

Four warriors appeared with a straight-backed stool mounted on poles to form a type of sedan chair. Jafa mounted it and sat upright, the warriors lifted and the procession of men slowly files from the village. Mande took them along the wall facing the river and eventually Pullen saw the large 'administration' building ahead. From there they made their way towards the fort.

The sentries were alert and by the time they arrived, Lynn, Soames, Thiago, and the others were waiting. Pullen noticed that the defenses had been improved. The walls were higher now, Up to a man's chest. The canoes had been moved and were covered with brush. A firepit had been dug and a spit to hang pans on had been installed. The opening had been widened. A big thorn bush which had been blocking it, was pulled over as they entered.

Lynn and Soames came forward. "John! We were worried. Thank God you're back! Now, you explain everything, and we will keep quiet while you do.

"Of course. This is Jafa," he indicated for the Chief to dismount. "He is the man in charge of the Piripkura that guard the City from intruders."

Then, pointing to Mande he said, "He will translate for us."

"Mande, please speak with Jafa and tell these men in their language, who Jafa is and why he is here."

Mande turned and addressed the Chief for a few moments and then listened to his reply.

"Here stands Jafa, head man of the tribe. He welcomes you to his City. He wants to know what you are doing here? Also he thanks you for lending us Pullen and the other men to help defeat the bad *poanjo's*. It would be polite to ask him to sit and to offer food and drink, then we can talk."

Soames immediately spoke to Thiago and in a few minutes, cans of beer were being offered. At the firepit more cans of food were being opened and water for tea boiled. A folding stool was fetched and Jafa sat down facing the group and was given a beer. He sipped it and a smile crossed his face as he nodded energetically and spoke briefly to Mande.

Pullen spoke. "Mande, I'll tell Lynn and Soames what has been happening while the food is prepared. Will you explain that to Jafa and please ask him to be patient with us."

Mande nodded, "He said the beer is very good" and started to converse with the elderly Chief.

Pullen told the group that Jafa would tell them the story of his tribe when they had eaten. It would be better that way as the old man had asked him to say nothing and let him tell the tale.

Hot canned chicken with dry biscuits were offered in tin plates and tea in mugs distributed. Mande told Jafa what they were to eat, and after trying the meat he commented to Mande.

"He said he does not understand how you get a whole chicken into one of those small tins. He said it's very good! However he would prefer chicha to the hot herbs and water. Do you have any more beer in cans?"

Pullen walked to a cold chest and took out a beer. Popping the tab he handed it to Jafa. The old man drank from the can and his face lit up as he called to Mande.

"Jafa said this is very good. Not as good as chicha but good all the same!"

They ate slowly, waiting for the moment when Jafa would start his story.

Finally he put down his plate and can. He beckoned to Mande and spoke a few words. Mande nodded.

"Jafa will tell the story of the Piripkura and the lost City. It is a long story he said so please sit comfortably and I will translate as best I can."

"What I tell you are the words of my ancestors. They repeated the story's, and they have been passed down over the years. Longer than anyone can recall a City was here before the trees grew. The river waters were much higher then but one day the level dropped and the earth all around here became bare. A people called Toltecs came, they built the City. Some called it '*Kupic*'. Many tribes came here. The Piripkura were one. For years the City thrived and the population, used the great river to trade. All was well, but then the gods sent to split the land. Huge fissures broke our City and knocked down many buildings and houses. Our tribe was small. We were workmen and lived where you saw us today outside the walls in a corner of the town. Most of us were spared when the cracks in the earth came. We lived in huts and when they fell we were hardly hurt although thousands in the City died from falling stones. After that the people left. We lived for many years in the jungle, traveling from constantly. We were called the Butterfly people because we flitted around to many places!" He laughed and pounded his knees for a moment. Then he became serious again.

"Finally, we returned. Our Chief had a dream that said we should protect the City from outsiders. That we have faithfully done. We are not craftsmen and cannot work the rock mines and build structures. The Piripkura are hunters and laborers, nothing more. Then Perfaw came and Zabe, the Chief, listened to his talk, drawn to him by the stories he told. Perfaw became sick, and Jak. Also, the one called Rim. Our women helped them, but Rim had the disease that eats the flesh and Rim died. Zabe wanted to know everything from Perfaw but he would not let him go into the City. I think Perfaw felt sure that one

179

day Zabe would relent, so he stayed. Then Zabe, Perfaw, and Jak, were taken out hunting eastwards. Perfaw got sick from slave traders who gave them all poisoned water. He died after two days from the drink. Jak was not hurt but Zabe never properly recovered and died two years later. Jak married a widow who had nursed him when he arrived sick. I am the son of her and Jak. I am ninety years alive and I am bewildered by what has happened here over the last days. It was never like that before you arrived. These bad *poanjo's* with the firesticks have killed our men and caused pain. Your soldier helped us kill many of them. We are grateful and that is why I have met with you today. I want you to tell me what is to happen because somehow, I think life as we understand it now, is about to change. You assisted us, I will show you what you want. The Perfaw and his son. We have them at our temple. But what comes next? What may happen to us? Are the bad poanjo's gone forever? Do you expect more people come now the City is known? I wish to understand what you think about all of these things? I invite you to my home where I will show you the temple and after we can eat and drink chicha and you can answer my questions." He sat back on the stool and stared at Lynn, who he obviously recognized as the leader.

"Please tell Jafa we will be happy to go with him immediately."

Mande translated, and everyone stood.

"Paul. You, John and I will go. Thiago stays in charge here with our five men and Teco. Keep a good watch. Thiago has a Bellini and we will leave a Glock. Take care!"

Jafa mounted his chair, and the procession passed the thorn bush and made its way through the jungle to the wall and back to the village.

CHAPTER XXVI

Secrets revealed

Five hundred yards to the east, Benicio hid in the reeds that topped the great wall diverting much of the Olgo's flow inland. His binoculars picked out the procession leaving the fort and winding its way up to the jungle.

"*Escorpião*! Look at that," he handed over the glasses. "They have an old man in a chair and they are going back, probably to where he lives. He has a jewel hanging from his neck! Now it's seven of them there with one shotgun. Good odds for us. We are fine here. Teco is with the group that have stayed. I want his heart cut out when we finish! We wait and see if they return with anything. Then we can attack the Fawcett's here early Friday morning from the cover of the wall or follow the Indians to their village and kill them in their homes."

The Scorpion nodded. "Yes *Patrão*. We wait. I promise you the heart of Teco. I will cut it out myself!" He grinned and Benicio patted his shoulder. The two of them climbed down the wall and into the small camp hidden below the structure.

Carrying Jafa, the group walked slowly back. Everyone had their own thoughts, and no conversation passed between them as they paced resolutely along the path until the village buildings came into sight.

Jafa was taken to his hut and Mande asked the others to sit in the shade until he returned. Pullen's watch showed twelve noon. The sun beat down but under the huge leaves of the palm tree they were not hot. A slight breeze came from the north, moving the white clouds that drifted high above the river. Soames drank from a water bottle. "I'm ready to call Victor and David when we get back later. He will need to know what's happening."

Lynn nodded. "Right. We must talk amongst ourselves. Let's see what Jafa has to show us, then we can converse with him and answer his questions. There's no doubt in my mind that this whole thing must be reported in detail. Let's start with Victor and David. The Ministry will be very involved in things once the news gets out. What say you John?"

"What do we tell Jafa? He is a very astute man and has obviously already gone over scenarios in his mind. He can have no idea of the scope of this find and what it may bring down on his head. There will be dozens of people flocking down here, hundreds perhaps. We need to make up our minds what we are going to say in advance. Personally, as a member of the armed forces, I can get by with quoting the military secrets act. I am not obligated to say a thing." He smiled at Sid and Paul.

"You two however are sure to be very much in demand. It's your expedition, and the press wants answers for a start. Then any fortune hunter that picks up the story will be here in a flash thinking something can be had. Victor has to have this area secured somehow. We must get the canoe's back along with the equipment. Everything is valuable now the City is discovered. It means a great deal of money coming in to the expedition coffers. Then there's movie and documentary rights. The expenses incurred are nothing compared with the income to be gained. I think a good financial advisory company with connections is needed."

Soames and Lynn were looking at him strangely. "Christ John," said Lynn. "We hadn't thought of that! You're right of course. Look. Hopefully we'll be back in England in a week or so. I don't want you running off back to your unit right away. We'll need your help for a few months to get things in hand. Will you allow me to handle that side after you report? I can talk to Bill Fredericks at Regiment and he can get you seconded to us for a while longer if that's all right with you?"

"Happy to leave it in your hands Sid. I agree, there's going to be a whole lot to take care of in a few days. We'll need everyone we have."

"Good. I'm glad we don't have to worry about that then! Poor Anastasia! All the publicity will drive her mad!" They laughed and at that moment, Jafa came out from his hut. He was dressed simply now as he led them towards the temple.

Mande translated for him.

"He says this temple is where the Piripkura always worshipped. Inside the City but not too large and did not attract much attention. The tribe lived outside the walls, so it wasn't hard to practice their religion. The City administration allowed, all to worship their own gods and there were many different sects. He will take you in now. I'll wait here. As I told Pullen, this is a very great honor."

They walked through, and Mande stayed at the entrance. In the anteroom all had to put on headdresses and cloaks. Jafa lead them to the narrow entrance, above which Soames saw the word '*Malchay*' and realized where they were going. Inside the hall Pullen hung back and let the other two gasp at the sights.

When they came to the Fawcett's he explained who they were. The two stared up at the mummified figures and Lynn took his camera and snapped dozens of pictures and then video-recorded everything. Jafa lead them forward again to the small room containing the emerald-filled stone tray. Lynn and Soames showed no emotion as he indicated the flowing water. When Pullen walked over, he realized why. The emeralds had gone and now he could see only the slate bottom of the sink. He immediately realized that Jafa had remained during the visit to get rid of the treasure. Where he had hidden it, Pullen had no idea. He looked towards the old Chief and was rewarded with a grin.

Turning, the group returned to the ante room and removed the headdresses and cloaks. Outside they met up with Mande again and walked slowly to Jafa's home.

Mande came out a few moments later.

"Jafa is very tired and asks if you can come early in the morning to talk?"

"Of course, said Soames. We will be here an hour after dawn."

Mande nodded and assigned a warrior to guide them back. As they paced, Lynn spoke.

"I would never have thought it. We must go back to camp and call Victor and David before anything else."

They passed through the thorn bush at four thirty. Once inside the fort, Lynn walked to one of the covered canoe's and looked for the sat-phone. He sat down with Soames and Pullen and Lynn handed the set to Soames who took a small card from his wallet and placed it in front of him. In a few moments he had his son, Victor on the line.

'Victor. It's me. The sun has been shining a lot. I found my sunglasses We ate fish last night. 8 space 40S Stop 53 space 61. That's all."

"I understand Dad. Everything's going to be fine I'm sure. Talk to you soon." The call finished.

"Interesting." Said Lynn. Now tell us what it means

Soames explained the late-night meeting he had had with his son at the Manaus base. "These are what those phrases meant." He read out the list.

- The sun has been shining a lot.–Enemies are here
- I found my sunglasses.-We found the lost City.
- We ate fish last night.–Secure area immediately.

"Those GPS coordinates have two numbers added to them. Victor will work the actual position out." He returned the card to his wallet.

"Victor now realizes we need military help here and we have problems. He knows we found the City and that the area has to be secured. He will call David and have the Ministry cooperate. The GPS coordinates are very useful."

"Well done Paul! That should do it!"

"I have no idea how long it might take. A chopper needs to refuel if it comes from Manaus. It will be at least twelve hours I'm sure. Quite a logistics problem!"!

Lynn had a small bottle of whiskey hidden away and they took turns to down a shot as they stowed the sat-phone and got ready for the evening meal. The guides had been fishing as usual and by luck had landed a 20lb Surubim on a strong handline. These sporting fish are excellent eating and Abilio had cleaned it and cut crossways into the backbone to allow it to be broiled and then the 'chops' served in that way. Dimas made rice and an hour later they were sitting in front of their plates. The guards patrolled and ate afterwards.

In Manaus, *La Fortaleza* had technicians watching communications along the Amazon. Most of the traffic seemed innocuous but once or twice every hour a message of interest would be intercepted. The operators were experienced and could pick out anything interesting. Once information about valuable shipments, routes, and arrival times were noticed, these were passed to a supervisor who decided if they should be sent to a convenient pirate launch who might be able to intercept. At four thirty-five an employee monitoring satellite's walked to the supervisor's desk.

"Boss, the commercial sat-phone channel was in use for a very short time a few minutes ago." He showed the man a print-out of the message. The supervisor nodded and picked up one of the telephones on his desk and dialed a number.

"Lorenzo here."

"Gustavo. This is Garces at *La Fortaleza.* We copied a satellite phone call from down south to a number in Manaus." He read the message and Lorenzo acknowledged it.

"Find out who owns that Manaus number and call me immediately." He hung up the 'phone. No one had called him via sat-phone and he had tried three times last night and twice this morning to get in touch. Benicio did not answer. That meant the telephone had to be out of service.

So, the Fawcett expedition had communicated with someone in Manaus. A very simple call. So simple it had to be a code of some kind. He realized that he would never be able to de-code a onetime message such as this. What about the GPS coordinates? Where were they? He called the supervisor back.

"Garces. The number? Who own it?"

"My contacts tell me it's an ABIN number *Chefe.**"

"Where are those GPS coordinates?"

"Sao Felix de Xingu *Chefe.*"

"The figures were disguised. They have to be well west of there! Start adding to those numbers until you get an area on the Olgo river about fifty miles north. That's where they must be. Call me right back with the information."

Something was wrong and *El Patrão* must be in trouble.

Shouting for his assistant he said he would need five men, fully armed for a seven-day trip, in fifteen minutes. Also, get food he heliport and told them to get the Sikorsky ready right away and arrange a refuel stop at Porto de Moz and another at Bello Horizonte. He would do his best to find Benicio to ask if he needed help.

*Chief

185

At ABIN headquarters, Major Victor Soames sat before General Leônidas Meneses, Head of the Brazilian Intelligence service.

"Holy Jesus Victor! This news will have an enormous impact on the country! We have to move quickly. Get two H225 Airbus choppers with fifty men down there right away. You go with them and take executive command. Arrange fueling stops. Those craft can do about five hundred miles on full tanks. That's a start. There isn't much time. This site will be overrun by tomorrow when the news leaks. I'll get onto Admiral Bonasera and ask what assets he has there. I must also get in touch with the President and tell him about this. Your brother? I suppose the Ministry of the Interior has to be involved?"

"Yes Sir. I will call him after I leave here."

"Stay in touch Victor. This is huge!"

Soames saluted and left the General's office.

Back in his own office he spoke with David.

"Everything is OK so don't worry. Dad called today. He is miles up the Olgo river and they found that lost city. It's a big story. I'm leaving in thirty minutes with troops to secure the place. It's going to take us at least twelve hours to arrive what with refueling. Please alert the people that handle lost cities, or whatever you call it, in your Ministry. Meneses is calling the President as we speak, and you need to tell your minister. It's important we keep visitors and press out. Can you get a 'no fly' order issued for these coordinates and the surrounding area?"

He gave David the figures. "Meneses has to call the Navy to find out what vessels are down that way. The *Vista* is at the Olgo. Everything must be controlled, or it will become a farce! Are you ok?"

"Yes, fine. Victor. I'll move right away. Call you back!" He hung up the 'phone.

At Renatto River Freight, Gustavo's telephone rang.

"Garces here *Chefe**. I've sent you a map to your cell phone where we are sure they are. Don't forget, *Touro Bravo* is at the mouth of the Olgo. She has radio's. They are out of range now but from Sao Felix you might get them on the air."

Gustavo thanked him and as he did so, his assistant advised the Sikorsky was ready, completely loaded and provisioned. Would he proceed to the pad right away? Gustavo called for his car.

It was going to be a race. The Sikorsky was slower than the Airbus but had a greater range. It remained to be seen who might arrive there first.

CHAPTER XXVII

A fight to the finish

Benicio watched the Fawcett group return to the fort shortly after four o'clock. They carried nothing, and the old man was not with them. He made his decision.

"*Escorpião.* We will attack the Indian village before dawn Friday. The Fawcett's will be here in their fort. The savages are armed with bows and spears and can be wiped out! You saw the old man? All dressed up with a head piece, a pretty spear, and a jewel hanging from his neck? They are hiding something, I swear! Get rid of them and we come back and kill the group in the fort or make them surrender when we tell them there's no Indian friends left." *Escorpião* nodded.

"I know how to find the village! Follow the wall on the inside all the way to the corner! No one can see us if we are careful. We sit outside and shoot anything that moves! It should take five minutes and we get our revenge at least, and we find out where these Piripkura hid their valuables. They have many for sure that's why they are talking to the Fawcett's! Go to sleep, we will leave at three."

The group of four lay down to rest. They could do nothing until morning.

Major Victor Soames, in full battle dress, sat in the H225 Airbus as it flew south. Looking out of the porthole, the flashing lights of their companion craft. A total of fifty men, armed to the teeth, flew in the two machines. They were quite fast, reaching about 150 knots but needed refueling every five hundred miles. He had arranged stops along the route where food, water, and fuel, would be available. The commander of troops, a Major in the Army, Enzo Murillo, was a hard-bitten veteran of many fights in the jungle against intruding groups from Bolivia, and Colombia. The latter, and the FARC organization continuously tried to establish bases in the Japura river area.

Soames told him all he had learned about the operation and stressed it was important to first find the Fawcett group and seek out about any hostiles. Once they were dealt with, they had to secure the area from civilian intruders and the press. He expected treasure hunters to make a dash for the area as soon it word got out and he felt sure that would be within twenty-four hours. Once they established themselves, Soames would call Manaus and give his estimate of what assets would be needed.

His cell phone rang, and he listened to Admiral Bonasera's aide who told him an SB90 fast amphibious patrol boat was on its way from Belo Monte on the Xingu. It had aboard a dozen marines. This craft would glide over rapids and other obstructions. With a speed for forty knots, it should arrive around noon the next day after a fuel stop at Bello Horizonte. It would also take on forty, five-gallon drums of additional oil. All good news so far! But now it was nearly seven o'clock, and they were due for the first refuel stop at Itacoataria.

The Sikorsky meanwhile had almost reached Urucuitiba. Unbeknown to either, both choppers had a second stop scheduled for Santorem at midnight. Soames dozed.

Pullen had guard duty from three to five in the morning. He was partnered with Gencio. Lots of rain and thunder accompanied a huge downpour. The two of them, ignoring the deluge, were staring out east and west, but Gencio found it difficult to make out the bend in the river from where he stood next to the canoes. Pullen watched to the west where the storm was concentrated. The lightning flashes illuminated the tops of the two retaining walls bringing in and taking out, water to the city. He wondered if it was really necessary for two guards to be posted. However, the old motto of better safe than sorry had been ingrained into him since his earliest soldiering days and he shrugged as he stared at the bright flashes. He closed his eyes for a moment and then opened them as a new strike hit the tree-line to the north. For a moment he thought he saw a flash of metal in the trees, but it vanished as the light died. Might that have been something? Why would there be anything there? He was imagining things. He turned south and looked across the river to the far bank. Another strike lit up the turbulent waters as they produced waves and carried the occasional uprooted tree west.

"Get back!", whispered Benicio as Joachim walked out from the jungle as lightning hit behind them. "Stay in the trees and then we head north to the wall in a few minutes." They finally made the turn and reached a collapsed section of the barrier. "Climb over and then we go west. When we find the wall turn north, the village is there. We have no hurry. It's sure to take us almost an hour walking slowly. Watch to see if they have anyone on lookout although in this rain I doubt they will be standing in the open." As he said this, the rain died away, and in two minutes they were pushing through wet brush with no downpour. Visibility improved but clouds rose from the stonework of the wall as the heat accumulated during the day, converted the wetness to steam. They pushed forward.

At Santorem the H225's were refueled at the airbase. A quick mechanical examination was made, and they were pronounced ready to go. With a range of five hundred miles, they would refuel again at Altamira and Soames called ahead asking Major Sanchez to meet him when they arrived about three thirty in the morning.

The Sikoursky landed at the same time, but at the civil airport. A sleepy crew from the fueling bay filled the regular and expanded tanks to capacity and it started its climb up to twelve thousand feet. It flew well below any commercial air traffic that they might encounter. They would top off the tanks again at Bello Horizonte before heading along the Olgo east. This next leg would consume only a third of the available fuel, the Sikoursky having a range of seven hundred miles with its modifications.

The SB90 was racing down the Xingu and would arrive at Bello Horizonte at two in the morning. It would be heading up the Olgo by five.

Benicio and his men had passed the 'administration' building, as the Fawcett group called it. They walked quietly. the only noise being the water dripping from tree leaves and hitting the stone wall with a soft splashing sound.

Escorpião held up a hand. There was a voice on the path ahead. He beckoned Joachim forward. He had the best ears. Looking at Joachim he listened and nodded.

He whispered in *Escorpião's* ear. "Chanting. One man. Probably a sentry trying to keep awake."

They backed up and Benicio was told of the guard's presence. He smiled and pointed to his own chest. Taking a knife from his belt he vanished into the brush. There was only the sound of the chanting for a minute or so and then a light cough. They waited for a few seconds and Benicio appeared. He held out his hand and showed the three waiting men a pair of bloody ears. Now they walked confidently, aware the sentry had been killed. They kept moving west passing ruined houses and collapsed portions of the wall. The first signs of the false dawn were seen in the sky behind them. Joachim moved forward as the residences seemed to thin out. They proceeded very slowly, stopping at regular intervals. Benicio was sure they might be close to the village. Joachim stopped and whispered to the others. "There's a large building ahead across this patch of cleared land. I would think they stationed a sentry there. We should go behind the building and approach from that side. It's not a regular trail and they will not expect visitors from that direction."

Benicio nodded, and they skirted the temple. On the other side, the village appeared. Women were starting fires for the early meal.

"Spread out. When I give the word, fire!"

The four pirates moved quietly into a line where they could observe all the structures. Then Benicio fired.

It was a massacre. The 7.62 loads mowed down the women and then the men as they came to the doorways of their homes. The ricochets from the stone walls doing terrible damage. Guns empty, the four men jammed in new magazines into the weapons and kept firing. Sentries from the west and north came running at the noise and were cut down, silhouetted by the cooking fires. The gunmen walked forward, shooting at anything that moved, but by now most of the Piripkura were dead or dying. The last two, Mande and Jafa died in Jafa's hut where Mande had gone to try to get him out. Benicio poured a burst of fire into the two of them as Mande supported the old man in an attempt to get to the door. They re-loaded again and fired off the thirty round clips in all directions to ensure no one remained living. Finally, the shooting ceased.

"Start with the Chief's house. That one there!" He pointed to where the Chief lay.

"Tell me what's inside there."

He walked in with Mateo. There was little to see except the ceremonial headdress and the spear they had noticed while watching previously. They did not find the hidden emerald.

"Look around, there has to be something here somewhere!"

But there wasn't. After ten minutes searching, they stopped. Benicio was angry. "Perhaps they took valuables to the fortress. We must find out. Let's go there now. They heard the shooting that's for sure. We have our AK's and can stay in the trees and get them from there. It won't take long, they've only got those short-range shotguns. They fire only twenty yards or so, we can keep out of range while we shoot." They moved out.

Pullen had noticed the shots. He looked at his watch. It was shortly after five in the morning.

He woke the others. "Gunfire from the village. That can mean only one thing. Those pirates came back!" There was more shooting and Thiago and Pullen checked their Bellini's and looked north-west.

"They'll be looking for anything valuable over there. Perhaps it's our chance Thiago. Earlier I thought I noticed a flash of metal in the tree-line to the east. I bet it was them coming from up-river."

They looked that way and saw the sky lightening, dawn was expected any minute. "I'm sure they doubled back and got past us in the dark either earlier today or even yesterday."

Soames and Lynn said nothing. This appeared to be a situation where the two jungle warfare men took charge.

"Let's go right now. Grab some ammo and we can move out of here. Sid, Paul. You stay put, Teco can do any translating if needed. There are only four of them. Keep the Glock's in case. When the shotguns fire, you know we are engaging them. That's when you need to be alert. Watch for us coming back through the tree-line and for Christ's sake don't fire!"

"Good luck to you both. We'll be careful," said Sid as the thorn bush was moved and they slipped out.

They moved through the brush and trees to the wall with Pullen leading. "That lot don't know the layout of the City, so they will follow the wall. They will probably return the same way and we'll be waiting. Let's get into one of the ruined houses below the big administration building. It's not far from the wall and we can pick out a field of fire for the ambush."

"Good idea John. Let's get as far west as we can, where the big building finishes it's more open down to the wall. We must ask for surrender you know. Those are the rules; however, the book doesn't say how long we wait for a reply!" He laughed and Pullen grinned. They understood the procedure.

They moved into position ten minutes later and waited for their visitors.

Victor Soames and the two H225's arrived at the Army base in Altamira at three in the morning. Crews waited, standing by for refueling. It took them forty minutes to get the fuel into the tanks while mechanics again checked the choppers and pronounced them airworthy. Soames met with Sanchez who elaborated on the Teco story. On the other side of town, the Sikorsky underwent a similar stop at the civil airport. The Assistant Manager came to meet the craft as Gustavo climbed down to the tarmac.

"Bom Dia Chefe! I have news. I looked at the radar. There are two military helicopters due to land at the Army base in five minutes. It's very unusual!

"Military eh? Big, small? What?"

"They are big Chefe. The kind that usually carries troops."

"Do we have a friend there?"

"Yes. The Safety Manager. I can call him."

"Hurry! Tell him we will take care of him as usual."

The organization had 'friends' everywhere that provided information in exchange for cash. The man returned to the main building. Gustavo waited as they continued fueling.

"*Chefe*. Our friend says two choppers with about fifty men. They wanted weather reports for the east Olgo."

Alarm bells sounded in Gustavo's head. This meant trouble for everyone.

"I need to use your radio. I want to contact our boat down there, the *Touro Bravo*. Wait a moment, I've got the call letters." He consulted a diary and after checking, provided the information.

Two minutes later he had the *Touro* on the radio.

"Gustavo here. Who is this?"

"*Chefe*, this is Manuel the communications operator. I've been waiting for any call to get through to us."

"Good. I am glad you are keeping watch. Is Dioneses there?"

A voice from the background answered.

"Here *Chefe*!"

"There may be a problem. I've not received a call from the *Patrão* and there's troops flying to the Olgo. I'll stay here in Altamira until the morning when we may learn more. Be ready to up-anchor and get out of there within five minutes from my call. It should be before noon. Return to Manaus at your best speed and don't stop for anything, understood?"

"We will stand by *Chefe*. Goodbye."

Gustavo walked outside and called the Assistant Manager.

"We are going to stay here until Friday morning and find out what's happening up the river. You must monitor the radar and the telephones and call me as soon as something is known. Where can we rest here?"

"At the back of the fuel shack *Chefe*. I'll take you now. As soon as anything comes through, I'll wake you."

He led them to a small back room and everyone, including the pilots, lay down on the packing rugs that stored there.

Back on the *Touro Bravo* Manuel, Dioneses and the two extra hands listened to the diesel motors on the river. They were anchored under the trees of the south bank and as they looked out, the moonlight reflected off a gray navy hovercraft as it sped east along the Olgo. They realized Gustavo's message probably had something to do with the sighting of the small warship.

At the City, Pullen and Thiago walked cautiously along the wall. The insects were awakening and the buzzing and clicking of the crickets was increasing. Birds started to fly, and the ant population was out hunting leaves underfoot. They found cover after ten minutes. A ruined residence with two windows facing east from which the wall could be seen for forty yards or so. Pullen whispered. "You call out for surrender first. Any reaction other than dropping their weapons, we open fire right away. I'm sure there's only four of them but they will have AK's, so we take no chances." Thiago nodded, made himself comfortable in the shadows and focused on the wall. Five minutes later there was a rustling and the first man appeared. They waited for five seconds more, and when everyone was in the open, Thiago called out.

"Pare! Mãos ao ar. Rendição ou atiramos*."

* *'Stop. Hands in the air. Surrender or we shoot!'*

194

The four men, surprised, stopped in their tracks and Pullen thought for a moment that they would obey Thiago's command. Finally the leader, realizing the voice came from the ruined house, opened fire from the hip as he fell to the ground.

Benicio shouted to the men. "Shoot them! Their guns have no range! We can easily kill them. They fire pellets, not bullets!"

Thiago and Pullen fired. The twelve-gauge shells from the Bellini's were accurate over fifty yards. With the Eotech 552 sight's, they were deadly. It was over in ten seconds after firing a six rounds apiece. In front of them four bodies sprawled. They moved forward, the jungle now silent after the explosions. Thiago turned to Pullen.

"The one in front told the others that our 'shotguns' fired pellets and had no range. Guess he had never seen an M4 in action."

Pullen laughed. "It's too late to learn now! Let's find out what we hit."

The effect of the twelve-gauge loads had shredded the chests of the pirates but they found wallets in the rear pockets of their pants and looked through them.

"I know who this one is!" said Thiago pointing down at Benicio. "He's Benicio Lorenzo the *Patrão*. He's like the chief pirate along the Amazon and runs most of the illegal activities." Pullen nodded. "Teco told me they shadowed us, hoping we would find something valuable here. If we did, they would take it and kill us. Fortunately it turned out differently! Let's go back to the fort. We need to tell the others and verify who caused earlier gunfire. I'm sure it was this lot who attacked the village."

They re-loaded and walked slowly back. The men in the fort noticed them and pulled back the thorn bush to let them enter.

"They're dead. Four of them. The remnants of the pirate group. Thiago recognized one of them from the name in his wallet. It's Benicio Lorenzo, and he said he's the leader of the Amazon Mafia."

"Well. What do we do now? Asked Lynn.

"We think they attacked the Indian village. If we go there, perhaps there's survivors."

"John. We had better call Victor." Said Soames.

Pullen agreed, and Soames made the call. In two minutes, a noisy connection was obtained.

"Victor. We are all fine here, but the shit has hit the fan. How long before you arrive?"

Pullen agreed, and Soames made the call. In two minutes, a noisy connection was obtained.

"Victor. We are all fine here, but the shit has hit the fan. How long before you arrive?"

"Leave the sat-phone on 'send'. We can watch you on GPS. Arrival fifteen minutes. Can we land?"

"Yes. In front of the camp. There's flat ground. Land there."

"Fine. See you momentarily."

Fifteen minutes afterwards the sounds of rotors was heard and the two H225's came into sight. They landed minutes later. Victor jumped from the first one and ran across to the fort. He was followed by forty-eight heavily armed Brazilian Special Forces marines, several of whom, Thiago recognized, waving his hat.

Victor introduced the troop commander, Enzo Murillo. Everyone spoke English.

"I'll make this quick," said Lynn, and gave a short version of the story. He explained that expedition sought the fate of Percy Fawcett and described briefly the canoe journey, Pullen's meeting with Teco and the visit with the Kayapo. He told of the attacks by Benicio Lorenzo and the pirates on the Piripkura and how the expedition helped them by dropping the snakes. The attack on the village and the probable massacre of the tribe earlier were mentioned and finally Pullen and Thiago's ambush.

The two Majors looked at each other in bewilderment and then Victor Soames spoke.

"John and Thiago had better go with Major Murillo and half of his men to the village and show them the site where you took on those gangsters on this morning. We will need a good supply of body bags. You realize there were rumors of Lorenzo being interested in the expedition. A friend of mine from ABIN inserted the undercover agent, Teco with the pirates, as he told John. I've spoken to David. He is on his way with a representative of the Indian Affairs Department. They have their own aircraft and he will come from Brasilia directly here. In the next days we are going to experience an enormous amount of government people arriving. The 'no fly' advisory is being issued as we speak but that won't stop the press from trying to get access. What about you Enzo?" he said addressing Major Murillo.

"Securing the area is the most important thing right now. I'll take thirty men with their equipment. All are CIGS graduates, trained jungle fighters. They'll be sent out in two-man teams along the City walls. They have food for a week and tents, so they will be fine until we get reinforcements. That ensures no one breaches the perimeter. Once done, I can call my Division headquarters for more support. We'll go now if Pullen and Sergeant Perez are ready? The communications team stays here with Lieutenant Andrade. He'll set up the comms center and when I get back, we can start."

The men picked up their gear and followed Pullen, Thiago, and Major Murillo, into the brush.

The Lieutenant proved to be an organizational genius and Lynn remarked to Soames that he wished he had been blessed with junior officers of that caliber when he was commanding. Men were dispatched to establish positions atop the two huge walls that diverted water into and out of the City. No one would be able to pass without permission from Major Soames. Portable tables were opened, and radios and auxiliary equipment installed and tested. The expedition generator was put to use, and the men sent to gather firewood until a commercial model could be delivered to heat food. Everyone cooperated. In an hour they had water boiling and Abilio, Dimas, and Erico fished for Piranha for lunch. These struck hungrily at the bait and Gencio and Marcelo cleaned them ready to broil on the military's compact grill once the big fire got hot.

An Army sentry reported a hovercraft turning the bend and a few minutes later the Navy SB90 rode up the beach on its air cushion. Lieutenant Silva reported to Major Soames he had twelve marines aboard as well large tents for the headquarters units. The marines got to pitching these immediately.

Then Pullen, Thiago, and Major Murillo, arrived back. Murillo made directly to the communications tent and issued orders to Andrade. Then he sat down with headphones on and a microphone in his hand. When he finished, Victor Soames took over and made his calls.

Pullen told Lynn and Soames he had seen the hut where Rimmell had died and had pictures of the structure and the scratched 'R' and arrow on the wall. Soames could give these to Drake Rimmell. Finally, the officers and the expedition leaders met together and one by one made their reports.

Murillo started.

"Thirty-seven villagers were killed. No wounded remained alive. I've asked for body bags. There will be no need for autopsy's. Four pirates killed, including two known to us. Benicio Renatto, *Patrão* of the Amazon Mafia and Cezar '*o Escorpião*' Costa, one of his assistants. Bad men! My men are spread out west and north along the wall in two-man teams. They've got everything they need for a few days. I've reported to base and requested more men, equipment, and a whole lot of other things!"

The Naval Lieutenant stood up and spoke. "My name is Silva. That's my hovercraft. We've pitched these HQ tents for the time being. I will need to refuel and once I do we can patrol up and down here a few miles in either direction to ensure security. My marines can help as you wish."

Lieutenant Andrade told everyone about the comms center and the guards on the walls entering and exiting the river. He said there would be food for everyone in an hour. Mr. Lynn's men were taking care of cooking.

Finally, Lynn spoke.

"Thank you everyone for what you have done. Obviously, we bow to your knowledge of what has to be accomplished here. All we require is transportation for my men and equipment back to Manaus when you are able. Myself and Mr. Soames have our own reports to make and then Sergeants Pullen and Perez can start loading our stuff. It all fits into cannisters so it's not difficult."

That of course caught the interest of the Brazilian officers who wanted to see how these men had traveled to the Olgo and what they had with them. Pullen and Thiago were detailed to handle this.

Then David Soames arrived with the Minister of the Interior and the Director of Indian Affairs. Their helicopter landed on the now crowded beach and they walked up to meet everyone and listen to a repeat of the stories.

The Minister took charge, thanked Lynn and Soames and said he would ensure they would get their transportation back to Manaus without delay. Would they please refrain from mentioning the unfortunate killings of the Indians and the pirates? The Government would take care of things. In a few days all restrictions would be lifted and apart from the slayings, they would be free to impart information. The Ministry would handle the press until then. The President wanted to meet them personally and that arrangement would be made after they got to Manaus. It was obvious the man had the respect of everyone and once the introductions were over, he headed straight to the radio.

Gustavo Lorenzo was awakened by the Assistant Airport Manager.

"*Chefe*. Wake up, please! There is news. Something big going on east up the Olgo. Rumors say a lot of Indians got killed along with the *Patrão!* The Army and the Navy sent men, and we have been alerted to expect heavy traffic, military helicopters, and troops. The Army base has no room for everything they are sending."

Gustavo was stunned. Renatto dead? He had to get back immediately. This could be a disaster if he wasn't in Manaus to take charge.

"Let me use the radio," he said, and walked to the waiting equipment.

"Manuel, Dioneses, Get out of there right away and back to Manaus with all speed. The *Patrão* they say is dead! We need to regroup so go back and come directly to headquarters when you arrive. Report to me. Take care!" He hung up the microphone.

"Is our chopper ready?"

"Yes *Chefe*."

"We leave immediately, file a flight plan for Manaus."

He walked over to rouse the pilots and his men for the long ride back.

CHAPTER XXVIII

Aftermath - Brazil

True to his word, the next day Saturday, two CH47 Chinook helicopters arrived carrying more troops and supplies. Amongst those was a heavy-duty generator to provide the power needed for the growing military presence.

The three expedition canoes, packed by Pullen, and Thiago, were easily stored aboard for the trip. Some of the men would be staying at the site. They said their goodbye's and thanked Teco for his help then climbed aboard for the flight. The Chinook rose into the sky and turned north-west. Below the beach was filled with supplies and more helicopters arrived by the hour. It was a huge operation.

They finally arrived back at the Manaus base after a couple of fueling stops. The equipment went in the hanger there. The men who had returned, showered and shaved, getting really clean for the first time in days and the others were sent on their way and promised a bonus once the administrative details got sorted out. Then the process of getting everything down on paper began.

Over the next few days, Lynn, and Soames traveled to Brasília where they met with the President at the Planalto Palace. There they were invested in the highest decoration available to foreigners, the National Order of the Southern Cross "As a token of gratitude and recognition for those who have rendered significant service to the Brazilian nation." The green leaves, bright stars, and a cross hanging below made it a handsome medal.

They returned after two days and read the newspapers for the first time. The Government had imposed restrictions on press releases for forty-eight hours, but now it was word-wide news. The discovery of a lost City didn't happen every day. Speculation was rife, and experts predicted the find would rival Peru's Machu Picchu. The Tourism Ministry announced plans to restore the City, a project they said would take ten years. An airstrip would be built to accommodate the expected influx of visitors. The Government basked in the international attention and finally relented to demands that the press be allowed to speak with the expedition leaders. There followed a week of interviews, TV appearances, and meetings, in Sao Paulo. Seven days later they were reunited in the Manaus hanger. Two canoes sat waiting to be packed and returned to the UK. One, with all its equipment inside, had been promised to the National Museum of Brazil*, in Rio.

The remaining two, along with everything else, were carefully stored by Pullen for shipment. With only a few items left, Thiago returned to his instructor's post after saying goodbye to the expedition members.

That Wednesday afternoon, with Lynn, and Soames off to an interview with a television station, Pullen sat alone, tidying up the final remains of their journey. In the quiet atmosphere of the large building he found a corner and a flat lidded box. There he spent two hours making an especially good job of packing and re-packing the Bellini's and Glocks in their special lockable cases.

largely destroyed by fire on September 2nd, 2018

He examined the remaining Bellini 12-gauge cartridge boxes, six of them half filled with live shells. The rounds were almost four inches long and .730 inches in diameter. They were in good condition and had not become damp from the humid conditions. He took some time filling the half empty boxes to their capacity and prepared to dispose of the others. Locking up, he took a half hour break and walked to the base commissary. He purchased a few souvenirs, four, one-pound jars of premium Brazil coffee, to take back to the UK. While there, he also picked up a roll of commercial adhesive tape.

Back at the hanger, Pullen had one last task to perform. He took the tape he had purchased and with the greatest of care, using his sheath knife to trim the ends down, sealed the boxes he had filled with unused shells. Everything fitted into the containers. These, labeled with the Reydon Hall address, were packed in the ULD's. They were put aboard trucks that evening and taken to the commercial airport under guard. The next day, Thursday, the equipment would leave for the UK.

Early in the morning on their last day, Major Victor Soames picked them up and took them on a tour of Manaus. At the base, the top military brass, the province Governor, and the Mayor, had gathered for a ceremony before they left. Here, Lynn, Soames, and Pullen, were invested with the Grand Cross of the National Order of Scientific Merit. Its maroon ribbon topped a similar colored cross.

The ceremony marked the end of their adventure and on the Friday morning, as a special recognition of their efforts, they boarded the Brazilian Air Force I. An Airbus A319 that usually transported the President. The Captain joked with them and said the unofficial name of the aircraft was 'Air Force 51', an allusion to former President Lula's preference for that brand of sugar cane brandy or '*chachaca*'.

CHAPTER XXIX

Aftermath - England

The luxurious aircraft took them to Miami where they were met by immigration officials and had their passports stamped and then hustled, without ceremony, across the runway to board a commercial flight to Heathrow.

When they arrived, crowds of reporters greeted them, and they were obliged to spend forty-five minutes answering questions in the VIP suite. Finally, they got away, and a limo drove them to Reydon Hall. The vehicle then took Soames home and dropped off Pullen in Southwold at his mother's house. She as usual, was very happy to see him. However, she read the tiredness in his eyes and told him to go to bed. He slept through until Sunday noon and by previous arrangement, strolled down to the Lord Nelson to meet his friends.

They arrived together at the pub and walked through to the snug. Everyone smiled as they ordered beers.

"I hope you all got some sleep last night, I certainly did," said Lynn. Soames and Pullen replied in the affirmative.

"Well, our 'vacation' is over," Lynn remarked. "Now it's down to the hard things! Let's talk about you John. I'll tell you up front that I would very much like you to help us out. There's an enormous amount of work to be done here. First, the disposal of equipment which of course has financial rewards."

He took out a notebook.

"FADE, for Fawcett Discovery Expedition, is the corporation name. We have to treat this as a business enterprise. We will need an accountant, legal representation, and help, with the public relations. People must be hired. My 'phone started ringing at six this morning with requests for interviews and even a call from New York to ask if we can appear on the 'Today' show. That's a start! We will have an awful lot more. The Parliamentary Office of Science and Technology called me on the way here! On a Sunday mind you! They want a meeting a soon as possible. Anastasia can help for a bit but the sooner we get organized, the better." He turned to Pullen.

"So you understand John, it's we three against the world! What I would like is for you to be assigned to us for a period of time. I can talk to the Regiment and the War Office and Paul here has all the ministry contacts we need to get this done very quickly. We would arrange compensation in accordance with military regulations, but I will say, you can expect to come out of this a wealthy man. Not that we think this would be your reason for joining us."

"Thanks Sid, Paul. I'm willing if you can do the necessary. We should start with the equipment I suppose. To be honest, I've no idea what it's worth but I have the purchase invoices. We can be sure people will pay a pretty penny to have something used in the discovery."

Soames grinned. "Look at this John, Sid. He took a newspaper from his jacket pocket and placed it on the bar. The headlines glared. 'LOST CITY DISCOVERED IN THE AMAZON BY BRITISH EXPLORERS'. I'm convinced we will find similar stories in every publication. It's world-wide news. I watched the BBC an hour back and they are promising interviews with the actual team!"

Lynn shook his head. "They have no idea of the extent of what's on the laptops. I'll must write a full report using the daily notes we made. Also, there's the photographs and video from my X100F and John's Coolpix. My guess is we've got about five hundred pictures and over three hours of video in total. Anyway. First things first. John, come to Reydon Hall tomorrow, say at nine, and we 'll wait for the equipment to get there. It should arrive early, and you can get started. Paul and myself will work on your assignment to us and also get moving on hiring a secretary and an administrator. As far as attorneys and accountants that will wait a day or so. Let's make it a point to get the three of us together every day from now on, say at noon, for lunch. Talk over what's going on and how we can help each other. No need for overlapping our tasks that would be counterproductive. Having said that, I had better move ahead with John's assignment while he sorts out the equipment. Find out who will pay what. That should keep us busy for a few days. Paul can start setting up interviews and TV appearances. I think I'll call a friend in the film business. They must know of a person who takes care of things after a movie has finished shooting. Perhaps that will help. Now, how about lunch?"

They picked up menu's, ordered another round of drinks and decided what they would eat.

Pullen arrived home at two thirty and was back in bed by three. He craved rest, those days in the rain forest really took a toll on the body. His mother seemed to understand and didn't wake him that's evening. Monday morning he got up early and took his mother tea in bed. She was overwhelmed, not being accustomed to this kind of treatment. He let her make him eggs and bacon and shortly before nine, carrying a plastic bag with two small packages inside, walked outside to find Douglas waiting in the Rolls. He politely said good morning and congratulated Pullen on his safe return. A few minutes later at the Hall, Anastasia greeted him.

"John. Great to have you back." She gave him a hug and kissed his cheek.

"I'm afraid we are a bit busy at the moment."

"Thanks. Here's a small gift from Brazil. It's a couple of jars of premium coffee."

"Wonderful. I'll get it to the kitchen. All the equipment arrived at seven this morning and the movers put it back in the big room. It's waiting for you there! There's a new laptop loaded with all the programs. You're going to need it!" She smiled.

"You have your work cut out! As we of course do. Paul will be here any minute and please don't worry about the telephone, Thursday I asked for another two lines to be installed. The Post Office people are doing it as we speak." She pointed to a small van parked over in the drive. "The 'phone doesn't stop ringing. That's not your problem. I'll send coffee to the room in a bit but now I must run! Good to see you John! Keep those blue eyes open wide!" She ran back into the house as the telephone sounded.

Pullen entered the house and made his way to the big room. He remembered the combination for the digital lock and keyed it. Everything was in the ULD's on the floor. They had plenty of UK Customs stamps. It looked like it had all be thoroughly examined. He took off his coat, put down his plastic shopping bag, and started work unloading. He opened an Excel file on the PC, naming it "Inventory". It listed quantities of remaining items. There was a column for the value and potential buyer name at the end. His coffee arrived, and he put it on the floor. There was no time to drink it right now.

By eleven the six big ULD's had been unloaded and by noon the containers were almost empty. The room was filling up with equipment. Everything was inventoried and listed on the PC. Much of the food and all the water had been consumed.

The two remaining Esquif's were battered and had lost a lot of paint. A seat was cracked in one and had been repaired with the epoxy resin. The tube and some fiberglass could be seen loose in the bottom of the canoe with half a dozen paddles and an anchor. One canoe had been given to the National Museum of Brazil before they left. The generator was donated, the Army using it on the Olgo.

The Limelite's got pushed to one side with the sleeping bags and deflated air mattresses. In a box there were several cans and jars of spices containing salt, peppercorns, curry, and paprika. In another, bottles of tabasco and tins of hot sauce with lurid labels stared up at him. Pullen sat the pepper jar aside. They had gifted the machetes to the guides and canoe men along with the first aid packs and cooking utensils. He would find out what the museums would offer for the other artifacts when they started to call, which he felt positive wouldn't be long. Sure enough, Douglas came in a few moments later with a list of museums and institutions who wanted to purchase equipment. It contained names and telephone numbers. That would be a job for the afternoon. As he prepared to leave, his cell-phone rang. It turned out to be a museum in New York. They wanted a tent! How they got his number he didn't know. He said he would be back to them later in the day.

Walking to the terrace he found Soames and Lynn drinking sherry.

"John, good news! I spoke to General Fredericks at Regiment. He said to tell you 'Great job!'. Tomorrow he'll be here in the morning, it's important to keep him happy! Expect no problems from his end assigning you. He'll sort out Division and they will take care of the War Office. The Minister was at Cambridge with Paul and he has already given his blessing. So one problem solved!" He nodded.

"More good news. Bill Fredericks has a retiring Major in his administration. Bill said he's what we want for our organization and would we be interested? He'll come with Bill tomorrow, so we can take a look at him. Anastasia is getting us a secretary. She still knows a lot of people from her days at UK Theater and when she called, her friend said they had recently turned down an excellent applicant for the top secretarial job. Seems the Director had 'a friend' who he wanted to place, so that stopped her from getting the position. She will be here tomorrow. Anastasia is setting up accommodations in Southwold for her." He consulted his notebook.

"We need offices. Much as I like working out of here we must have a business organization. We'll wait until we meet the retiring Major tomorrow and if all goes well, he can see about space in town. Now Paul, what about you?"

"Oh dear! It's incredible the number of people that want to talk with us! We can't do all the TV here, so some will be in London. Probably at least one day a week for the next month. I've arranged everything else to take place locally. Can we use John's equipment room for the interviews if there's space?"

Pullen answered. "No problem. Most of the stuff will go out this week. I've got to start answering calls about purchases this afternoon. There's a New York museum that has offered us $150K for a tent! It has to include an air mattress and sleeping bag. They intend building an Amazon river set around it! Amazing!"

Soames laughed. "That's a lot of money John! I think we should take it. What do you say Sid?"

"Without a doubt! Make sure they are the ones who pay for shipping it John, then go ahead!" They ate a sandwich and started talking again.

Soames spoke again.

"I've called Halesworth and spoken to Drake Rimmell. I've made an appointment to meet next week and give him some photographs. We owe him our thanks for what he provided us."

They finished up, and Pullen returned to the equipment room. Once inside, he shut the door. The bolt clicked, and he realized he was safely alone. Crossing to the arms chest he pushed three keys in turn and unlocked it. There rested the two shotguns and two pistols. The Benelli M4 with Eotech 552 sight and the two Glock 17's.

They were cleaned in Manaus before leaving so nothing remained to be done. He added them to the inventory list. Finally, there was a plastic container with ammunition. He put this on a small table where some sheets of paper rested and pulled up a chair. The seal was broken meaning Customs had taken a look. Inside, the Glock ammunition cartons were loosely closed. The shotgun shells themselves looked undisturbed though. It was only the tape he used to close the boxes with that was broken. He looked around the room, nothing was disturbed. Walking over to the plastic bag he had carried with him that morning, he removed one of the pound jars of coffee, taking it back to his small table. With his sheath knife he cut through the strip around the lid and opened the screw-top jar. The odor of fresh coffee drifted deliciously up to his nostrils. He poured half of it onto a sheet of paper, careful not to spill any on the floor. Then, peeling back the loose tape on a 12gauge box, he stared at the twenty cartridges. One by one he removed them, and held each one up close to his eyes, looking for a tiny mark made in Manaus. Soon, six of them came out of the box. Searching in his pants pocket he took out a small pair of needle-nosed pliers.

With great care Pullen used the sheath knife and pliers to loosen the cartridge from the charge. When he loosened all of them, he took out their contents and slipped them into the half-empty jar of coffee. Then he returned as much of the coffee powder as would fit into the vacant spaces, making sure the emeralds were completely covered. He resealed the lid with a roll of tape he carried with him and put the extra coffee in a paper twist on top of his coat.

It took thirty minutes to refill the cartridges with the buckshot from inside the peppercorn jar but eventually he finished. The indents in the cartridge where it joined the charge were all squeezed tight. Everything was tidied up, and he left the room with the laptop in his hand and a paper twist in his pocket. He was now about $150K richer than when he arrived that morning. Outside he stopped at a small bathroom, emptied the loose coffee into the toilet bowl, and flushed.

Removing the list that he had been provided with, he walked out to search for a telephone from which he might call the various museums. As he strolled through the door, he thought of Kipling's words. *'Now remember when you're hacking round a gilded Burma God, that his eyes is very often precious stones;*'*
Now how did Kipling know that?

Rudyard Kipling 1865/1936
From the poem 'Loot'

CHAPTER XXX

Where are they now?

<u>Abilio–A Guide.</u>

Abilio hitched a ride back to his village on the Xingu after a month when the SB90 hovercraft returned to its base. He was hired again by SIGS for a special assignment and was killed in 2020 while accompanying a group of Academy troops making a raid on the Vila Cruziero favela in Rio de Janeiro. He was 36. The Army arranged a pension for his widow.

<u>Bernardo Lorenzo–El Chefe.</u>

Lorenzo inherited the leadership of the Amazon Mafia when Benicio Renatto died. He ruled for only six months but, realizing he didn't have the killer instincts of his former boss, he took over two million dollars of the organizations funds and moved to Punta del Este in Uruguay. Unfortunately, his avarice caught up with him and he was shot dead on the stroke of midnight at 'The Moby Dick', the towns iconic pub, in November 2018, a warning perhaps for others with ideas of stealing from the group. The hit was carried out on the orders of Ignacio Garces, Communications Chief of La Fortaleza, who became the new *Patrão*.

<u>Erico–A canoe man.</u>

Erico stayed on as an assistant cook for the Army at the Lost City. He did well financially over the next year, clandestinely showing workers, bought in for the restoration, around the area. He returned to his village in 2021 after getting a call from Thiago Perez. Today he works for Perez as a guide with the Lost City company.

<u>Sydney-The Viscount Lynn-Landowner, Peer of the Realm.</u>

Sid Lynn became famous as the man who had found Percy Fawcett's resting place and discovered the Lost City. His book was published in 2019 He was frequently seen on television programs about the expedition. Lynn died in July 2020 from complications following an attack of malaria, probably contracted in the Matto Grosso during his Brazil journey.

<u>Sir Paul Soames-Diplomat and businessman.</u>

Paul Soames left the Diplomatic Corps at the end of 2018 to become Executive Director of FADE. He turned it into a very wealthy organization which supported viable exploratory groups world-wide. Many said he was too much of a showman but there's no denying he could make money. The two movies and over a dozen television informative documentary's, using the extensive videos and photographs taken by the expedition in Brazil, were huge financial successes.

<u>Major Victor Soames-ABIN Brazilian Army Intelligence Service.</u>

Advanced to Lt. Colonel in late 2018 and made Assistant Director of ABIN. Chosen by the Defense Ministry for promotion to Colonel in 2020, he became Chief of Government Information Services.

<u>David Soames–Ministry of the Interior, Brazil.</u>

Made Principal of the Lost City Project after its discovery and responsible for the initial planning of the restoration. Became Director of Indian Affairs in 2022.

<u>Thiago Perez–Sergeant Brazilian Army.</u>

Promoted to Warrant Officer upon his return to duty. Appointed Chief Instructor at CIGS January 2019. Retired from the Army at the end of 2020. Became a well-known TV personality after numerous appearances on programs regarding the Lost City. Obtained a grant from FADE in early 2021 which helped him buy the vessels needed for his company 'Lost City Guide Service' based in Sáo Felix de Xingu which offers airboat trips along the Olgo to the Lost City.

Teco–An employee of ABIN.

Stayed at the City sight working directly for Victor Soames. Then became an investigator for Paul Soames when Paul was put in charge of the Lost City project. Was successful in routing out much of the corruption during the restoration work. Instrumental in bringing the Kayapo into the modern world after talks with his father, the Chief. Awarded the Amazonic Service Medal in 2019.

Ado–Sub-Chief of the Kayapo.

Became Chief when Ako died at the end of 2018. Was reunited with his son, Teco that year. The two talked at length about the future of their tribe whose lands bordered the Lost City. For the good, or the bad, Ako decided to make the Dolphin legend into a tourist attraction. It became a great success once the City was opened to tourists in 2021 and was a favorite overnight stopping point for the Lost City Guide Service owned by Thiago Perez.

Staff Sergeant John Pullen-British Army.

Stayed a year with FADE after being seconded to them by the Ministry of Defense. Returned to duty with the Army and attended the Short Course for senior NCO's and qualified for a commission. Promoted to Lieutenant in early 2020. In July of the year, Pullen was a pallbearer at the funeral of Viscount Sidney Lynn. Appointed Assistant Commandant, Jungle Warfare (JWS) School in Seria, Brunei January 2021, he flew from Mildenhall along with luggage which contained an old jar of Brazilian coffee. Step cut emeralds are much sought after in Bandar Seri Bagawan, the capital. On leave in 2023, and now a retired, and wealthy man, he re-united with Anastasia, widow of Viscount Lynn. They married in September of that year.

The Piripkura tribe

Sadly, the massacre of Jafa and Mande, along with the remaining tribesmen, seemed to signal the extinction of the Piripkura peoples. However, late in November 2021, two natives, a male and a female, walked into the village of Ado and the Kayapo along the Olgo. They explained they need a midwife for the woman. They said they had been hunting on that fateful March day and when they returned, they saw the death at their village, and fled back to the bush. They had been living alone there for more than three years. Ado radioed Thiago Perez. On his next airboat trip, three days later, Perez was accompanied by an Indian Affairs Bureau medic who examined the woman and delivered her of a baby boy the next day. The Piripkura expressed their desire to return to the jungle and continue their simple lives there. Two days later, they walked out of the village into the greenery and have not been seen since.

A NEW EPITAPH

Percy Fawcett discovered

In 1925, ninety-four years ago to the day, Percy Harrison Fawcett DSO, disappeared while exploring the forests of the Mato Grosso in north-eastern Brazil. A somewhat mocking epitaph was written by a fellow officer at that time. Today, now the mystery of his disappearance has been solved, another is offered:

Percy Fawcett has been found,
His bones not buried in the ground.
But standing tall with Jak and Rim,
The men that did accompany him.
He found his City, jungle covered,
That for years was undiscovered.
All hail to Percy for this feat,
He fought the rain and conquered heat.
And the Indians he found there,
Honored him, compassionate, fair.
His green eyes watch. What does he see?
Some say it is men's apathy.

The bodies of Fawcett and his two accomplices were found on Thursday March 22nd, 2018.

* From 'The Westminster Gazette.' - April 22nd, 2019.

213

Printed in Great Britain
by Amazon

43766233R00129